SPY, INTERRUPTED

The Waiting Wife

T. Dasu

For my parents,

Madhura Bharathi and Krishnamoorty

ACKNOWLEDGEMENTS

I would like to thank Kumar for reading the manuscript multiple times and making substantive suggestions that vastly improved the novel. He is also responsible for the book's main title and cover photo. I deeply appreciate Dr. D. S. Rao's comprehensive reading and his invaluable advice and encouragement.

CONTENTS

THE PARTY

Nina stared at the mirror. She'd better go downstairs soon if she didn't want to appear rude to her hosts. She'd met them last year at her friend Amy's wedding. Even though she'd barely exchanged a word with the Alis at that time, here she was, their guest for three long days. She adjusted her dress and sighed.

"Smile," she said to her reflection. "They're being so nice to you. Be good."

A wave of babble washed over her as she went down the staircase to the large, high-ceilinged living room. All the guests there seemed to know each other. Some sat on sofas and chairs scattered across the room, engaged in animated conversation. Others stood around, drinking, arguing, and laughing. On the far side, a long wall of glass doors opened onto the lawn, where the overflow from the house congregated. A hundred yards beyond, the ocean was a vast darkness at the foot of the sloping lawn.

"Nina! Come on over here. Sit down," Sid Ali's voice boomed at her. He was in his element, mixing drinks behind the wide kitchen counter.

"Hi, Sid." Nina was glad to find a friendly person in the sea of strangers. She perched on a stool at the counter and looked around. Everything in the house was modern and chic—steel, glass, concrete, designer lighting in surreal shapes and colors.

Sid slid a pale-pink drink in front of her with a flourish.

"What's this?" she asked.

"It's a lychee martini. Trust me; you'll like it." He winked at her. "Drink up!"

Beyond the kitchen counter and to the right, an enormous table was set for dinner with thirty place settings. It occupied an entire side of the huge room. An array of dishes fit for the cover of a glossy food magazine sat at the center of the table. Their aromas wafted around the room, circulated by a fan churning overhead.

"What a lot of food!" Nina said.

Sid looked over his shoulder at the table behind him. "Sheri and I love to cook. We made *all* of it."

Nina sipped her drink and snacked on the nuts in a bowl in front of her. The mix was seasoned with such surprising finesse that she examined the bowl closely to figure out what Sid had put in it.

"Thanks for inviting me."

"We've heard so much about you from Amy." He leaned across the counter toward her. "It shouldn't have taken us this long."

Nina and Amy had been childhood friends, together from preschool all the way to high school. They had remained close even when college and careers took them in different directions. Amy had gotten married last year, leaving Nina lonely and friendless. Last week, while her husband, Jeff, was photographing locals in some remote jungle, Amy had asked Nina to join her on a visit to the Alis' beachfront home. Nina had accepted eagerly.

"How did you spend the day?" Sid leaned closer and gave her a wide grin that crinkled the corners of his eyes. He was a big man, more than six feet tall, with a propensity to corpulence. "You should've come with us to the seafood place. It was delicious."

"I'm a vegetarian. A seafood place is pretty useless to me." She smiled to soften the effect of her words. "I had a great time walking around your neighborhood, though, looking for a nice spot to sketch."

"Did you find it?"

"Yes! The Victorian mansion next door, with that lovely garden."

"Ah, the haunted James mansion, as I call it. Make sure the redoubtable Mr. Stephen James doesn't catch you. He might come after you with a gun."

Nina raised her eyebrows and put her glass down. "Really? But he was quite nice. He showed me around."

Sid stared at her, first in disbelief and then with amusement. "Sheri. Come here. *Sheri*," he bellowed.

A tall woman skimmed across the room, trailing white chiffon, and appeared at his side. She frowned at him but not without affection. Her face and arms were freckled from the sun—the bane of redheads.

"Sid, my love, you need to stop yelling like that. People will think you're a bully."

He wasn't in the least bit bothered by his wife's scolding and pulled her closer to stand next to him.

"What's up?" she asked with a proprietary arm around him.

"Guess who Nina ran into? Stee-phen!" He dragged out the syllables.

"Oh my God, really? That's too bad. I hope he wasn't rude."

Stephen James had struck Nina as slightly brusque but not unfriendly and certainly not rude. On the contrary he'd been courteous in an old-fashioned way: quick to open doors and to offer his hand to help her get in and out of a golf cart.

She replied, "No, no, he was quite nice. He drove me around the orchards and greenhouses and showed me the orchid atrium inside the house. It was stunning."

"You were actually inside the house?" Sheri asked.

"Yes."

Sid and Sheri stared at Nina and then at each other.

"He must really like you," Sheri said. "We've lived here for three years. He has never invited us or offered to show us around his place, even though he's had dinner at our home many times." She looked Nina up and down. "All we get from him is a bottle of wine."

Sid jumped in. "Well, he spends most of his time on his boats. No friends, family, or visitors, just the staff who take care of the property. Oh yes, then there's a tall, old guy who shows up occasionally. You remember, Sheri. Weird guy...Looks like Henry Kissinger and smokes like a maniac?"

"I remember. Well, well! Stevie gave you a tour, huh? We need to get to the bottom of this." Her green eyes lit up. "Let's invite Stephen for dinner tomorrow. He never says no."

"No, no," Nina begged, half afraid they might actually do it. She gulped down her drink and excused herself to go look for Amy. A young man spotted her and headed purposefully in her direction. She was in no mood to talk to him. He had been pestering her for an introduction to a friend of hers. It was tricky but she managed to duck in and out of the crowd without making it obvious that she was trying to avoid him—she didn't want to offend a guest of the Alis.

Finally dinner was announced. Nina sat down at the table, relieved that she could go back upstairs as soon as the meal was over and return to her book.

Sid had made a special vegetable dish for her with okra, mustard, and yogurt.

"It's my mother's favorite," he shouted to be heard across the table. "She is vegetarian, just like you." His mother was Indian and his father was Pakistani, both doctors with a flourishing practice in Michigan.

Nina was seated between Amy and a voluble Pakistani writer named Tariq Rehman. The man had a lovely voice, but she wished he would stop his incessant self-promotion. Did it really matter how many books he had written or how many departments he chaired?

Unlike Nina the other guests were in full party mode. Wine disappeared by the case, and a constant stream of dishes came out of the ovens, steaming, sizzling, smoking. The room was soon saturated with the aromas of lamb kebabs, roasted potatoes and freshly baked flatbread. A small band set up in the living room for postdinner dancing. Sid and Sheri dashed around, filling glasses and piling food onto the plates of their guests.

Sid stopped and lingered next to Nina every chance he got. Sheri noticed it, and a familiar insecurity gripped her. Perhaps Sid missed being with his people. But she quickly pushed away such thoughts because she knew how unfair it was to him. It was in his nature to be an attentive host—he wanted everyone to feel at home, eat well, and have a great time.

Recently, though, Sid had been making a lot of new friends. Tariq Rehman had persuaded him to help raise funds for several Pakistani charities, and Sid had thrown himself into the task with his usual energy. He spent hours on the phone and computer, talking to bank managers, sending out e-mails, and meeting new friends he did not bother to introduce to Sheri. It was unlike him. He usually shared every little detail with her. Things were changing between them now. He seemed to be drifting away on a dark tide, propelled by this Rehman character.

But this was a party. With effort Sheri shook off her gloomy thoughts and walked over to Nina.

"Would you like some more wine?" Sheri asked with a smile.

Nina shook her head and concentrated on her food. She hated large gatherings, especially when she did not know anyone. She longed to be back in her apartment, snuggled under her freshly washed comforter, reading her favorite magazine, or talking on Skype with her mother.

When it was time for dessert and coffee, Nina picked up her untouched glass of wine, went out to the lawn, and walked toward the ocean. The guests were all inside the house, huddled in intimate groups in dimly lit corners, their faces warm and glowing.

A beaming moon cast a silvery glow over the bay. She sank down into an Adirondack chair, slipped off her sandals and looked at the moonlit water. Seagulls squawked in the distance in pursuit of fishy treats. She closed her eyes and took a deep breath of the cool, fresh air. Her nerves settled down, and the beauty of her surroundings filled her with peace and gratitude.

Then something moved in the trees. Her first impulse was to shout for help. Before she could do so, a figure stepped out from behind the trees and waved to her. There was something familiar about the ramrod posture and quick movements.

It was Stephen James of the haunted James mansion, as Sid had put it. He gestured to her to come closer, but she hesitated. Sid and Sheri hadn't been exactly complimentary of him. What if he really carried a gun? And what was he doing lurking in the bushes like that?

His waving became more insistent. Nina took a deep breath, rose from her chair and walked toward him.

"Hello," he said. His starched white shirt glowed in the moonlight and his round, metal rimmed glasses reflected the moon.

"Sorry to drag you out here. I didn't want to crash the party."

"That's fine. I was fed up inside anyway." Her eyes remained glued to the wine glass in her hand.

He hung back for a second. "What are you doing tomorrow, Nina?"

Her stomach did a little somersault. He had paused before he said her name, as if to accord it a special weight. And the way he said it would have sent Sid and Sheri into a frenzy of speculation.

But she was in no mood to care about what the Alis might think; she was busy hanging on every word he said.

"Nothing much. Why do you ask?"

"You don't have any plans with your friends?"

"Not really."

"Would you like to go sailing with me?"

Despite Sid and Sheri's prescient remarks, and despite what had been a clear lead-up, Nina was taken aback. Maybe it was the suddenness of it. She had met him barely seven hours ago, and the meeting—touring his high-tech greenhouses and orchards, listening to his scholarly account of self-sustaining cultivation—had been unremarkable, except for one instant when he had given her a candid summary of his family's sordid history and watched her reaction with unnerving intensity.

She stood in the moonlight now and stared down at her glass, trying to get a grip on her thoughts, which raced in every direction like a swarm of excited bees. Usually she was quite good at brushing off a guy with a polite no. But now all she could do was dig her toes into the soft, springy grass.

"I've never been on a sailboat before."

"All the more reason," he handed her a piece of paper. "That's my cell phone number. Call me tonight."

She took it without thinking.

"Good night." He gave a quick bow and walked away.

Nina was irritated with herself. Why hadn't she just said no? She trudged back to the party and cornered Amy.

"We need to talk."

Amy knew Nina's body language better than anyone did. "Some poor guy tried to ask you out, didn't he?"

They walked back out on the lawn, to the Adirondack chairs. Amy wasn't surprised at all when Nina described the bizarre encounter with Stephen. Men often found Nina's air of innocence irresistible, only to be quelled by her extreme uptightness. Nina was paralyzed by excessive caution. A misguided entanglement during her college years had turned her off romance completely. Upon graduation from college, she had joined a skyrocketing tech company and had been so consumed by work that she had become even more unapproachable.

Amy tried to persuade Nina to get out and socialize more, to try to be friendly. "Don't turn into a female Unabomber," she had warned. But Nina was either too lazy or too paranoid. Even Nina's mother, Deepa, had begun to drop hints, like, "I'm going to start looking for a suitable boy." Nina, lost in her own fanciful world, paid no attention to Amy or Deepa.

"You should go out with him," Amy said now. "For heaven's sake, Nina. Have some fun, girl! In another four years, you'll be thirty, and nobody will ask you out if you keep pushing away men like this. What's the big deal about going sailing? It's not like you're going to marry him, for God's sake."

Nina listened to the lecture with her eyes fixed on the black ocean. She hated to admit it but her friend was right. Perhaps she'd read too many Jane Austen novels and had unrealistic dreams of love. Perhaps her first boyfriend's infidelity had soured her view of men. Anyway, she'd better take control of her personal life rather than wait for fate or other people to shape it.

Amy threw the final punch. "Look, we'll be gone in two days, and you never have to see him again. Come on, Nina. You've got to do it. It'll be fun, and you'll be outdoors, so it won't be too awkward. You'll love it."

"OK, OK, I'll do it," Nina muttered.

Before going to bed that night, she picked up her phone to call Stephen. She opened his slip of paper. Underneath the number, precisely and perfectly formed, was the phrase, "See you tomorrow."

SAILING

Stephen sprinted toward the dock at just before seven in the morning. The air was already warm and heavy with moisture. Nina should be showing up at any minute.

According to his boss, old George Applegate, Nina Sharma came highly recommended. "Her former professor said she'd be a terrific recruit to the CIA. He's sent many good candidates our way in the past. Here's the opportunity you've been waiting for, Stephen, to start your operation on the Indian subcontinent," George had drawled in his Louisiana accent. "There's something nasty brewing out there. We need to find it before it comes here. Why don't you meet Nina, check out the usual things: Is she trustworthy? Does she have

13

the skills? It couldn't be more convenient since she's visiting your neighbor."

To Stephen's surprise, Nina was already there, sitting on the stone bench and watching the sparkling ocean. At the sound of his footsteps on the gravel, she turned around and smiled.

"Hello. Did I keep you waiting?" he asked.

"No, I was early. I thought I'd wait here instead of waking everyone at the house." She had slept poorly but managed to look fresh and scrubbed from her morning shower. Her skin glistened.

"The marina is just a few minutes away." Stephen started to walk toward it. He slowed his pace when he saw her struggling to keep up with him. She carried a very large tote bag. It hit the ground when she took it off her shoulder and carried it in her hand. He thought of offering to carry it but decided against it, unsure how she would interpret such a gesture. She had bristled when he'd opened the door for her yesterday.

A narrow sidewalk wound its way along the water's edge to the marina. Gentle waves sloshed against the concrete retaining wall. Sailboats, yachts, and motorboats bobbed together in a scenic jumble.

"Please wait here," Stephen said when they arrived at the marina. "I'll be right back." He disappeared inside a small shack.

Nina waited, feeling a little self-conscious. The locals stared at her and averted their eyes when she looked at them. It wasn't often that Stephen was seen with company, especially with a woman. He emerged after a few minutes carrying an oversized gym bag in his hand. Right behind him, a young fellow came lugging a picnic basket and a cooler. The three of them made their way down the pier to a white sailboat with blue, rolled-up sails. Nina stepped in gingerly and steadied herself as the boat rocked. The boy put down the basket and cooler. He looked at her with wide eyes, and hung around and watched them even after his errand was done.

Stephen followed Nina onto the vessel and pulled in the last line behind him, and got ready to push off.

"Please put this on." He gave her a bulky life vest.

"Do I have to?" She was quite warm as it was.

"Yes. We can't leave until you do."

She strapped it on, and the boat started to move slowly. Stephen maneuvered it away from the dock, expertly dodging nearby vessels. He described to Nina what he was doing, but she was so overcome by admiration, she barely heard a word. The boat launch was an impressive bit of showmanship, although it wasn't clear to her whether it was his natural style or put on for her benefit.

The water was smooth and blue, like the sky above. Other boats with delicate, petallike sails dotted the bay. Everyone seemed to know everyone else and shouted and waved as they passed one another. An occasional speedboat caused Stephen's vessel to wobble in its wake.

He wore sunglasses, a baseball cap, and a white T-shirt and cargo shorts that were already damp from the spray. His hands rested lightly on the wheel. The sun got warmer; the deck got hotter. Nina's lips felt dry and salty. She pulled a water bottle from her bag.

Stephen turned to her. "There are drinks in the cooler downstairs. Feel free to help yourself. Could you get me a bottle of water, please?"

She went belowdecks and returned with two bottles of water. Her legs were stiff from too much sitting, so she decided to risk standing at the helm, near the steering wheel. The boat sliced through the water and raised a cool mist.

Farther from town the bay was less crowded. Stephen lashed down the wheel to take a break. It was quite comfortable in the shade of the jib.

"What do you do, Nina?" He looked at her as he drank from his water bottle in short, greedy gulps.

"I work for BigSearch, at their Chelsea office in Manhattan."

"And what do you do there?"

"I manage nonprofit projects—their funding, implementation, and supervision. Particularly ones that focus on education for children from rural areas in third-world countries."

Her managers at BigSearch had propelled her at a rapid clip, impressed by her energy, drive, and commitment. She could switch from scientist to spokesperson to activist in seconds. She was BigSearch's person on the ground in disaster-struck areas like Haiti, where she set up communication centers to coordinate re- sources for relief and rescue efforts.

The more she tried to keep her answers brief, the more questions he asked—not in a nosy, abrasive way but with a natural desire to know. What kind of projects did she fund? How long did it take for a project to take off?

"I'll give you an example." She turned to face him. "We just approved a grant for an NGO in India that designs and manufactures mobile schools to educate children in remote rural areas. By rotating through many villages, they can cover a large area and help many children."

This was a different Nina from the one he had seen thus far. This Nina was impassioned and determined.

"What other countries do you work with?" he asked.

"I've focused mostly on India because I know the culture and a couple of the languages spoken there. I might consider Bangladesh or Sri Lanka next year."

"What about Pakistan?"

"Pakistan and Afghanistan are harder to tackle be- cause of their political situations. But they really need our help. It's tragic how little some of those kids have. And the conditions they live in are terrible, especially the girls. Their prospects are bleak, but the slightest ef- fort on our part could make huge differences in their lives. Education is their only way out."

She stopped, arrested by Stephen's unblinking gaze.

"Sorry, I get carried away." She smiled.

"It sounds fantastic. Where can I read about these projects?"

"I'll send you a link."

He nodded and took a quick survey of the surroundings to check for other boats.

"So, what do *you* do?" she asked.

"Nothing so interesting, I'm afraid. I'm a marine engineer. I specialize in design and materials. I advise the US government—my only client."

"Do you like what you do?"

"Very much. I grew up around boats and the ocean. It doesn't feel like work at all."

She was about to ask another question when he cocked his head to one side and listened to the sound of a faraway motor.

"I'd better get back." He returned to the wheel.

While they drifted along the coast, Stephen pointed out the sights—historic New England buildings, the graceful lines of a long bridge. Stately homes rose behind trees and gates, and exuded privilege from every brick. Soon the coast became rocky and stark, and the water got livelier, flecked with white. In the distance a lighthouse came into view.

"That's where we're headed." He pointed to it and turned around to catch Nina's eye. "And in the evening, if we go out a little farther into the ocean, we'll get a great view of the sunset."

She leaned out to get a better look. The red and white lighthouse stood on a rocky landmass that jutted out into the ocean. The beach was littered with stones and boulders and gave way to a grassy stretch culminating at a gray, rocky slope. The shoreline turned a sudden corner and revealed a sheltered, sandy cove the size of a soccer field. It had a dilapidated dock toward which Stephen turned the boat. There was not a soul to be seen.

Nina felt apprehensive for the first time. She had not planned on such isolation. But she took his proffered hand and stepped off the boat with her bag. She walked ahead as he busied himself with securing the boat.

Her phone pinged—a text message from Amy: "How's it going?"

Nina could have cried with relief that there was reception in this lonely corner of the world. "Picnic at lighthouse!" she texted back.

It was a picturesque spot sheltered by the rocky slope on three sides. The sea lapped at the opening on the fourth side while the lighthouse stood sentinel near the edge of the cove. Wildflowers and grasses grew between rocks and at the foot of the granite hill. The sand in the clearing was dotted with patches of a weedy groundcover in full bloom, with tiny, pink blossoms on dark-green leaves. Clouds of small, white butterflies rose up wherever she set foot.

While Nina texted, Stephen had set up a large, blue blanket under the shade of a white beach umbrella. A big cooler and an equally big picnic basket sat at one end along with the gym bag. He lay back on a huge, puffy pillow, getting ready to read a book.

"This place is beautiful," Nina said. She put away her phone and went to the blanket. "What's the name of those pink flowers?"

"Beach pea, and some red clover. I thought you might like it here. You told me yesterday you were look-ing for scenic spots to sketch."

He placed the book facedown on his chest and clasped his hands behind his head. The fleeting ex-pression of alarm on Nina's face as soon as she'd seen this secluded place had not escaped him. He had de-cided that lying in full view in the middle of the clear-ing was the best way to make her comfortable.

It was a rare opportunity for Nina to get a full-length view of him. He now wore a red polo shirt; he must have changed after docking the boat. His long, tanned legs were crossed at the ankles, and he wore brown-leather flip-flops that marked time to a beat in his head. Round, metal rimmed glasses and a mass of brown curls on his head reinforced his look of careless ease. He squinted at her through half-closed eyes, with his lips pressed together in a thin, straight line.

"What are you reading?" she asked.

He handed her the book—*Complications*, by Atul Gawande. She inspected it and handed it back to him without comment. She started to empty her handbag so she could carry her sketchbook and pencils in it.

"How did you discover this spot?" she asked while she discarded things in a big but neat pile on one corner of the blanket—two water bottles, several books, a couple of cereal bars.

"I grew up around here. I know this place inside out." He smiled when he saw the cereal bars. "I see you came prepared."

"Insurance. I'll be back soon."

He watched her walk across the field batting away impertinent butterflies. What a strange girl. Very prim; never got within two feet of him; independent, with strongly held views that she expressed only when asked. But she was easygoing, quick to smile, and perfectly natural with him, like an old friend. There were no efforts to impress, flirt, or entertain. She was happy to let long stretches of silence go by without inane remarks. In fact there was nothing date-like about their time together so far.

He sighed and examined the books she had left behind. One was in Hindi, but he was not yet facile enough in the language to read the cover. He had been concentrating on his Urdu and Pashto skills. The other book was *Baltasar and Blimunda*. He read the first few pages but found it too freewheeling, with a lack of punctuation. Fiction wasn't his thing anyway. He picked up his book to look for where he had left off.

Nina walked across the field, searching for interesting subjects. The lighthouse was gorgeous but such a stereotype—there were millions of postcards celebrating lighthouses. She made a desultory attempt to draw the wild grasses and flowers, but they too failed to inspire her. Having arrived at the edge of the clearing, she decided to walk back.

As soon as she turned around, she glimpsed the perfect composition framed for her by the granite slopes: a white beach umbrella against a backdrop of gray, jagged rocks; a man in a bright-red shirt on a pale-blue blanket in a sea of bleached-white sand and flowering groundcover. The reflection of the harsh summer sun off the sand and water sharpened the colors to a surreal, metallic brightness.

A couple of hours later, Stephen looked up from his book. It was well past noon. Where was Nina? He sat up, slightly worried, and looked around. What if she had fallen off a rock or slipped into the water? But there she was in the far corner, sitting on a rock in the shade of the hillside, drawing with intense concentration.

He walked over with a bottle of water. She closed her sketchbook at his approach and greeted him with a smile from underneath an atrocious straw hat. She was flushed red from the heat.

"Be careful. You'll get dehydrated." He gave her the water bottle.

She took it gratefully, poured some water on her face and arms, and wiped the excess off with a tissue from her pocket.

"Let's walk back along the beach. It'll be much nicer by the shore." He led the way.

Stephen was right. It was at least ten degrees cooler by the water, in the humid, dark shadow of the rock. Small pools collected in the shallows and rock hollows, populated by algae and other water fauna. Tiny black tadpoles flitted in the water in busy, swirling groups. A briny, pungent smell hung thickly in the air.

He walked slowly to keep pace with her as she picked her way carefully between the boulders and stones. She soon felt tired. Her feet were sore from the uneven surface, and she had twisted her ankle several times. He noticed her discomfort and led the way back to the clearing.

It was bright and hot in the open field after the shade of the rock, but a cool breeze tempered the heat. Nina plopped down under the umbrella. She was exhausted. Stephen felt sorry for her—she was clearly not used to the heat and physical exertion. Not an outdoors type.

"We should go back into town. You look very tired. I didn't realize it would be so hot." He looked down at her.

"I'm fine. Don't worry." Nina sat up. She shielded her eyes to look at him. The glare was too much even though they were both in the shade of the umbrella.

She didn't seem fine at all. The problem was that she was too heavily dressed. She wore full-length, olive-green cotton pants with sneakers and socks.

"We can have a really nice picnic in the garden at home."

"No! You promised me a sunset."

"Are you sure you're OK? We can come back later for the sunset."

"Yes, I am sure."

They had another staring contest. Stephen couldn't reconcile the girl in front of him with the picture his boss had painted. George must have been crazy. Did he seriously expect this girl to go to hostile, remote places in Pakistan? It would be madness to send her out to hobnob with spies, informants, and jihadis. She could barely walk in the sun.

"She can help us," George had said. "She speaks Hindi, Gujarati, and Urdu. She works for BigSearch, Inc., and as a part of her job travels to remote villages—particularly in Gujarat and Rajasthan, near the Indo-Pak border. They're popular points of entry for terrorists, second only to the Kashmir border. And nobody would suspect her! Her boss swears by her smarts. She is exactly what we need."

She might be sharp, but she was not their type at all. Deceit and distrust were prerequisites of the life of an undercover CIA agent. She hadn't shown either of those traits.

"Well, at least take off your sneakers to cool down."

It was a perfectly innocuous statement, but Nina looked away, momentarily thrown off balance.

"Let's eat," she replied. "I'm starving."

The picnic basket was packed with sandwiches, cold noodles, salad, cookies, pie, preserves, pickles, fruit, wine, juice, and water.

"Are you sure there's enough?" she joked. "How did you get all this food?"

"I have my ways." He took a big helping of noodles. "Mrs. Brown, the housekeeper."

It was well past lunchtime and they were both hungry from the long walk. They ate in companionable silence.

"That was the best meal I've had in a very long time," Nina said.

"Glad you liked it." Stephen smiled and leaned back against the cooler. Nina sat cross-legged on the huge pillow, a few feet away from him.

"How long have you known the Alis?" he asked while he filled two wine glasses.

George had told him to find out if Nina could get close to Sid, who George believed had taken up with very questionable characters.

"To tell you the truth, I don't know them at all. My friend, Amy, asked me if I'd like to come for a long weekend with her to visit her friends from college. Her husband, Jeff, is away so I thought I'd keep her company." She gestured for him to stop when her glass was half full. "I agreed, and when she mentioned it to the Alis, they were kind enough to invite me."

"I know Jeff quite well. We've sailed and raced against each other many times. He's a good guy." Stephen went silent, sipped his wine, and stared into the distance.

"The Alis seem like nice people," Nina couldn't think of anything more substantial.

"Yes, very social. They entertain constantly." Stephen looked at her from over the rim of his wineglass. "I enjoy their parties. Always an interesting cast of characters."

"But you have your reservations."

He was surprised that she had guessed. But he recovered with a quick shrug. "The glare and the noise get to me occasionally, that's all."

Nina could see his point. Last night the party had gone on well past four in the morning. It could be a nuisance to the neighbors.

They sipped the wine in silence. It was a dessert wine, the only kind she liked—almost as if he had known because who brought dessert wine to a picnic anyway? The heat and the wine soon made her light-headed. She could feel herself slipping into a state of giggling silliness.

"No more for me, please." She stopped him when he tried to top off her glass.

He pushed his plate away and settled back, his hands under his head for support. George had said to find out if she had met Tariq Rehman, the Pakistani writer. Rehman was traveling quite a bit lately. He had been spotted by electronic eyes at crowded venues all over the world—at airports, sporting events and music festivals—within hours of sightings of suspected terrorists at those very locations. But there was no concrete evidence of Rehman meeting with the suspects, or indulging in other criminal or terror activity. And now Rehman and Sid seemed to have become best buddies. They talked several times a day. George wanted to know about what.

"I'm going to take a nap," Stephen said.

Really? Nina was taken aback. What kind of date was this?

"It's too hot right now. We have another hour before it cools down." He glanced at his watch. "We can see the lighthouse and head out to the open sea for the sunset after that. There are newspapers and magazines in the gym bag if you'd like to read."

He saw the look on her face and laughed. "Trust me. You won't last until sunset without a nap. I highly recommend one." With that he covered his face with a newspaper and fell asleep almost instantly.

Nina shook her head. What was the point of going all the way there to take a nap like a couple of toddlers? She fished for the *New York Times* in the gym bag. It was surprisingly heavy when she tried to push it away. What did he have in it, a nuclear reactor? She threw the pillow on it and leaned against it to read.

When Stephen woke up, the day was cooler, the sun less fierce and much lower in the sky. Nina had fallen asleep despite scoffing at his advice. He rolled over on his belly to take a closer look at her. She wore no make-up. Her skin was the color of molten honey with a faint blush from the heat and wine. Large eyelids lay closed under long, arching brows. It was a tranquil, contented face; her lips curved with the hint of a smile even in sleep.

He remained like that for a few minutes with his face barely inches away from hers. A faint perfume rose and ebbed with her breathing. He had a wicked impulse to kiss her. But his inherent decency prevailed, and he rolled away and sat up. His eyes were instantly drawn to her feet. Earlier he had watched surreptitiously while she'd removed her shoes and her feet emerged, soft and brown, with glorious metallic-peach nails—a welcome surprise given how severe the rest of her outfit was.

"Nina," he said loudly. "Wake up."

She woke with a start. Stephen was squatting on his heels next to her. She sat up and straightened herself. It was embarrassing beyond words, not to mention shocking, that she had fallen asleep within feet of him.

"There's a restroom in the lighthouse if you'd like to freshen up." He broke into a wide grin and discomposed her even more. She looked away quickly. He was different when he smiled—younger and not so hard edged, almost charming.

They climbed the rough-hewn rock steps to the lighthouse. It wasn't very tall. Inside, a spiral staircase led to the top, where a makeshift viewing platform encircled the lighthouse.

The view was breathtaking. To the left the bay stretched out to the town they had left behind earlier that morning. In front of them and to the right, the open sea shimmered. The sun had acquired an orange glow as it made its slow descent in the west. Seabirds rode invisible air currents and glided past their heads.

Stephen looked at the boats that plied the ocean below and began to whistle an old rowing song his grandfather had taught him. Could it be that he was actually happy? When was the last time *that* had happened? More than twenty years ago, when his grandfather was still alive, and his parents, although alienated and distrustful, still lived under the same roof.

"Look." He grabbed Nina's arm. "Dolphins!" He took a pair of compact binoculars from his pocket, unfolded them, and gave them to her.

"Where? Where?"

He turned her impatiently by the shoulders to point her in the right direction. The dolphins must have just had a good meal. They were lively and playful. They circled, jumped, and rolled, solo and in pairs.

Nina forgot her fear and leaned precariously over the rail with the binoculars. "Oh my God, they're beautiful!"

They shared the binoculars and took turns watching the dolphins. They didn't notice how low the sun had sunk in the meantime.

"We should leave," Stephen said abruptly.

They raced down the stairs, packed their things, and boarded the boat. It chugged along slowly into the open water, where they could get a clear view of the sun's disappearing into the fiery ocean.

Stephen killed the motor. The boat rocked gently with the waves. They were bathed in the glow of the sun and the sea. It was a spectacular show—the water swallowed the orange orb bit by bit until there was only a ghostly, crepuscular light left in the sky.

Stephen turned the boat around and headed back to town. Lights came on one by one along the shore, and dusk gave way to a star-filled sky. Neither he nor Nina uttered a word.

He returned the boat to the marina, and they walked home in continued silence, completely content-ed. When they got to Stephen's dock, Nina stretched out her hand.

"Thank you. I had an absolutely fantastic time."

He took her hand but, instead of shaking it, leaned forward on an impulse and kissed her—a soft, long kiss on the lips. She was startled. There had been no hint or warning.

"I should go," she said quietly.

"Of course." He released her and buried his hands deep in his pockets.

The moon shone down on her as she walked back to the Alis' place with her head bowed. When she got to the door, she turned around to see if he was still there. He was.

GEORGE PAYS A VISIT

George was irritated. He tried to find a comfortable position on the hard bench of the motorboat. He wanted to smoke his freshly lit cigarette.

"What do you mean it won't work?" he asked.

Stephen sat with his hand on the tiller and stared sullenly into the distance. It was mid-September. The air was cool, and the vegetation blushed with hints of orange and gold.

"I don't think it's a good idea to approach her," Stephen said without looking at George. He hated cigarette smoke.

"Why not?"

"It just won't work, OK?"

"Would you care to elaborate?" George asked.

He had first met Stephen fifteen years earlier, when he'd bee Stephen's undergraduate advisor at MIT. Stephen had been an arrogant eighteen-year-old, the sole heir to his grandfather's considerable fortune and barely on speaking terms with his mother and siblings. To George's great surprise, Stephen had a first-rate work ethic despite his privileged upbringing; he also possessed a tremendous curiosity and an aggressively competitive personality. While his friends partied most of the semester away, Stephen spent his time in George's office, haranguing him with long discussions on whatever happened to take his fancy at that moment—psychology, poetry, mysticism, philosophy. George, with a canny eye on the future, had indulged him patiently and imposed order on young Stephen's chaotic intellect.

The wind picked up a little. George watched the curling cigarette smoke and shifted his weight on the bench. Stephen pushed his patience to the breaking point like no other agent could. The boat's movement was making him sick. He tried a different tack.

"Look, Stephen, this is the perfect opportunity. We really need a source in India, close to the scene, and I want our own person, damn it! I'm fed up with collaborating with other agencies. There's so much shit flooding in every day. We don't have much time. Nina has access to key border areas in India. She talks routinely to the villagers, who know exactly what's going on but aren't willing to talk to authorities. And she could easily work her way into Sid's confidence. It really can't get any better. Just imagine if we can place her undercover in Pakistan. Wouldn't that be something? We hardly have any women agents there."

"For good reason," Stephen muttered and continued to stare at the horizon. George could see he was headed into one of his black moods where he would go completely off the grid, disappearing at sea and anchoring off a godforsaken beach in the middle of nowhere, doing nothing but reading and swimming.

At their very first meeting, George had sensed Stephen's intensity, his desire to do something of consequence. To *matter*. Upon graduation working for a top-secret intelligence organization was the perfect choice for him. He was naturally reticent, confided in no one, and was quite fearless. And he had a formidable memory. When George had broached the subject of becoming an undercover officer for the CIA at the end of senior year, Stephen had agreed eagerly.

In George's defense he had a great deal of affection for Stephen. He had stepped in when the young man had sorely needed a father figure. In the months after his father's suicide and his grandfather's death, Stephen had had to handle decisions that were far beyond even the most precocious eighteen-year-old.

George had helped him sift through the wreckage and find counsel in the right quarters.

Over the years George had come to realize it was not easy to manage Stephen. The sole heir to the James fortune was imperious and willful and couldn't be made to do anything he didn't want to do. He was reckless and took inordinate risks. And, despite their long history, George could never breach the wall that guarded Stephen's private life. That was how it had been to the present day.

Maybe there was something out of whack on the personal front.

"Stephen, tell me what's wrong."

"Put out that bloody cigarette, will you?" He turned to glare at George, who flicked the cigarette into the water, pleased that Stephen had been goaded out of his silence.

"Look, we've had indications from many independent sources. We need to get to the bottom of it."

Stephen nodded. He knew George was right.

"Let's recap the facts," George continued. "First, Tariq Rehman and your neighbor, Sid Ali, have been very cozy lately. Second, we suspect that Rehman is somehow connected to Zia Akhtar, a bigwig in the world's worst terror network. Third, these three characters are somehow involved in a major attack that is about to happen on the Indian subcontinent, most likely in India."

George paused to light another cigarette but remembered Stephen's admonition and put it back inside the carton.

"Stephen, you know that whatever they pull off in India will be a dress rehearsal for what they want to do here in the United States: coordinated bombings, shooting rampages, airplane hijackings. I think Nina can help us connect the intelligence in India to Sid Ali and Tariq Rehman. You must tell me what makes you hesitate—if there is any inherent flaw in the girl or in the plan."

George sat back and drank from a water bottle without taking his eyes off his protégé. When there was no answer, he continued.

"I know she is not physically tough, and she tends to be too open and trusting. But those are her strengths. Nobody would suspect her. She's a good listener and very likable. Bureaucrats in India cut through formalities and procedures to help her out. She's fearless in her own way. Look, she even spent a whole summer in the jungles of southern India, setting up schools for children of sex workers."

George was getting exasperated but forced himself to speak evenly.

"Stephen, if we can get her into Pakistan undercover, she will be able to reach Pakistani women. Imagine what we could do with that opportunity!"

A willingness to tread questionable ethical ground was the key to George's success—coercion, kidnapping, torture, even assassination. He was a ruthless Louisiana aristocrat who was rumored to have done it all. Stephen had a guilty admiration for the man even though part of him vigorously questioned George's "ends justify the means" approach. In Stephen's opinion Nina wouldn't last an hour out in the field. It was shocking how trusting she was. He had been a total stranger, and she had walked into his house without hesitation just because he had mentioned his collection of orchids.

George looked at him through narrowed eyes. Perhaps Stephen didn't want to deal with Nina for some reason. Maybe he was a closet racist or sexist or both.

He was about to say so when Stephen turned to him and said, "OK. I will try." Without warning, he turned the motorboat around and pointed it toward the shore.

Stephen knew he had no choice. Zia Akhtar was a valuable target: a powerful broker who arranged operations and took care of visas, finances, and fake passports. He oversaw all the complicated logistics of a terror attack. He was the conduit between the high command and foot soldiers. Eliminating him would be a huge blow to the enemy.

But he would never be able to convince George that it would mean needlessly endangering Nina and that she seemed incapable of deceit, the bread and butter of the spy trade. She didn't have the wherewithal to defend herself. George would simply shrug it off as collateral damage and continue with his plan. And he would find other ways to get to her if Stephen didn't agree. He would probably have done the same in George's position. Zia Akhtar was worth risking some serious collateral damage, and, clinically speaking, Nina's safety was relatively insignificant.

George already had visions of her deep undercover in Pakistan in a few years. With her caramel complexion, dark hair, and dark eyes, not to mention her language skills, she'd blend in beautifully in a city like Karachi, where there was a large overlap with the Indian gene pool.

He was puzzled afresh at this uncharacteristic diffidence and lack of enthusiasm on Stephen's part. Something was off, but he couldn't place it. Anyway Stephen had agreed, and that was enough for now.

RECONNAISSANCE

The Newport PATH station in Jersey City was relatively quiet on Tuesday afternoon. A handful of people waited watching the TV monitors that beamed cheery trivia at them. Stephen made his way along the dank platform. He was deep in thought but got distracted for a moment by the gaudy coral and green pillars.

A long escalator disgorged him into the daylight, right in the middle of Jersey City's glass and concrete waterfront. A dense cluster of high-rise buildings towered a few yards away. He entered one of them and, after a brief conversation with the doorman, took the elevator to the twenty-third floor. As expected no one answered the doorbell of apartment 2306. He dumped his gym bag on the floor and leaned against the wall to read his newspaper, prepared for a long wait. Each time the elevator bell chimed, he looked expectantly down the hallway.

Stephen had persuaded himself that his interest in Nina was purely professional, and that he wouldn't get too personally involved–just enough to keep her interested until he found an opportunity to spring the recruiting proposal on her. They had met several times since the sailing date, usually over dinner at the end of the workday. He'd sought her out under the pretext of getting her advice on funding projects in South Asia. She had played along. Neither of them had ever mentioned the word date.

George, on the other hand, had made it clear he would hand the assignment to someone else if Stephen dawdled any longer. Even after agreeing to recruit Nina, Stephen had tried to slow things down and had driven George to exasperated fits of muttering.

But George knew Stephen too well to push him. Instead he subtly pressured Stephen by sending him every scrap of information on Nina he could find. As a result Stephen knew more about her life than perhaps even she did. As he'd read George's little treatise on her habits and routine, he'd become a ghostly presence at her side. He'd stood watch over her when she took the PATH train to Fourteenth Street in Manhattan in the morning; had been her companion while she worked in the office she shared with her Beach Boy coworker; had watched her eat lunch in BigSearch's gourmet cafeteria; had accompanied her home in the evening while she gossiped with her mother on the phone; and had left her safely asleep in her bed in her studio apartment in Jersey City.

Stephen looked at his watch now. It was almost six o'clock in the evening. She should be there any minute. The elevator bell rang, and this time it was Nina. An attractive Indian man in a well-cut suit stood next to her. He was quite tall, taller than Stephen, and was leaning down to listen to her when the elevator doors opened.

Stephen's blood pressure shot up. *Who's this prick?* He bristled. George's folder hadn't said anything about a boyfriend. Why was he standing so close to her?

"Stephen!" Nina exclaimed when she saw him. "What a wonderful surprise."

"Hello, Nina."

She made the introductions. Samir was Nina's neighbor and friend who, if Stephen's reading of his body language were correct, wanted to be more. Nina was either unaware or did not care. She explained enthusiastically how she had met Stephen. Samir and Stephen dutifully shook hands and shared a brief, stilted exchange. Samir stood around for a few seconds longer and then left.

"Come in." Nina smiled at Stephen over her shoulder and opened her apartment door. The place was spacious, with floor-to-ceiling windows that framed views of the Hudson and Lower Manhattan, the Freedom Tower at the center. There was a large painting between the two windows, a small kitchen and a living area to the right and an alcove on the left with a minimalist platform bed.

Nina threw her bag down on the sofa and rushed to the kitchen, saying, "I'll make tea."

Stephen wandered around the apartment while she was busy putting on the kettle. A couple of photos stood on the nightstand by her bed: one with parents and kid brother, another with just the brother on some sort of vacation. In yet another photo, he recognized Amy with Nina. The girls stood smiling in the Caribbean sun.

Nina watched him from the corner of her eye. The summer tan had faded and drained his face of warmth. His gray eyes stared coldly at the world from behind stern, efficient glasses. A dark suit and red tie with a long overcoat draped on his left arm screamed young Republican; all that was missing was the flag pin. He was even more remote and aloof than she remembered, but she was excited to see him in her apartment, among her books and paintings, sliding his long fingers along the top of her sofa.

She had been daydreaming these past few months, thinking of that hot, lovely day at sea when he had so unexpectedly kissed her. Their subsequent dinners had been enjoyable if a bit formal. She'd never felt that sun-fuelled rush again. Which was probably for the best; they had no future together other than a short-lived romance. And *that* was a nuisance she could do without. Nina wanted to find the One and get married—that was it. No complications, no broken heart, no secret longings.

Yet, she hadn't been able to refuse his invitations to dinner each time he had called, even though she had known that his interest in non-profit projects was just an excuse to meet her. And because he had never made any move beyond a friendly peck on the cheek, she had felt quite comfortable going out with him. Perhaps keeping that distance was a deliberate strategy on his part not to spook her, or, who knows, to get *her* to make the first move. Whatever his motive, he had succeeded in occupying her thoughts. Lying in bed at night, she'd imagined how it would be to lie next to him, to feel his skin against hers, to have him come bearing down on her. It had been tough, to push such thoughts away. And today he had appeared outside the elevator doors like a magician, and her feckless heart hadn't stopped racing since.

Stephen continued his examination of the room and soon came face to face with the painting between the two windows. It took him a few moments to realize what it was, and when he did he was stunned. It was vaguely impressionistic in style and measured around four feet by five. A man in a red polo shirt and khaki shorts lay in the center on a pale-blue blanket under a white beach umbrella, his face hidden by a book. A craggy, granite slope rose behind him, bathed in harsh sunlight. White seagulls froze in midflight in the small strip of sky at the top. A flowering vine spread its tendrils over the sand near the man's feet, and a sliver of ocean glimmered a brilliant blue at the extreme right. The artist had done a superb job of capturing the bright, metallic light of that afternoon.

Stephen stood paralyzed in front of the painting. Nina looked up from the kettle and saw his expression. *Good God, what must he think?* She sat down at the table, confused about what to do next. An occasional ding from the elevator floated inside and remained suspended in the quiet stillness of the room.

A slow smile spread across Stephen's austere face. He finally understood the reason for his reluctance to do George's recruiting errand. It had been just an unsettling, amorphous feeling that had never left him since the day he had met Nina. He should have realized it sooner. But this was strange, new terrain for him.

Nina felt deeply embarrassed, and she concentrated on her tea, afraid to look up. She had never expected he would show up at her door unannounced, although she had fantasized about it many times. She wished she had never put up that stupid painting on the wall. But it was really good—her best probably. While time had dulled the intensity of her feelings, that painting, made during the days when her head had still been full of him, was as strident as ever, a naked confession in red, white, and blue.

He walked over and sat down at the table across from her. She pushed a cup of tea toward him. They drank in silence, without looking at each other.

"Want to go for a walk?" A change of scene would break the awkwardness perhaps. She nodded and disappeared behind the double doors next to the bed to change. Stephen returned to the painting, captivated by the colors, enormously pleased that his recently acknowledged feelings were returned in equal measure. But, the specter of George's wrath killed the buzz. What a fucking mess.

It was still light outside but cool. A gusty wind was amplified and channeled by the tall buildings. The riverside promenade was hopping. A predominantly young and South Asian crowd occupied the plaza. People were on their ways home from work or heading out to dinner.

"Do you like it here?" he asked.

"It's OK. My parents want me to live here."

"Why is that? Is it safer than other areas?"

"I guess so. Usually South Asian communities are family oriented. And of course my mom hopes I'll meet a nice Indian boy one day." She laughed.

"Samir?" He stopped and stared at her.

"God, no!" She shook her head. Stephen looked at her for another instant before resuming the walk.

Older people who had come from the Indian sub-continent to visit their children and grandchildren sat on benches. Deprived of their familiar routines and surroundings, stuck inside claustrophobic apartments all day with fussy infants, time passed slowly for them. They complained to each other and compared their return dates. Nannies looked on in boredom as their charges played near the strollers. Young rakes whizzed past in flashy cars with mandatory Bluetooth headsets blinking in their ears.

"This place is so different from where you live," she said.

He nodded absentmindedly.

Nina bit her lip. *How embarrassing.* He had already tuned her out.

But that was not the case. Stephen was grappling with the task of keeping George and Nina in separate compartments so as not to raise George's suspicions or alarm Nina with the truth.

People began to drift indoors as the wind picked up. Unmarred by milling crowds, the views of the sky-line and river opened up. Nina and Stephen sat on a bench by the water with a panoramic night view of the city. A tugboat went past with a graceful arc of lights.

"Something wrong?" she asked after a prolonged stretch of silence. He was deep in thought and stared at the skyline, seemingly oblivious to her presence.

No, nothing's wrong. His conscience was trying to rein him in; that was all. He had become an expert at ignoring it for the greater good, for a higher cause, but he could not use that excuse this time around. It was completely in his selfish interest.

He turned to look at her. She was huddled in her sweatshirt and looked cold.

"It must be past your dinnertime. Let's go in." On the way back to the building, he asked, "Is there anyplace here we can have dinner?"

"Why don't we order in?" It was too late to go wandering around looking for a place to eat. After a brief debate about the virtues of Thai versus Indian, they settled on Indian.

The apartment was bright and warm after the chill of the autumn night. They had fifteen to twenty minutes to kill before their food would arrive. Stephen draped his overcoat and jacket neatly on the sofa, rolled up his tie in a perfect spiral, and tucked it inside the jacket pocket. Nina felt ashamed at having flung her sweatshirt on the chair in the face of such a persnickety demonstration. She picked it up and went to the closet to put it away.

They sat across from each other at the dining table and waited. Nina doodled on a writing pad. Stephen looked at her, trying to compose in his head what he wanted to say and how he wanted to say it. The lamp above shone brightly on her bowed head and the little red flowers she was drawing.

"Oh, I forgot," he said abruptly. "I brought you something."

He took out a large, cardboard package from his gym bag and placed it in front of her. A delicate fragrance seeped out of the box and soon filled the room. Stalks of stargazer lilies, each in a glass tube of water to keep it fresh, lay inside, carefully wrapped.

"They're gorgeous!" Nina filled her lungs with their perfume and looked up at him. "Are they from your greenhouse?"

"Yes, the very last batch of this season."

She located her biggest vase under the kitchen sink and filled it halfway with water. He followed her and leaned against the counter with his hands in his pockets while she clipped the stalks. There was hardly any space between them in that tiny kitchen. Her elbow would touch him if she moved a fraction of an inch to the left. Even though she couldn't see his face, she knew he was looking at her.

"I came here today to apologize in person for not calling sooner. It's been almost a month since we last spoke," he said before his conscience could get the upper hand. *Don't do it. Don't drag her into the mess. Do the right thing. Walk away*, it tried to interject.

"I didn't call either." Did he really think that she'd been sitting around waiting for him to call?

"Why didn't you?" He looked at her head bent over the sink. She had stuck a pencil in the twisted rope of her hair to hold it in place.

"I don't know."

She straightened up to put the flowers in the vase and juggle them into position. Bright-orange pollen smudged her nose and cheek like clumsily applied makeup.

He stretched out a finger and wiped the pollen off her cheek.

Just then the doorbell rang. Nina ran to open it. Stephen heard her talking to the delivery boy in Hindi. She returned with two big bags of food and placed them on the table.

"Could you please get the plates from the cabinet behind you?" She busied herself with unpacking the food.

Stephen brought the plates over to her. She was struggling to get the lid off a plastic container. A graceful tendril had escaped from her knotted hair and curled on the nape of her neck. He couldn't resist any more. He slid the pencil out of her hair. Without the restraint, the thick, coiled mass tumbled down and fell forward. It was precariously close to the food. He gathered it back gently and turned her to face him.

"May I?" he asked and, before she could answer, pulled her close and kissed her.

THE CALL

"Are you serious?" Amy asked. Nina, who took umbrage if a guy sat too close. The ice princess who had fended off the attentions of eager young men since her first and only boyfriend had dumped her in college.

Amy and Nina sat at a picnic table in Central Park, but their lunch remained untouched. Dog walkers, skaters, Frisbee players, bicyclists, runners, strollers—the sea of Manhattan humanity rose and ebbed around them. Cars whizzed by on Fifth Avenue. Nina had just recounted last night's surreal happening.

"I don't know. You're the one who encouraged me." Nina reached for the potato chips.

"I know, but I encouraged you to go on a date, not invite him inside your apartment and jump into bed with him. That's a big leap." Amy bit into her veggie wrap. "He could be a serial killer or a pervert. You know nothing about him. Other than that he's handy with the Zagat survey and has philanthropic aspirations."

"I trust him."

"Why?" Amy worried about Nina's reckless behavior. Her friend had been cautious to the point of paralysis ever since her breakup during their sophomore year in college. Besides, Stephen was not the classic Nina type: soulful, poetry quoting, literary—your typical brainy engineering nerd. He was a supercilious, overprivileged layabout who whiled away his time puttering around his precious boats. At least that was the impression Amy had gotten from Sid.

She had thought it was safe for Nina to go out with Stephen because the chance of any long-term success was quite low. Nina needed to get out of her little world, and Stephen seemed as good a candidate as any to help her with that. Amy had been surprised when Stephen and Nina continued to meet after the girls had returned from their visit to the Alis. But, to the best of her knowledge, *nothing* had happened so far. Nina would have told her if there had been any interest.

According to Nina's own account, the dates were quite uneventful—dinners at stuffy restaurants, lengthy discussions of funding non-profit projects, debates about politics, with occasional digressions to talk about books and museums. Amy had fully expected the connection between Nina and Stephen to follow Nina's usual dating pattern and fizzle out in a few weeks when Nina rebuffed the inevitable sexual advances. There had been absolutely nothing to presage last night's shocking episode.

Now she really regretted having pushed Nina into Stephen's arms. This man had mesmerized her. He must have had some secret agenda, or he was just cruelly taking advantage of her friend's trusting nature.

"When are you supposed to see him next?" Amy asked.

"He said he would call tonight."

Amy frowned at her. "Call me if you need to talk."

Nina nodded. Her confidence wavered under Amy's interrogation. Amy saw the look on her face and gave her friend an affectionate hug.

"Don't worry. It'll be fine."

Later that evening Nina walked from work to the Fourteenth Street PATH station. Normally she would have enjoyed the bustle of the Chelsea neighborhood, the busy cafés and delis, the young and the hip at their stylish best, even the never-ending roadwork. But today none of them made an impression on her. She walked with her head down, with just one thought in her mind: Why hadn't he called? *Why* hadn't he called?

The station was packed with homebound throngs carrying shopping bags, groceries, laptops, backpacks, babies, and briefcases. A young man played the clarinet. His instrument case was open at his feet. Nina stopped for a few seconds to listen to him, but the music couldn't divert her mind from Stephen and his silence. She looked at her cell phone for the hundredth time. She would be quite disappointed if the call didn't materialize. She checked again when she got off the train at Newport. Nothing.

The apartment was dark and cold. She switched on the lights and looked at the mail—all junk and bills, nothing personal. Who wrote letters anyway? People could barely write. She chucked the envelopes on the coffee table and wondered what to do. The gym! That would be the best way to get all this nonsense out of her head.

The gym bustled with energy and activity. Sweaty people puffed and pumped. She worked out halfheartedly on an elliptical machine. She had deliberately left her phone at home, and now it drew her like an evil magnet. There was no way to resist it; she might as well go home. When she got there, the phone was as unhelpful as ever. It revealed no new information, no missed calls, no voicemail, and no text messages.

Nina forced herself to get up from the sofa, change into her favorite cotton nightdress, and warm up leftovers in preparation for a marathon binge-watching of

BBC's six hour production of *Pride and Prejudice*. This was her pacifier, a surefire remedy to calm her down. The costumes, the scenery, the diction, the dialogue—she loved every bit of it.

She dozed off on the couch hugging her big, puffy pillow. It was around four thirty in the morning when she woke with her heart pounding. There was a loud knocking on the apartment door. The TV screen was aglow with Mr. Darcy and Elizabeth Bennett reconciling on the English moors. She turned off the TV, gathered her nightgown around her, and went to the door with her cell phone in hand.

"Who is it?" she asked loudly.

"It's Stephen."

She looked through the peephole. The hallway lights shed a creepy yellow glow on him and glinted off the rim of his glasses.

"Please, open the door. I need to talk to you."

How on Earth had he gotten past the doorman? She opened the door and stood aside. Stephen strode in, paused to look at her, and sat down hard on the corner armchair. She hesitated and wondered if she should change out of her threadbare nightgown or at least find her robe.

"Please, sit down." He pointed to the sofa. "We need to talk."

He was on edge and in no mood for pleasantries or formalities. It was a cold night, and he had spent the last four hours wandering around windswept Manhattan to make sure George's hounds couldn't track him down.

Stephen waited impatiently for Nina. She sat down. Her legs were a little unsteady from being startled out of a deep sleep.

He looked at her as if for the first time. Her nightgown looked soft and white, with tiny roses faded and frayed under the assault of a hundred washes. Thin spaghetti straps showed off her shoulders and long arms. She was flustered by his stare and demurely pulled the hem down over her knees.

The minutes ticked by, and he didn't say a word. She looked at him in vexation. What was he up to? He looked different. For one, he sported a fresh haircut, the curls cropped close to his head. That gave him a younger but more ascetic look, the gaunt lines of his cheeks and jaw more prominent than ever. Dressed in a dark sports jacket, a starched white shirt, and dark pants, with his shoes shined to a dazzle, he looked ready to party.

"You're all dressed up," she said.

He got up from the chair and went over to sit on the coffee table in front of her. He felt calmer now, after a very trying day of self-examination and reevaluation. A momentous day. How should he begin?

"Let's get married. This Saturday."

Nina looked up at him sharply. She was about to say this was no time for stupid jokes when he reached for her hand and slipped a ring on her finger. It was warm from being in his fist and glinted with a spectral light.

She looked at it in shock. She had to be dreaming. But his hands were real, cool from the night, with strong fingers that squeezed hers to stop them from trembling. He raised her hand to his cheek and closed his eyes—an uncharacteristic display.

After several minutes, when she hadn't said a word, he opened his eyes. Nina looked bewildered. The strap on her nightgown was twisted. He straightened it out and let his hand slide slowly down her shoulder and arm, arriving at her newly adorned finger.

It was a silver rolling ring with three interlocking rings. Nina stared at it in disbelief.

"I made it when I was seventeen." He remembered it well. His parents had fought like savages, and he'd been the constant witness. His two older siblings had long ago disappeared from home. His grandfather had accused them of not being his son's children and threatened to disinherit them. It had been a miserable time. Stephen had made the ring in metal shop in school, hammering away at it to chase away his unhappiness.

And after all these years, fate had brought this strange girl into his life. He could think of nothing but wanting to spend every minute with her.

"You made this?" she asked.

"I ask you to marry me, and you ask whether I made the ring." He wanted to make her laugh and relax. She looked shell-shocked, and her voice was barely audible as she tried to find her composure.

"It's beautiful."

"Does that mean yes?" He moved closer and rested his forehead on hers.

"We hardly know each other."

"Even after last night?"

Nina stared wordlessly at her fingers imprisoned in his hand. He ran his index finger along her jaw and lifted her chin to make her look at him. She brushed off his hand.

During the course of his self-examination, when he had tried to trace back to when the idea had begun to take shape in his head, he had arrived at that instant atop the lighthouse, standing next to her, when he had heard the tentative knock of long-lost happiness.

"Why? Why did you choose me? Why not Samir?" he insisted.

She had no reply. He answered for her.

"Because you cannot be with someone you don't respect, someone who is intimidated by you and for whom you have to pretend to be less than what you are."

"I am not that special." She frowned and turned away.

"Rubbish! Your good friend, Samir, eats his heart out for you, yet you barely look at him when he talks."

"Not true." How dare he comment on her behavior toward Samir?

"Completely true. I watched you yesterday when you stepped out of the elevator with him. You were bored to tears. Your face lit up when you saw me."

She didn't say anything. He pressed his advantage.

"The Samirs of the world don't have a chance. You would rather be alone than waste your time in such company."

The closer he was to the truth, the angrier she got. She wanted to get up, but there was no way of getting past him; his knees blocked her. He was very animated now, bubbling with mischief and fun—quite the change from his usual air of cynical detachment.

"You're afraid you'll be sucked into the ordinariness of his life, one day exactly like the next. Samir has nothing to offer you, and you know it, my dear Nina." He said her name with such sweetness that she got goose bumps.

Nina racked her brain for a comeback but failed to find one. She glared at him, which made him smile even more.

He got up to stretch his legs. Nina took the opportunity to escape from the sofa and walk over to the window. The Empire State Building glowed against the dark sky. He came over and stood next to her.

"I offer you my respect and loyalty and to support you in whatever you do. There's so much good we can do. You know it better than I. And it would be much more fun to do it together than to do it alone."

It was an oddly pragmatic proposal with no mention of love or hearts, almost like a corporate mission statement. Nina, being somewhat odd as well, found it appealing. If he had said, "I'm madly in love with you. I cannot live without you," she would have dismissed him right away on grounds of insincerity.

"Why this Saturday? That's the day after tomorrow."

"What's the point of waiting? Doesn't your culture frown upon living in sin?"

He smiled because she had said so during one of their dinner dates. Her mother had brought her up with very orthodox values where dating was concerned. It wasn't unusual in the South Asian community.

They went back and forth for another hour:

"I have to tell my parents. I'm very close to my family."

"Of course. Let's call them now."

"But I need time to prepare them."

"Let's go right now and see them. Why wait around?"

"My parents can't plan a wedding in two days."

"Here's an idea: why don't we have a civil wedding on Saturday and then you can take your time preparing your parents?"

"That's crazy!"

And so on until finally he threw up his hands. "Nina, why are you stalling? Tell me what's stopping you."

The building stirred with the early morning symphony of running water, flushing toilets, and elevator chimes. Eager joggers and workout maniacs were headed out.

Stephen and Nina were both exhausted.

They looked at each other for a long time, she with anxiety and he with longing, locked in silent communion.

She hardly knew him. But all she could think was yes. She could not resist the hypnotic man standing in front of her.

He waited with his hands in his pockets. His eyes never left her face. Stephen had an aggressive determination—a winning trait of robber barons—and when he wanted something, there was hardly anyone or anything that could stop him. Poor Nina. She had no chance against such an overwhelming force of persuasion.

As if propelled by his will, she stepped up to him, stood on tiptoe, and whispered in his ear, "Fine."

Even as he gathered her in his arms, his conscience interrupted. *This is not fair. She doesn't know the truth. You must tell her. Tell her the whole truth at once!*

But he paid no attention to it. He was happy beyond words in the warmth of her embrace.

COUNSEL

Stephen was on his way back from Nina's apartment, speeding down the scenic highway, hoping he hadn't tripped up and left a trail for George's minions. His immediate concern was getting the wedding out of the way without alerting them, or George would do whatever it took to stop it. Luckily Nina too wanted to keep things quiet until she had an opportunity to break the news to her parents. He had to be careful and not do anything stupid before Saturday.

He parked his car in the garage and stopped to talk to the groundskeeper, who was in the tool shed nearby. Apparently there was a gentleman waiting for him on the porch. Had to be George. For the first time, Stephen was worried.

He ran up the house's steps. George was settled back in a chair on the sweeping porch, staring at the dock and the ocean beyond, his newspaper neatly folded on his lap. Mrs. Brown was in the process of clearing away a coffee tray.

"May I get you some coffee, Mr. James?" she asked. Stephen shook his head. The two men waited until she was out of earshot.

George took Stephen in—the sharp outfit, shiny shoes, and tired eyes with a hint of bags under them.

"Out partying?"

"Yes," Stephen replied without looking at him. He was quite certain George had had him followed.

"How did it go?" George watched Stephen sit down and take off his shoes and throw them in a corner— quite out of character for the obsessively orderly young man.

"Well enough. Things might move faster than I thought." He sat back in his chair and fixed George with a cold stare.

George knew that look well. It said, "Back off." George let him get away with it because Stephen was very good at what he did and would do it no other way. But George had made his expectations clear at their last meeting: Stephen had two more weeks to recruit Nina. And one week was almost up.

His guess was there must have been a setback, but Stephen was too egotistical to admit it.

"How is Nina?"

"She's fine."

"Have you asked her?"

"No."

"Do you think she'll agree?"

"I don't *know*, George."

George ran the South Asia desk for the CIA, and hoped that one day Stephen would take over. In fact, he had higher, much higher ambitions, for his young friend. Stephen was the perfect presidential candidate—from the right stock with the right connections. But the trajectory from an undercover agent to the highest office in the land had to be meticulously planned and executed. And, that's exactly what George intended to do on Stephen's behalf.

"Anyway, I was just passing by on my way to the campus. I thought I'd drop in and see how things were going." Particularly since Stephen hadn't bothered to return his calls in two days.

"Thanks, George." Stephen stood up.

"Where were you, Stephen? Where was this party?" George ignored the invitation to leave.

"Nowhere."

"When are you going to ask her?"

"You gave me a deadline, George. Have I ever missed one?" Stephen shook his head in exasperation.

George rose to his feet. He allowed Stephen liberties for which he would fire others. Why? Because he needed Stephen. The final stage of his career hinged on Stephen Edward James III.

"Something wrong?" George asked while he buttoned his overcoat. Stephen was more standoffish than usual. He was either lying or hiding something.

"No, nothing." Stephen shook George's hand. He need not have worried—while George suspected there was something amiss, he never would have dreamed of anything even remotely close to the truth. His conjecture was that Stephen had difficulty connecting with Nina and was not sufficiently confident of her reaction to broach the subject of her working for the CIA.

George put on his hat and walked down the porch steps. He turned around when he reached his car and waved to Stephen.

With great relief Stephen waved back and watched him get into his car and drive away.

Amy and Jeff had invited Nina to dinner at their place. Jeff had just returned after a long absence, and Nina hadn't wanted to infringe on the couple's precious time together, but they had insisted.

Amy had been chewing off Jeff's ear with her commentary on Nina's strange and reckless saga. That morning Nina had called to announce that she and Stephen were getting married in two days, and she wanted them to be the witnesses at the civil ceremony. And no one, not even her family, was to know. Despite Jeff's protests Amy wanted to talk her out of it.

Amy and Jeff had a small apartment on the Upper West Side with a great view of the Hudson River. They were a happy couple. Jeff was the perfect foil to Amy's boisterous personality. She bullied and mothered him, just like she did Nina. He played along most of the time but reined her in when she lost all sense of proportion—as she was on the verge of doing on this occasion.

The doorbell rang. Nina walked in all smiles. "Hi, Jeff. Hi, Amy."

Jeff, perpetually sunburned from his trips, was dressed in dramatic black. He had thick, black hair, bright eyes, and a sparkling smile. His facial hair had gone through every possible incarnation from mustache to beard to goatee to Vandyke to soul patch.

Nina and Jeff had an easy relationship. He seemed to be able to say the most outrageous things to her with a straight face and not offend her.

"You look uncommonly happy today, Nina. Anything I should know?" Jeff asked.

"Just that I'm getting married."

Nina beamed at both of them, unable to hide her excitement. Jeff gave her a big hug. He was happy to see her looking so lively. She was a big part of Amy's life and, therefore, his.

During dinner Jeff entertained the women with stories of the strange characters he met on his trips as a professional wildlife photographer. He was a natural raconteur with a remarkable ability to recreate the atmosphere of any place with his words. He populated his narrative with characters, sounds, and smells. The two women listened, entranced like little children.

After dinner they pored over the photos on his MacBook while they sat in front of the fake fireplace and ate almond cookies Amy had baked. The photographs were, of course, spectacular, but as he explained, each photo represented hours and days of patient waiting in the heat, in the rain, surrounded by poisonous insects, while danger lurked under every rock and behind every bush. But he loved every minute of it. Once in a while, he tried to convince Amy to accompany him, but she couldn't live without a bed and a clean bathroom—unheard of luxuries in the places to which he travelled.

The conversation slowed down after a while.

"OK, guys, you can give me the sermon now," Nina said.

Amy looked at Jeff, but he hesitated. It was rude to interfere in Nina's personal life.

"It's fine, Jeff. I know you're concerned. Tell me why."

He continued to look uncomfortable. Amy poked him in the ribs to get him going.

"I would like to say up front," he said, "that Stephen is a good man. I know him from sailing and squash."

Jeff paused and smiled at Nina. She smiled in return but her heart skipped a beat with apprehension. She wondered what he'd say next.

"I like the fact that even though he comes from extreme privilege, he doesn't wear it on his sleeve." He picked up a cookie, examined it and put it down. "However, there is one thing I find troubling," he turned to Nina, "and it's not a reflection on you in any way. I probably know more about him than most people, having seen him regularly at the sailing club. You're unlike any girl he's dated in the past. Over the last fifteen years, I've seen him with three different women: all archetypal WASPs, typically blond, daughters of senators, members of DAR, Harvard Law, and so on. I thought he'd marry one of them and run for president one day. You are such an outlier. What do you two have in common? Why do you like him? Why do you think he likes you?"

Amy was taken aback by Jeff's bluntness.

Nina tugged at the cushion on her lap. She struggled to find words. "I can only speak for myself. I admire the fact that he's willing to make such a huge commitment. That he knows what he wants, that he's decisive and doesn't wait around for permission from others. Others have professed their love to me over the years, but no one has ever stepped up to commit to anything, not even dinner with my parents." That was a dig at Samir. "Yet here's a man who has known me just a few months and knows he wants to be with me for life."

"You want to marry him because you're flattered that he asked you?" Jeff said.

Amy interrupted. "No. She wants to marry him because she slept with him. You don't have to, Nina. Things have changed since the 60's."

"Don't be silly, Amy. Anyway, you have it backward. The reason I was comfortable being with him was because I felt we had a future together. The thought of marriage *had* crossed my mind. Of course, I didn't think it would happen this soon."

"Being with him!" Amy rolled her eyes at Nina's euphemism for sex.

Nina ignored her and continued. "And Jeff, no, it wasn't flattery. I genuinely like him. He's a lot of fun even though he has had such a lonely life. I never get bored in his company. And, I have the greatest respect for the fact that he's a productive human being and doesn't sponge off the wealth of his family."

"Big deal," Amy said.

"Come on, Amy, give credit where it's due. It would've been so easy for him to coast on his inheritance. But he chose to put his energies into studying and building an engineering company. Don't you find that admirable? I do."

Amy sighed. Academic credentials were Nina's blind spot, she could never see beyond them. It was an Asian trait inherited from her parents—nobody with good academic standing could be a bad person.

"And I love being with him. He's very sweet and considerate."

Jeff stared at her. He could not imagine associating the word "sweet" with Stephen, who would probably die of embarrassment if he heard himself described in that manner.

Nina continued, unaware of the effects of her words. "I hope what Stephen sees in me is a partner who shares similar values and can make life more interesting and enjoyable. I can't think of any other motive, can you?"

She looked from Amy to Jeff and back to Amy.

"Nina, aren't you afraid your parents will disapprove?" Amy asked.

"I don't want to think about it now. They'll come around eventually."

Amy shook her head. Why was Nina rushing in without her parents' blessing, without even telling them about it? Was she worried that they would object to her marrying outside the Indian community, that she would actually have to defy them to marry Stephen, and she didn't have the courage to do that?

Jeff had other questions. "But why the secrecy and hurry? Why doesn't he want anyone to know about the wedding? Why a civil ceremony?"

"The secrecy is my doing. I don't want my parents to find out and go crazy. I'll tell them in the next couple of weeks. I'm too overwhelmed right now. I can't deal with the endless debate, discussions, and arguments that will surely happen."

"And the hurry? Why is he in such a hurry?"

Nina shrugged. "I don't know. I think it's some quaint notion of chivalry—to make a respectable woman of me."

Amy looked at her. Maybe he's worried Nina might change her mind and foil whatever strange plans he had. How he had managed to have so much influence over Nina in such a short time? Nina was easygoing but certainly not docile, and when she felt strongly about something there was nothing anyone could do to convince her otherwise. But there she was, doing Stephen's bidding without thinking about her parents or the consequences.

She could not to let Stephen alienate Nina from her. He had to be a very controlling man; how else could he get Nina to do all these insane things? But right now all she could do was pray. Because by tomorrow morning, Nina's fate would be inextricably tied to his, and nothing that Amy could say or do would matter.

SIGNED, SEALED, DELIVERED

Stephen was to drive down from Massachusetts on Friday night and stay with Jeff in New York City. They had to be at City Hall early next morning.

Amy was already in Nina's apartment in Jersey City, to have one last chance to make sense of the puzzling situation. Nina was in a trance, alternately happy and anxious but mostly excited.

They stayed up most of the night. They giggled as they recounted their teenage years and all the boys they'd had secret crushes on, high school romances that never materialized. Amy was glad she could be a part of Nina's day tomorrow because she knew that Nina sorely missed her parents and her brother, Neel. This was the most important event in Nina's life, and she had chosen to exclude the people she loved most. Amy could not understand why it had to be this way.

Nina kept repeating: it is for the best, it is for the best. Maybe she was worried that a delay would cause the whole thing to unravel, but why was she so taken with Stephen?

"Nina, my love, are you sure you want to go through with this? There's still time to change your mind."

Nina nodded. "Yes! Absolutely! Amy, you know me. I don't compromise. I don't settle. Not even while buying a dress. Why would I be any less picky while choosing a husband?"

Amy wasn't sure.

"Stephen understands what I want to do with my life. He doesn't think I am showing off when I talk about my projects, nor does he feel threatened by my ambition. I know it sounds arrogant but that's how I used to feel on those dates with other men."

Amy pursed her lips.

"Amy, you *have* to believe me."

"Then why didn't you tell your parents?"

"Because, dear Amy, while *I* know I have the right man, convincing my parents is going to take a whole lot longer. I can't even convince you!" Nina laughed.

And suddenly it struck Amy: Stephen had courted Nina very shrewdly—with subtle flattery to appeal to her self-image as an intelligent and ambitious woman, and by cultivating her bookishly like a Jane Austen hero until she was impatient to be made love to.

She arranged the pillows on the sofa and lay down, pulled the blanket around her, and turned to Nina. "I hope you know what you're doing. But remember that no matter what happens, Jeff and I are always there for you." She blew a kiss to Nina. "Good night, old friend."

When Amy finally fell asleep on the couch, Nina got out of bed and went to sit on the windowsill. The river looked beautiful, reflecting the city lights. If only the clock would move faster—she could put all this angst behind her once and for all. Once it was done, she could not feel guilty about not calling her mother and telling her everything, about not asking her family to show up at city hall. At this moment, though, the window of opportunity was still open, and every passing minute required an effort on her part to fight the guilt and not make that call.

Friday evening traffic was its usual snarled mess. By the time Stephen arrived at Jeff and Amy's, it was well past ten at night. Stephen and Jeff had a late dinner. The two men did not have much to say to each other—mostly small talk about the weather, politics, and sports. They talked a little about their sailing days. Soon Stephen rose from the table saying he was tired and wanted to go to sleep. Jeff showed him to the guest bedroom and went back to the kitchen to clean up.

While he washed the dishes, Jeff pondered how best to approach the task with which his wife had charged him. It went against his better judgment, but he felt he owed it to Nina. After he finished putting the kitchen in order, he knocked on Stephen's door. It flew open to reveal Stephen in an unusual state of discomposure. He had changed into pajamas; his hair was disheveled and his face flushed. It seemed as though he had been clutching his head.

Jeff knew that expression. *Cold feet.*

He was wrong. Stephen was afflicted by guilt, not cold feet. He was about to drag Nina into a difficult, violent, and dangerous life and didn't have the courage to tell her. It was unfair, and she was too trusting to suspect him of deception. But he couldn't tell her because he couldn't take the chance of jeopardizing his own happiness. He needed her. If she knew the truth, she would either refuse outright to marry him or at least want to wait and think about it. He couldn't afford the delay, not with George breathing down his neck.

Without preamble Jeff asked, "Why do you want to marry Nina?"

He thought Stephen would politely tell him to fuck off. But he didn't. He waved Jeff into the room. Jeff sat on the bench at the foot of the bed while Stephen stood near the window and looked out.

"Jeff, you probably know me as well as anyone. I am not impulsive. But for the first time in my life, I can think of no reason except that I really want to."

He paused to look for Jeff's reaction. When none was in evidence, he continued.

"Long ago I read somewhere that man and woman are the two halves of a monster. They spend their lives looking for the other half and are not at peace until the monster is made whole. Well, that is Nina and me. The minute I saw her, the monster was made whole. There was no escape for either of us. I can't stop thinking of her."

Jeff looked at him in surprise. What an odd analogy. Monster, escape—were these the words of a man about to marry the woman he claimed was the love of his life? Stephen paced the tiny room, pausing now and then to look at Jeff, who listened intently.

"I know that Amy and you are worried. I can assure you this is not an idle whim. I have never been married or engaged. I am not in the habit of doing this sort of thing. I will do everything in my capacity to keep Nina safe and happy."

Safe? The word jarred on Jeff's ears. Another odd word choice, when there were so many beautiful words to choose from: passion, magic, fire, love, poetry, desire. How come none of those came to his lips?

Jeff watched him closely. Stephen was uncharacteristically worked up. There was no questioning the genuineness of his emotion. But what was that emotion? Was it love? Lust? There was some of that for sure. But there was something else buried several layers beneath. It was as though this was some abstract, intellectual exercise in the service of a grand goal, and he and Nina were actors in that drama. Whatever he was orchestrating, it was clear Stephen was not entirely forthcoming about his motives. What was he up to?

"Do you love her?" Jeff asked.

Stephen looked uncertain. "What is love? Is it blind infatuation? I'm too practical for that. What I do know..." He paused. "What I do know is that I feel easy and happy when I'm with Nina."

By the time he finished the sentence, his face was red, and he couldn't bear to look at Jeff.

Jeff smiled. Nina was right after all. Stephen *was* quite romantic. Who would have thought?

But with a straight face, he warned, "I have to tell you—Nina takes this seriously. She has very strong notions of marriage and believes that it's a lifelong commitment. I hope you understand that. It's not something to be terminated once the fun goes out. I know I sound like a pompous uncle, but I owe it to Nina to say this to you."

Stephen had recovered his composure by then. He stopped his pacing and sat down next to Jeff on the bench.

"Why are you in such a hurry to get married anyway?" Jeff asked. "Why don't you move in together or continue to see each other until the two of you are sure this is what you want?"

Stephen's face took on a sly, mischievous look. He echoed Jeff's words. "What can I say? I have very strong notions of marriage as well. I believe that if you like someone enough to live together, you should be able to commit to getting married."

THE WEDDING

N ina was the perfect bride—elegant, pretty, and nervous. Stephen looked sharp in his smartly tailored suit and trim haircut. He held Nina's hand tightly with her arm under his. They made a striking couple, he pale and erect in dark attire, she a dusky apparition, shimmering in her white-silk sari with a fiery-red border. Jeff, in his customary all-black ensemble, stood to Stephen's left while Amy, in a red *salwaar kameez*, flanked Nina on the right. The municipal clerk checked the license and identification documents. The judge read a brief pronouncement, inquired whether the bride and groom were willing, and pronounced them man and wife. He concluded with a cursory "you may kiss the bride" and waited impatiently for the next pair of matrimonial hopefuls. Just another Saturday at city hall.

The two couples tumbled out into the sunshine, onto the barricaded steps of the beautiful old building in Manhattan. Stephen and Nina sported shiny gold bands that Jeff and Amy had given them as gifts. Amy was busy snapping photos with her little camera.

Jeff nudged her aside. "Let the pro do it, sweetheart." Off came his backpack, and out his equipment. He clicked away at lightning speed—move right, closer, yes, yes, that's great.

"We need to leave," Amy said at last. "We'll be late for our lunch reservation."

Jeff put away his equipment, zipped up his backpack, and looked up. He stopped, riveted by the scene in front of him. Damn. What a shot.

Nina was awash in sunlight while she adjusted the folds of her sari. Stephen stood on the step behind her with his hands in his pockets, a picture of casual elegance. But it was the expression on his face that caught Jeff's eye. Stephen stood looking at Nina with a helpless tenderness—a look full of love, longing, and cutting sadness. It filled Jeff with an unreasonable fear. What made Stephen so sad?

Amy was also studying the couple closely. This was the first time she had seen them together. Nina looked deliriously happy; her smile alone could light up the entire city. She kept stealing looks at her new husband, who couldn't stop smiling either—a miracle for a guy whose normal look was one of prim superiority. He had not taken his eyes off of Nina from the time they had first seen each other in front of city hall that morning.

I hope this works out, Amy prayed. *I hope they're always this happy. I hope he is everything Nina deserves, and I hope he never hurts her in any way.*

They piled into a taxi. Jeff sat in front with the driver. Nina was sandwiched between the two people she loved dearly. Stephen was still holding her hand hostage.

Although it was the first time that Stephen and Nina were together in public, they were neither self-consciously shy nor unnaturally bright. Stephen was relaxed and charming; he spoke fluently about a wide variety of topics and smiled constantly. This was completely new to Jeff, and he wasn't sure that he liked such a 180-degree turn in personality. Then again, who was Jeff to begrudge this groom his happiness? It was his wedding day. He had married the woman he loved and had every right to be happy.

When it was time to go their separate ways, Nina and Amy were locked in a tearful embrace. Jeff too was unusually emotional in his good-bye. He gave Nina a big hug.

"We are here for you," he said quietly, so only she could hear. "You can call us anytime, anywhere, for any reason big or small. Don't hesitate to call us if you're in trouble."

Nina was puzzled. Why would she be in trouble?

Amy was more direct with Stephen. "Take good care of Nina, or you'll have to answer to me."

"Yes, ma'am," Stephen replied with affected courtesy.

"You're a very lucky man, Stephen James, to marry Nina."

"I know." He shook her hand without a smile.

The cars headed in opposite directions, with Nina and Amy waving to each other until they were out of view.

Stephen and Nina arrived late that evening at his home. They passed through the orchid atrium; climbed past the second floor, which had once housed Stephen's parents and their three growing children; and went up to the third floor, which Grandfather James had used. Stephen occupied it now, all three thousand square feet. The master suite stretched across the rear half of the house and overlooked the garden below as well as the dock and the ocean in the distance.

Nina was intimidated by the scale of everything: the high ceilings, large rooms that could contain multiples of her entire apartment, but most of all the huge canopy bed—it was five feet high, and she wouldn't be able to get on without a running start. This was Stephen's home, his domain, where he was the undisputed lord and master. She could see it in him—the immediate sense of authority and belonging and the strength he drew from it. He seemed to grow more powerful with every minute he spent in the house.

Stephen showed Nina around.

"Here is the bathroom…and here is your part of the closet."

"*Closet?* I can fit my whole apartment into it!"

"Here's the living room, and there, across the atrium, that's my office and workshop. It runs all along the front of the house. You can see it tomorrow."

As it was quite late, they got ready for bed. While he leaned against the bathroom doorway to watch her brush her teeth, their eyes met in the mirror, and they were both overcome by a sudden awkwardness. He went away and lay down on the bed while she finished.

Nina climbed onto the bed with some effort, even with the help of the wooden stepstool Stephen had placed at her side of the bed. That made him laugh, and he watched her with a smile as she navigated the expanse of bed between them to arrive—squeaky clean and sparkling—at his side.

She sat cross-legged, like a Girl Scout ready for a story by the campfire, and asked, "Is that your grandfather's portrait above the mantel?"

Thus began the longest conversation of Stephen's life. He talked more in the following hours than he ever had before. He spoke naturally, as if they had done this every night, the two of them. He lay on his back with his hands clasped under the back of his head on that extravagant, plush bed and looked up at Nina. He spoke about his childhood, about the things he and his grandfather had done together, how his grandfather had inspired him, and how Stephen had spent all his waking hours with him.

"My grandfather took me everywhere with him anytime I was out of school. He taught me how to ride a bike, how to ride a horse, how to sail, how to shoot, how to tie my tie…"

Nina leaned forward to hear him better. She listened with her entire body, asking an occasional question that opened yet another door. He must have missed his grandfather so much, and there was no one to fill that vacuum for him. Each time she looked into his eyes that night, she saw something new: pain, hurt, anger, bitterness, sorrow, innocence—emotions that were accustomed to visiting him at that hour in that bed, returning now out of habit. He was surprised by the torrent that poured out of him like a noisy, racing brook, calm when it flowed through flatland but angry and foaming when it hit rocks.

At last he stopped, exhausted and empty, wondering how many hours he had been going on. Nina must have been bored, but when he came out of his trance and looked at her, she was as attentive as ever, her face a mirror of his feelings.

She wasn't bored at all. She wanted to know everything about him and familiarize herself with every nook of his lonely life. She had sensed the depth of that sadness during their very first meeting, and now she wanted to share with him the affection and unqualified support she had received so abundantly from her family. She smoothed the curls off his forehead and, along with them, the little furrow on his brow.

"It's OK. I'm here to share it, whatever it is. You are not alone." She smiled her infectious smile, and the old demons that were so entrenched in Stephen's head went into hiding, unable to stand up to its warmth and brightness.

He smiled back at her. "I'm in your hands now. Do what you want with me. I'm tired of being in charge, being responsible, running the show, planning, doing, striving, struggling. I am tired. I need a rest, and I need you to take control of me."

He *was* tired. At the age of eighteen, he had been left to handle the aftermath of his father's and grandfather's deaths, barely days apart—the lawyers, relatives, hangers-on, hustlers, and shysters that had tried to take advantage of a vulnerable, inexperienced youth and the stream of flattering, silver-tongued women attracted to his fortune. And the day just a few months ago, when Stephen had come across Nina on his garden bench, he had been truly tired after all the years of going it alone, carrying the world on his shoulders, keeping the wheels moving. Even as he plotted to start his new operation on the Indian subcontinent, he could feel the claws of that tiredness dig into his chest and pull him down, with loneliness hard on its heels.

That day, when Nina had listened to his impulsive confession about his family's history, she had looked at him with an instinctive empathy. That look that had ignited a spark in him that had grown into a five-alarm fire by the time they had returned from the sailing trip. He had watched over it and analyzed it for four long weeks, curious to see if it would die down or change, but it hadn't. He needed her and had pursued her with an absurd single-mindedness. And now she was here, right next to him, all his to have and to hold, 'til death would they part.

Nina fell asleep with her head on his shoulder. Out of habit he fell into a quiet conversation with the portrait of Grandfather James, lit by the dim nightlight.

"Here I am, Grandfather, a married man. I remember those long, dark nights—too many of them—when I lay on this bed and looked up at you, drained by the incessant gnawing of loneliness. I despaired that all life had to offer was an endless succession of minutes, hours, and days filled with striving and purpose but in the end devoid of any meaning. If I were to stop breathing, I wondered, would I be missed? No matter how hard I looked, there was no one bright enough to light up my world day after day, no one worthy of sharing this bed, this room, this home, my body, my mind, my life. Until now."

"Grandfather, I married Nina a few hours ago, this woman asleep next to me on your bed. I think she cares for me. I think she will make me happy. I wish you could meet her. You would like her. You would see beyond the color of her skin, unlike the others in our family. Please, give me a sign. I want to know that you approve."

It was almost dawn when Stephen woke to the sound of birds chirping in the trees outside the windows to the balcony. He looked at Nina by his side, fast asleep, her legs wrapped tightly around his thigh. He was sprawled on his back as usual but with a protective arm around her, keeping her close lest some inauspicious demon pry her away.

He kissed the tip of her ear. Is this happiness? This feeling of warmth, of wanting to keep things exactly like this, to bring time to a standstill in this beautiful room filled with memories sweet and sad; the weight of her leg on his and her body so close it felt like a part of him, one body in which both of them lived. And his grandfather blessing them from atop the mantel, happy in their happiness.

Stephen's eyes were drawn to the pale-golden pool of light that had just appeared on the floor under the heavy drapes. The sun was up.

⊫⊣ ⊢⊨

"Mrs. Brown, I need coffee for two," Stephen said over the intercom.

"Of course, Mr. James."

Coffee for two? This early? That too upstairs? Mrs. Brown turned off the intercom speaker and forced herself to get out of bed. The intercom buzzed again.

"Could you please bring up some fruit and yogurt as well?"

"Yes, Mr. James. We have plenty of fresh fruit. But we don't have any yogurt. I could send out for some if you'd like."

"Please do." He hung up.

What's going on? Who's up there? Mrs. Brown was completely confused. After grandfather's passing, Stephen had forbidden anybody (other than staff) from entering the mansion. Even Professor George Applegate wasn't allowed in beyond the porch.

She took out a breakfast tray from the closet and set it down on the counter. While the coffee percolated, Mrs. Brown arranged a milk carafe and sugar bowl on the tray, laid out cups and silverware. She washed the strawberries and grapes, and sliced a ripe honey-dew melon.

There was a knock on the side door; a sales clerk from the organic store down the road dropped off a case of yogurt. She opened a carton and scooped out the contents into a bowl. With a final look of satisfaction, she transferred the tray onto a steel food cart. A quick look in the mirror assured her that she was presentable. She pushed the cart out of the kitchen toward the butler's elevator.

A few minutes later, Mrs. Brown exited at the third floor, navigated the back hallways and came to a stop in front of Stephen's suite. The ornate double doors were shut. She knocked.

"Come in," he called out.

She nudged open the doors curious as to what or whom she'd see. The foyer appeared unchanged with its mahogany console table and an elaborate flower arrangement on top of it. The doors to his bedroom on the left were shut, but the double doors on the right that led to the living area were wide open. She entered and turned the corner with the cart in front of her.

The living room was awash in early morning sunshine. At the center of the room, a slender woman with beautiful, bright eyes sat in Grandpa's leather armchair. Her long dark hair was combed straight down to her waist. She wore a pale pink silk dress. Stephen stood behind her with his hand on her shoulder.

Mrs. Brown lowered her eyes quickly before Stephen could catch her staring. A colored woman! What kind of perversion was this?

"Nina, this is Mrs. Brown, our housekeeper."

The young woman shook Mrs. Brown's extended hand. "How do you do, Mrs. Brown?"

"Mrs. Brown, meet Nina Sharma. We were married yesterday."

Mrs. Brown's heart stopped for a second. Her eyes fell on the wedding band on Stephen's finger, which she hadn't noticed until then.

"Congratulations, Mr. and Mrs. James!" She managed to say it without stumbling over the words. Her mind raced. What a story! She couldn't wait to get back to her room and call up her friends.

"Thank you, Mrs. Brown." Stephen dismissed her.

Back in her quarters, after the initial excitement subsided, Mrs. Brown began to worry. She had gotten accustomed to a fat paycheck and negligible workload. What if the new mistress decided to get rid of the current staff and replace them with her people? Who was this Nina Sharma anyway?

She switched on her computer and groped around for her reading glasses. They were hidden under a bunch of old issues of People magazine she had been reading the previous night. A quick Google search spewed pages and pages on Nina Sharma—some sort of computer person and community organizer, it turned out.

Mrs. Brown wasn't impressed. She had hoped that Nina might be the daughter of a maharajah or something—People magazine was full of Indian princes and rajas driving bespoke automobiles—but, no, Nina wasn't royalty. It saddened her that young Mr. James had married outside the charmed circle he was born into.

At least she could be sure of one thing—he would definitely have had Nina sign a prenuptial agreement. Being an avid reader of celebrity magazines, Mrs. Brown knew all about divorces and foolish men who neglected to get legal protection. Stephen Edward James III was no fool.

"Would you like some more coffee?" Nina asked Stephen. They had just finished their first breakfast as husband and wife. It felt surreal and quite wonderful.

"No, thanks. I need to make a few calls. It shouldn't take very long. Will you be OK being on your own until I'm done?"

"Of course! I'll explore the rest of the house."

"Here, take this master key with you. It has all the security codes." She took the key from him and watched him stride away. He turned around at the door and winked at her before closing it behind him.

After a quick check of her phone for mail and messages, she got up from grandfather's armchair and went to the atrium. Filtered sunshine streamed in through a stained glass cupola above and dappled the space with rainbow sparks. The staircase spiraled down in graceful sweeping arcs.

She decided to start with the wing of the house directly beneath their suite, where Stephen's childhood room was located. The stairs led down to a broad landing. Heavy wooden doors on her right guarded the entrance to the wing. She looked up the security code on the master key and typed it on the keypad.

The doors swung open to reveal the interior. It had Stephen's imprimatur all over it. She had expected a Dickensian vista of cobwebs and dust like Miss Havisham's home, but the place was spotless. The furniture was wrapped in clear plastic and arranged methodically inside tall glass-front cabinets along the walls. Each closet had an inventory posted on it. Surveillance cameras blinked from every corner.

She wandered from room to room. Everything was impersonal and sanitized—cold, cavernous spaces with polished wood flooring and high ornate ceilings, lined with floor-to-ceiling clinical glass cases full of plastic-wrapped objects. It reminded her of lost-and-found cages at airports where misplaced baggage was stored.

At last she came to a room that had some personality—a sort of a library. Here the glass cases contained cataloged manuscripts, scrapbooks, albums and bound documents. An entire wall was devoted to leather-bound albums. A large reading table occupied the center of the room. It was the only piece of furniture that wasn't entombed in the glass cabinets. Even the chairs hadn't been spared.

She texted Stephen: "I'm near the albums. Which one has your baby pictures?"

"Check out SEJ: 1984, SEJ: 1990 and SEJ: 1995," came the immediate reply.

The albums were heavy. She spread them out on the table and leafed through them in chronological order; Stephen morphed from a baby to toddler to boy, looking increasingly sullen with each passing year. Many photos featured grandpa James, and some were of Stephen with his father, but there was not a single one of his mother or siblings—they had been edited out of his life. The albums ended abruptly in 1999, the year Stephen's father had killed himself. The last picture was of a teenage Stephen gazing out of the window of his grandfather's bedroom balcony while the old man lay on the huge canopy bed looking very ill.

She had never seen anyone so young look so sorrowful. In the photo, Stephen's lanky frame was weighed down with grief. His head rested against the window as if he hadn't the will to hold it up. Nina was so engrossed that she didn't hear Stephen enter the room.

He watched her while she lingered over the last photo. Nina had a very expressive face and her eyebrows alone could convey many emotions. The sadness in the photo had seeped into her eyes.

He couldn't bear to see her like that.

"Nina, time to head out."

She was startled out of her trance and looked at him blankly for a second, and then quickly turned away pretending to close the albums. It took her a few seconds to compose herself. She stacked the albums neatly and smiled at him. "Help me put these away—they are so heavy!"

But that look in her eyes continued to haunt Stephen. Over the next few days, he tried his best to keep her smiling and happy. He got a local Indian chef to deliver fresh food every day, but he could see that Nina didn't like the meals even though she said they were delicious. And on the fourth day, she stumped him by asking where the washing machine was. He had no idea. His laundry was washed and ironed by unseen hands. All he knew was that it went down a chute in his bathroom and reappeared neatly ironed and folded in his closet.

"It's not a problem, Stephen," she said, but he wouldn't listen—he spent the next few hours calling every appliance shop in town. After that, Nina had no ambitions beyond getting through the rest of her stay without making any demands that would send Stephen into a frenzy.

In fact, there was nothing to complain about. The surroundings were beautiful; everything was taken care of, and all she had to do was say the word and anything she wanted would materialize. It was like living in an exclusive resort. She hated it.

She missed the small things she had taken for granted, like cooking or singing along to the songs on her iPod. It made her homesick for noisy Jersey City, where she never had to worry about curious eyes observing, assessing, and analyzing her every move. But in Stephen's home, the staff were constantly watching her and whispering. Even at night, the large portrait of Grandfather James looked down upon them from above the mantle opposite the bed.

So it was a relief for Nina when it was time for them to return to her place toward the end of the week. That night, after dinner, she began packing.

Stephen lay on the bed propped up against a pile of pillows and watched her in silence.

It was then she first noticed the change in his mood, and that he wasn't packing.

"Aren't you coming with me?" she asked him while she folded her clothes.

"No, I'll come next week," he replied. She was taken aback because she had assumed that they would be together and that they'd alternate between their two places.

"Would you like me to stay on? I can work remotely from here."

"No, I don't want to disrupt your work."

He replied with such finality that she couldn't pursue the discussion. She tried to hide her disappointment and look normal. He switched off the lamp on his side of the bed and shut his eyes.

She finished her packing, changed into her nightdress and slipped under the covers next to him. He was unnaturally still, too still to be asleep. She put her arm around his waist and pressed her face into his back between his shoulder blades. Normally, he would have grabbed her hand and pulled her on top of him. After a few minutes when there was no response from him, she withdrew her hand and turned away.

The next morning he drove her to the train station. The air was crisp and cold, but the sun shone brightly from a stunning blue sky. The parking lot was empty except for Stephen's car.

Nina turned to Stephen. He had been moody and distant all morning. Now he stood frowning in the direction the train was supposed to come from.

"Stephen, I'd like to say something." She didn't want to part on such a cold note.

He turned to her with the frown still in place. She rallied her courage and continued.

"I love being with you. If you're unable to get away I'd be delighted to work from here. It's easy."

He was about to say something but she raised her hand to stop him.

"However, I understand completely if you need to be by yourself. I'll not be offended or hurt. All you have to do is tell me that you want some space."

"That's not the case at all," he said and looked away. *I know you hate it here.*

The train's whistle gave a long blast as the locomotive approached the station. She kissed him goodbye and boarded the train, and watched him recede. He stood without moving, like a stubborn child with his hands folded across his chest, staring at her.

It was late by the time she reached her apartment that evening. She put her things away and looked in the fridge to see if there was anything worth eating. All she could find was a box of frozen quinoa. She heated it in the microwave and sat down at the table.

It was such an anticlimax to be sitting in her apartment, eating dinner all alone, as if nothing had changed. Did the last ten days really happen? But the rings on her fingers gleamed under the lamp, the silver-rolling ring on her right hand and the gold band on her left, proof that she hadn't dreamed the whole thing. She put down her spoon and called Stephen's cell phone, but there was no response. She called his home, and got the same result. He wasn't taking her calls.

What had she done? She'd married a man she hardly knew. And now he didn't want to be with her. She got up and started pacing the room.

"It's not true that he doesn't want to be with me," she said aloud. "I shouldn't blow it out of proportion. It's not like he said he didn't want to see me, or live with me. He has been nothing but attentive and considerate. There is no reason to doubt him. I just have to give him time and try not to be so clingy."

She wanted to talk to him. Should she try his cell phone once more?

The doorbell interrupted her frenzied soliloquy. She wiped her face, took a deep breath and went to open the door. She looked through the peephole but couldn't see anyone. Must be the dry-cleaning guy. She opened the door and jumped back startled.

"Stephen!"

He pushed past her carrying two large cardboard boxes. A big suitcase, several suits and the familiar black gym bag sat on a bellboy's cart in the hallway outside. She stepped into the corridor to get out of Stephen's way while he moved his things inside the apartment. When he was done, he pushed the empty cart out into the hallway and closed the door.

He turned to her, hands on hips. "I am moving in."

She gave a squeal and hugged him. "Thank you, thank you, thank you!"

⚑⚑

During Nina's second visit to his home, Stephen installed a shiny, new washer-dryer next to the kitchenette in the passageway between the bedroom and living room of their master suite. He wanted to build a proper kitchen by claiming space from the giant closets, but Nina vetoed that firmly. The living room got a makeover, with a love seat to complement grandfather's leather armchairs, which were straight out of the smoking room of a fusty old country club. Stephen brought in flowering plants, a big screen TV and music system to hook up her iPod to—anything he thought would make Nina feel more at home.

Mrs. Brown watched in amazement. She had known Stephen from the time he was twelve years old. He was by far the coldest, most distant member of the James household. He'd had no attachment to anyone other than his grandfather and retreated into his own world after the death of grandfather James.

It was a shock, therefore, for Mrs. Brown to see the frosty Stephen agonize over every little detail—whether a certain plant would please Nina, whether she would prefer beige over ivory for the furnishings, and whether Mrs. Brown could find a good personal chef who could cook vegetarian food for Nina. The refrigerator had to be stocked with fruit and yogurt, and the meats had to be carefully wrapped and sealed so as not to offend Nina's sensibilities! She was frightened by how much power Nina had over Stephen.

The staff covertly watched Nina on her subsequent visits and tried to guess what changes she would make and how it would affect them. An eager young maid commented that they had nothing to worry about—Nina did not even have a proper engagement ring, just a plain gold wedding band and an old weird looking mismatched silver ring. The younger members of the staff started an over-under betting pool on how long the marriage would last—two years, they said.

Mrs. Brown knew better. She had seen that weird silver ring enshrined in a glass box next to grandfather's pipe right by Stephen's bedside, for as long as she could remember. She knew it had a special significance for him and meant more than any diamond ring. "Stop the silliness," she warned the staff, "if you want to hang on to your jobs."

And Nina tried her best to settle in and please Stephen. It was important to him that she be happy in his home. But despite her best efforts, she could never feel completely at ease—the very air in the mansion was heavy with all the cruelty, heartache and condemnations that had passed under its roof.

FLEEING THE NIGHT

Stephen kicked off the sheets. It was past midnight in muggy New Delhi. The air conditioning system was on full duty to keep the deluxe suite at the Hotel Le Méridien at a nice, cool temperature. He looked over at Nina, who seemed to have fallen asleep instantaneously. She was curled up at his side, holding on to his arm with both hands. He pulled the covers over her shoulders when he felt her shiver. He was always too warm, and she was always too cold; they had yet to find a temperature that worked for both of them.

Stephen and Nina had been traveling up and down India's western border, combining work and pleasure—a delayed honeymoon six months after their wedding.

Nina was on a business trip to assess projects for funding. Stephen tagged along, allegedly to tour and enjoy India through her eyes. In reality he was on the job. There had been chatter around the terrorist network about an impending attack in India, and George had asked Stephen to investigate.

Under the pretext of accompanying his wife, Stephen had been poking around for information. Sid Ali had made many trips to India in the last six months and seemed to be scouting Mumbai sea routes on behalf of Tariq Rehman. Stephen had been re-creating those routes and inferring different ways they could be used for an attack. His inquiries in Gujarat and Rajasthan, states along India's border with Pakistan, had not yielded any leads. After weeks of dusty villages and barely usable toilets, he and Nina were now enjoying a few days of pampered luxury before their next foray into rural India.

Suddenly he was wide awake. His ears had picked up a very small sound that didn't belong in the symphony of room noises. He got out of bed and walked quietly through the living room to the front door of the suite. A folded piece of paper lay at the foot of the door. Someone had slipped it through the crack underneath with a knock just loud enough to wake Stephen. He picked it up and then opened the door and looked up and down the wide hallway. No activity, just the chandeliers dimmed for the night, their light glinting off the occasional bronze sculpture.

He closed the door softly, went back inside to the living room desk, turned on the table lamp, and opened the slip. The light shone brightly on it. Written on the hotel stationery in black ink were just two words: "LEAVE <u>NOW</u>." No signature, no salutation, nothing. He picked up the phone to call the front desk. No dial tone, not even static. It was completely dead.

By that time his internal antenna had started to buzz like mad. He walked across the plush carpeting and pulled back the heavy, silk drapes. The landscaping lights in the garden blinked a couple of times and went out. He was certain now: something terrible was about to happen.

He quickly pushed the panic code on his emergency cell phone and sent an SOS to George. As soon as he got an acknowledgement back, he yanked out the batteries from both his phone and Nina's and rushed over to her.

"Nina. Nina! Wake up. We need to leave."

She sat up in bed. "What?" She squinted at the clock—1:33 a.m.

Stephen was frantically pulling clothes from the dresser and stuffing them into her suitcase. His bag was already packed.

"Stephen! What's going on? I can't leave. I have meetings all day tomorrow."

A pair of jeans and a shirt landed on her.

"Get dressed," he snapped.

"Stephen! What's wrong?"

He grabbed her by the arms. "We have to leave *now*. Get dressed."

"Why? You're hurting me!" She wriggled free.

"Nina, I can't explain now. You have to trust me. We're in danger. *Move*!"

She stared at him for a moment and then, without a word, changed into the clothes, threw the nightgown into his waiting hands, and ran to the bathroom. Her head was full of unsettling thoughts. Stephen had never behaved like this before. He was annoyingly calm during crises. She had never seen him panic, not even when they had been caught in a massive squall on a sailing trip. Something awful must have happened to rattle him. When she came out of the bathroom, the bags had disappeared.

Stephen gestured for her to be quiet and switched off the lights. He opened the door of the suite, and a dim glow entered from the hallway. He stepped out and scanned the corridor.

The lights flickered. Far away someone shouted.

"Let's go," he whispered.

They slipped through a door at the end of the hallway and then a smaller door. A nasty smell hit them as soon as they entered the stairwell. It was dirty and dark, meant for carting garbage, hardly ever used by anyone else. Stephen broke into a sprint, taking the steps two at a time, a flashlight in his hand. Nina was slower, hanging on to the guide rail because she could barely see. He muttered something, grabbed her arm, and rushed on, half carrying, half dragging her.

"Move, move," he said between clenched teeth. At the bottom of the stairs, they came out into a huge, cluttered warehouse piled with mounds of trash shredded for recycling.

Stephen looked around for a second and then raced ahead, pulling Nina with him. A red "EXIT" sign blinked in the distance. There was a faint shout behind them; a door slammed shut, and the lights went off. Total darkness. All gadgets, gizmos, and appliances suddenly fell silent. The electricity was out.

She was about to call out his name when his hand landed on her mouth.

"Quiet," he whispered and held her crunched to his side so she couldn't move, her face smothered under his armpit. The voices behind them grew louder.

He stopped and pushed her against the wall, shielding her with his body. The voices were now barely twenty feet away. A man said in Urdu, "Asad, *miya*. There is no one here. We need to get back upstairs."

A flashlight danced on the ceiling. Nina's knees buckled. She wanted to sit down, but Stephen had her firmly pinned behind him.

The voices were very close now. Stephen pushed her down to the floor. She felt a metallic object brush against her cheek briefly. In the feeble light reflected on the ceiling from the distant flashlight, she saw him pull out a gun and heard the click as he released the safety latch. Her heart stopped. Even to her untrained eyes, it was obviously no ordinary gun but a special professional one that could blow off someone's head in a flash.

The disembodied voice repeated its plea: "Asad, we are needed upstairs. We have to go now. The boss wants us."

Someone kicked at the teetering walls of trash with a curse, and an avalanche crashed down. When the clatter ceased, the voices had receded to the other end of the warehouse.

The footsteps got fainter, and the far door of the storage area opened and then slammed shut.

Nina felt Stephen's shoulders relax just a little. In their six months together, she had not seen such rough behavior from him. He had never raised his voice at her. Even at his moodiest, he was unfailingly affection- ate toward her. So what had turned him into this rag- ing madman?

She tried to free her arm once more, but his grip tightened in reply. He waited for what seemed like a very long time and then pushed open the nearby exit door. They stumbled out.

Nina had hoped for relief outdoors but a hot, pu- trid night greeted them. The air was radioactive with the stench of decaying offal.

A vast garbage dump stretched out in front of them, almost to the horizon. Occasional street lamps rose over a jungle of rotting trash mounds. Stephen took off at a quick sprint, exhorting her in a low voice when she failed to keep up.

"Stephen, I can't run anymore," she pleaded. He ran back to her, slung her over his shoulder, and began to sprint once more.

His head was filled with just one thought: he had to get her out of there. He couldn't let her fall into their hands. If they were to get hold of her, they would inflict every perversion and cruelty upon her just because she was his wife. He *had* to get her out.

Nina struggled to breathe. Why were they running? Why did he have a gun? She swatted away the flies that tried to settle on her lips. Her eyes and nose watered from the fumes. He charged ahead, deaf to her questions and pleas. She tried to slide to the ground because he was breathing hard now, struggling to carry her while keeping up the pace. But he curtly told her to stop it.

A hundred yards later, he veered to the side and pulled her toward a chain-link fence at the edge of the garbage field. A large clump of trees rose darkly beyond it. He hoisted her to the top.

"Jump," he said. He climbed up next to her, and when she remained perched there, hesitating, he grabbed her and jumped down. She landed at an odd

angle, twisted her ankle, and cried out in pain. He immediately clamped his hand down on her mouth and
dragged her to the shelter of the trees.

Nina was too afraid even to cry. It seemed like a
dream, the last six months of almost perfect happiness. What had happened to her sweet, sexy husband
who smiled at the mere sight of her? Who was this fear-
some man?

They waited deep inside the stand of trees. Stephen
scanned the darkness anxiously. As the precious seconds ticked by, his tension increased, his fingers digging into Nina's wrist. The more she squirmed, the
tighter he gripped it, oblivious to the force of his fingers. Muffled sounds came regularly from the direction of the hotel. He pulled her closer.

He was worried. Perhaps George was not able to put
his plan in motion. Was this going to be the end, the
two of them shot dead in a garbage field? This would
be Stephen's legacy, his gift to his wife of six months.

Finally a short burst of light flashed from beyond
the trees. A black, dilapidated ambassador car pulled
up in front with its lights switched off. Stephen lunged
toward it.

"Come on, come on, Nina." They tumbled into the
car, and as soon as he shut the door it lurched into motion. "*Jaldi!*" he told the driver. "Go!"

The car careened through slums and back roads,
leaving a trail of enraged mongrels in its wake. Stephen

grabbed a rag from the driver and wiped down the filth on his and Nina's legs and shoes. A siren mourned in the distance.

Stephen turned to the driver. "Go faster. *Jaldi chalo!*"

They hurtled through the night in that jarring, jolting vehicle and then arrived quite suddenly at a small, private airport. A tiny plane idled on the runway, and scattered the smell of burning diesel. Before the car could come to a total halt, Stephen rushed out and pulled Nina to the plane. The driver scampered after them with their bags.

As soon as Stephen closed the door, the plane taxied to the runway and was airborne. Nina had barely enough time to sit down. Her hands trembled while she tried to click her seatbelt into place. Stephen snatched the buckle from her and snapped it together violently. The ground slipped away below.

What on Earth is going on? Her mind was in complete disarray. She clutched the armrest tightly to stop her hands from shaking. Crazy, garbled questions rose to her lips, but she couldn't get them out. She took a deep breath and closed her eyes. It took her a few minutes to master her panic. It wasn't easy, with the plane rattling and shuddering precariously.

Nina opened her eyes and looked at Stephen. She was completely mystified. Why was he so furious? What had happened? Why wouldn't he tell her? After a while she picked up the courage to disturb his silence.

"What's going on, Stephen? Where are we going? Why?" She tried to sound normal. Any show of emotion would only infuriate him further.

He looked at her—really looked at her for the first time that night. He had been too preoccupied to worry about how she must have felt. With an effort he calmed down and put his arms around her. What a jerk he was. She was terrified, and he was unable to get a grip on his temper. But words failed him, trapped by the rage in his chest, and all he could do was squeeze her shoulders in reassurance.

"Why do you have a gun? What's going on? Are we in danger?" she asked.

"It's a long story. But we will be OK. I'll tell you when we get home. We need to get out as fast as we can. The embassy called to warn that we should leave immediately. You have to trust me." In the plane's dim light, his face looked ravaged by worry.

"Why? What did the embassy say?"

"Some political turmoil." He shrugged. He didn't want to use the words "terrorist attack" and conjure up visions of the World Trade Center towers crumbling like columns of dust.

Nina didn't press him further. He turned away to look out of the window. The flight seemed interminable, but they finally landed at a busy, brightly lit airport. She peeked out. Surely they must have left India; they could have covered the length and breadth of it in less than four hours. Were they in Bangkok? Manila?

But she didn't have time to figure it out. As soon as they landed, a cart drove up and took them, along with their bags, to a larger, modern plane that was already lined up on the runway, ready to take off. It was not a commercial airliner. A ladder on wheels leaned against the entrance.

Stephen and Nina entered the airplane. She went in first, and a young man in military fatigues led her to a seat in a curtained-off area. From there she saw Stephen outside, at the bottom of the ladder, talking on a phone. And then he smashed it against the railing and lobbed the broken instrument away into the bushes. What had gotten into him?

He came inside and sat next to her. He was more relaxed now. George had assured him the plan was going smoothly so far. No sign that Stephen and Nina had been followed or detected. The plane began to move on the runway in preparation for takeoff.

Nina closed her eyes, feeling exhausted and overwhelmed. When she had to go to the bathroom, Stephen insisted on standing outside the door.

"Aren't you being a bit paranoid? If it's political turmoil in India, aren't we safe now?" she asked. He didn't say anything, just gave her a faint, forced smile. He could have told her the truth but decided to wait until they got home. It would be easier on her there.

"Go to sleep," he said when they returned to their seats. "We'll be home soon. I'll explain then. Please, bear with me for a few hours more."

Before she could ask any questions, he tucked a blanket around her and kissed her good night. Her cheek felt soft and warm against his. Her perfume soothed him for an instant. He rested his forehead briefly on her shoulder and then turned off the light and closed the door on any further conversation.

The plane wobbled and shook in an effort to slice through an agitated airstream. Stephen bent down and picked up a magazine that had fallen off Nina's lap earlier. She deserved a ton of credit for following him without hesitation, and for keeping her cool. The last thing he needed at a time like this was hysterics. He had grown very fond of her in the six months they had been married. An impulsive gamble on his part had turned out to be the best decision of his life. He had hidden nothing from her—not his family history, not his brief bout with alcoholism, not his finances, and not his past relationships. Just the one inconvenient fact that he was a spy and that his intention when he had introduced himself was to recruit her into America's premier intelligence agency, the CIA.

As they had spent time together, he'd discovered things he must have known instinctively when he'd decided to marry her. She was gentle, incapable of meanness or cruelty, and took such delight in pampering him. It had been a foreign experience for him to be the center of so much care and concern, to have every need and whim of his given such weight and preference. Then there was her irritatingly optimistic view of the world—everything would be fine, everyone was good. It was the source of her happiness, the secret why she woke up every morning with a proverbial song on her lips, ready to smile, smile, smile, and be happy.

Stephen sighed, unable to sleep despite the soporific drone of the airplane. The hours went by slowly.

Nina woke up and looked around. Nothing had changed. Stephen sat like a sphinx, upright and fiercely alert, as if he were afraid she might evaporate and disappear.

"Stephen, who were those guys in the warehouse?" she asked.

He looked haggard, with red-rimmed eyes. He had not let down his guard since they had left the hotel.

"I don't know," he replied truthfully. He removed his glasses and rubbed his eyes. "I wish I did."

"Are we in trouble?"

"No, we are not." He was emphatic. "We will be home in a few hours. It will all be over."

Nina looked at him with wide eyes. "Are you in trouble?" she asked. But what kind? He wasn't very political.

"No, not at all. You have to trust me, Nina." He replaced his glasses and turned away to look out the window across the aisle.

Trust? That was a tall order today. The gun had rankled her. Where was it now? Did he have it on him? He must have. Strange fears started to take shape. Was he some kind of an arms dealer? An international drug lord? A smuggler? Was the mafia after him? Couldn't be.

The steward informed them they would be landing soon. To Nina's surprise they didn't land at Newark Liberty International but at a small county airport. Just before they got off the plane, Stephen borrowed the steward's phone and made a call. Nina saw him nodding and listening. He returned the phone, and as they deplaned, a limo drove up right to the wheels of the landing gear.

Instead of going to her apartment in Jersey City, they drove to some kind of luxury spa resort in central Jersey. Stephen sat like a marble statue, immobile and silent, for the entire forty-five minute ride. The car pulled up to the entrance. Stephen grabbed their bags and hurried Nina into the elaborate foyer, where a waiting attendant gave him a set of keys. He then broke into a run until they arrived at their room. Once inside, he slammed the door shut and fell on the bed face down, exhausted.

Nina stood in the room without taking off her coat. She didn't know what to do next or where or how to begin being normal.

Stephen sat up after a minute and, with great effort, like an old man, walked over to the TV. He stared at it, remote in hand, unable to switch it on. Finally he pressed the button, and the TV popped on with a blink. Nina found his behavior increasingly bizarre but took her eyes off him and looked at the TV.

It was tuned to CNN. Some big news was breaking, with a solemn announcer, graphics, and sound effects. On the screen a tall building was on fire, with black-ops commandos positioned all around it. Gunfire rattled offscreen. The camera cut to close-ups of gunmen in the windows and on the roof of the building. "BREAKING NEWS: TERROR IN NEW DELHI," the ticker screamed.

Nina's hand flew to her mouth. The building was Le Méridien, the hotel they had fled fewer than twenty-four hours ago. Terrorists had taken it over. Masked men had locked it down and were going from floor to floor, killing the sleeping guests. According to the announcer, 166 had been confirmed dead, their bodies tossed out of the broken glass windows. There were another estimated two hundred people still inside— guests, hotel staff, and other crew. The siege had been underway for more than twenty hours.

Nina went numb, unable to think, say, or hear anything. Stephen switched off the TV, but she continued to stare at it, transfixed.

"Nina, look at me. Talk to me." He turned her to face him.

"Did you know about this?" she asked after a minute.

"I wish I had. I could have tried to stop it."

That was the cause of his rage—that he had failed to prevent it and had been forced to flee like a coward, leaving innocent people to die at the hands of the butchers. What was worse, Nina had barely escaped the same fate thanks to the incompetence of the world's premier intelligence community.

But Nina could not understand what he was saying. It made no sense. How could he have stopped it? He was a marine engineer.

"I don't understand how." Then she remembered that he still had that gun.

"I should have suspected. It wasn't supposed to happen for at least another three months, and it was supposed to be in Mumbai, not Delhi. I never would've let you get within a hundred miles of that place if I had known."

"What do you mean, 'supposed to be'? How do you know what was supposed to be?" Nina struggled to keep her thoughts together, but she was tired and in shock. The smell of the garbage field lingered on their clothes and shoes.

Stephen had no choice at this juncture. He had to tell her the truth. He should have told her long ago, when things were normal, not in the middle of this horror. But he had to tell her now. He couldn't lie anymore.

"It is my job to know these things. I am an under-cover officer for the CIA. George Applegate recruited me in my senior year of college." He looked at her, his gray eyes locked on hers. She didn't understand at first and listened with a tense, tight smile. Then she lowered her eyes and sat down on the edge of the bed with great formality, and her clasped her hands in her lap.

"Come on, Nina, don't be like that." He kneeled in front of her and took her hands in his. "I've been meaning to tell you. Every day. But I couldn't get up the courage."

"Is that why you married me? Am I a part of the job? Your cover?" she asked in a small voice, still not looking at him.

"Of course not! How can you think that? I broke every rule in the book to marry you and almost got kicked out for it."

What else had he kept from her? What else had he lied about? She didn't bother to wipe her tears, which were falling quite freely. *What's the point?*

He had never seen her cry, not even during their worst arguments, when he had slammed the door and stalked out in a fit of temper.

"Look at me, Nina, my love. Please, look at me." He got up from the floor and sat beside her and tried to bend down and look into her face. It was hot and streaked with moisture. He wiped it with a handkerchief. "Come on, dear Nina. You know me better than that."

She looked at him finally, but her tears continued to flow.

"Do I?" she asked. "I don't think so, Stephen. I don't know you at all."

He didn't know how to console her.

"Amy warned me," she said. He stiffened at the mention of Amy's name.

"She was right. I knew nothing about you then, and I know nothing about you now." Nina looked up at him. "Such a big secret, Stephen? And you didn't think that I deserved to know?"

He was ashamed but also angry that Nina had brought up Amy at this moment when he'd spent the last twenty hours killing himself to get her to safety. He controlled his irritation and said, "Nina, you have to trust me that I had my reasons for not telling you sooner."

"No, Stephen, *you* are the one who doesn't trust me with your secrets." She walked away to the bathroom and slammed the door.

GEORGE'S THEORY

The morning after their return from New Delhi, Stephen and Nina took a limo to her parents' home in New Jersey. Stephen was scheduled to go on to meet George in Virginia, where a big crisis meeting had been convened.

The first time Stephen had visited Nina's parents, barely a couple of weeks had elapsed since their secret civil wedding. Nina had wanted to put off the moment of confession and confrontation a little longer, but Stephen had insisted. He'd wanted to meet her parents and get it out in the open. He'd had enough secrets as it was.

They had driven through picturesque woods and horse country, up a hill to a large Frank Lloyd Wright-style home built to disappear into nature. Nina's parents had received them at the front door. Stephen had been courteous but reserved, a little overwhelmed by the hyperkinetic family and its hovering hospitality. Nina's grandparents, who lived with her parents, had greeted Stephen with a ceremonial courtesy reserved for sons-in-law in India. He'd felt like the sun god, the center of the universe; all that had been missing was rose petals strewn in his path. And to add to the chaos, this had been on Diwali, the Hindu festival of lights. The sprawling home had glittered with candles, lamps, and lights; mountains of food in elaborate silverware had occupied every table and counter.

Stephen had been struck by how much Nina resembled her mother, Deepa; they had the same dark, darting eyes and wide smile. Deepa was a natural host, with an instinctive need to take care of everyone and make sure they were happy. Stephen had liked her immediately and sensed she approved of him. Nina's father, Ravi, had been more of a challenge. He was the same height as Stephen, well built, with a thick moustache. He had been concerned about this rapidly moving romance and had told Stephen so almost immediately after being introduced. Stephen had neutralized the concern by suggesting he and Nina get married as soon as it was convenient for the family. He had promised Nina that he would keep up the pretense of not being married. It was very important to Nina; her parents would feel very hurt if they find out she had gotten married without telling them, she'd said, so she was going to introduce Stephen as her fiancé.

Over time Stephen had gotten used to the family dynamic, where everyone was involved in everyone's life and decisions. It came from a deep affection and loyalty to each other, not from a desire to interfere or control. It was the key to Nina's happiness and strength. He had appreciated her all the more for taking the giant leap of faith in marrying him without letting her family know.

In the driveway of her parents' house now, Stephen opened the car door for her and watched her step out. She was composed but deeply hurt and angry. Nina's mother stood at the top of the stoop and waved to them. She must have heard their car pull up.

He put his arm around Nina on their way up the front steps and gave her a quick hug. She didn't pull away but didn't look at him either. Deepa embraced her daughter tightly. They were all glad that Stephen and Nina had made it out of Delhi just in time. The city was shut down, with a three-day curfew, shoot-on-sight orders, and the military out in full force on the streets. The family didn't know that Nina and Stephen had actually been staying at Le Méridien; otherwise they would have been frantic.

Stephen left Nina in her family's care, fully aware it would be years before he could comfort her at the organic level they could. Nina saw him off at the door. She wanted to say so many things—that she was angry but loved him and trusted him despite the doubts that were beginning to take root. But her pride got in the way and she could not say the words. All she managed was a cold good-bye.

It was lunchtime when Stephen got to Virginia. He made a beeline for George's office. It was bereft of any ornamentation or personal touches, almost like a prison cell. George had been in meeting after meeting for the last thirty hours. He looked spent and old, his head bent forward as if he didn't have the strength to hold it up. He had been under attack from all directions, from up and down the chain of command. At least fourteen American citizens were unaccounted for at Le Méridien, all presumed dead. Stephen was scheduled to meet a battery of officers over the next few days, to see if there were anything he could report that could shed new light.

"George, what happened? How come we were all so wrong?" he demanded as soon as they were alone. What an understatement. They got killed, flattened, hit by a ten-ton truck while crossing the street looking in the wrong direction.

"So many things," George replied. He leaned back in his chair and closed his eyes. "The terrorists found out that we knew about the Mumbai plan, so they used it as a red herring. They changed their real plan, changed the time and place. They stopped the use of cell phones and satellite phones, did everything by courier and hand delivery. We couldn't monitor the real operation. We didn't even know it existed. We were too busy monitoring the Mumbai charade that they kept up for our benefit."

"How is that possible? We are the premier intelligence agency, with billions of dollars and the best technology in the world. We can intercept anything, anywhere, anytime—e-mail, phone calls, conversations. We have informants everywhere. How could we let it happen, George?" He leaned forward and glared at him.

George did not react. "We also think they figured out your real identity and advanced the date of the attack so they could take you out with the rest of the guests."

"What? How is that possible?" Stephen jumped up from his chair. He hadn't expected his identity to become known to the enemy so early in the game. But how had they found out?

"Sit down, Stephen," George said wearily. He had ordered two boxed lunches and a pot of coffee. He pushed one box toward Stephen, poured out the coffee into two paper cups and opened his lunch box.

But Stephen couldn't sit. He paced the room and scanned his brain for faces and voices at Le Méridien that might offer a clue. There must have been some hint, some inconsistency, some cue he had missed.

George took a bite of his sandwich and put it down. It was a cold, soggy mess that oozed mayo and mustard. He swallowed it with difficulty and took a big gulp of coffee to help it go down. "We think Sid arranged for the note to be delivered to you through some intermediary."

Stephen whipped around and looked at him. "Sid? My neighbor? How? Why? What makes you say that?"

"Sid actively scouted Mumbai locales and worked on instructions from Tariq Rehman, you knew that. Sid must have heard there was a mad scramble to advance the attack to coincide with the presence of a valuable American target, an intelligence officer. I don't think Rehman would have told him. Sid is too low on the food chain. But someone somewhere brags, and word gets out."

"Except to us," Stephen said. They had gotten no word, no whisper, not even a wink. Nothing. He sat down and tried to focus on George's story, but his brain went back to New Delhi once more to look for clues, swooping like a helicopter around the hotel hallways and rooms. He saw the young people at the front desk, the staff at the health club, the other guests. No one stood out. The only person he'd had some concerns about was the *sardar* who manned the breakfast buffet every morning, but nothing had come of that.

The strapping Sikh had checked out clean in all the agency's databases.

George's voice interrupted Stephen's thoughts once more.

"When Sid heard about the scramble to launch the attack at Le Méridien, he did some digging of his own to guess who the target was. He found out Nina and you were there at that time. Maybe Tariq Rehman showed a sudden interest in you and started asking questions. Maybe Sid's wife heard it through Nina's friend, Amy, or maybe through some other friend at BigSearch. We haven't figured out that piece yet. He must have thought there was a good chance you were the intelligence officer in question. Or perhaps Sid was just being neighborly. Who knows?"

George closed his eyes and paused. He continued without opening them. "After he tipped you off, Sid must have waited to see whether you'd made it out. Only a person with special skills and logistical support could have gotten out of the hotel and the country that fast. Now he can approach you with certainty, knowing you are indeed an intelligence officer, and you can possibly get him out of the mess he is in."

"What mess?" Stephen asked. He was shocked that Sid had connected the dots so effectively while the agency had been caught off guard.

George squinted at Stephen over the top of his glasses. "Well, you remember he made those large contributions to charitable foundations. They turned out to be fronts for other dubious activities. And there was a long paper trail that connected him to them. His newfound friends, who he thought were helping orphaned kids in Pakistan, turned out to be crooks, and they blackmailed him into cooperating with them."

Stephen sat still and listened. Is that how they recruited their jihadis? Blackmail? Drugs? The whole world had watched in horror the security camera tapes from Le Méridien, the chilling sight of a young man, barely nineteen years old, walking around and talking on a phone to an unseen supervisor. "Shall I shoot?" he would ask and then shoot innocent hostages. How did they teach such a young person to hate like that? They must have filled him up with so much cocaine, he couldn't tell the difference between a real human being and a video game.

George's voice brought him back. "But Sid has grown increasingly afraid. He wants out, especially with a baby on the way. He knows the FBI is investigating his finances and charitable contributions. He's been trying to figure out how to approach us, I guess. Luckily there you were, right next door—his neighbor of three years. This was his way. First confirm your credentials and then reach out."

Stephen listened without any reaction.

George looked at him. Come on. Say something. Enough with the stiff upper lip. Wasn't Stephen shocked, surprised, worried?

He continued when Stephen didn't say anything. "What a delicious victory if they had gotten you in addition to those poor bastards in the hotel. They would have gloated that they took out a top American intelligence officer. They would have dragged you around like an animal."

"And they very nearly did."

It wasn't the dying that bothered Stephen but the thought of Nina and what would have happened to her if they had not managed to escape. She would have been a very special hostage. They would not have killed her. That would have been too easy and too kind. They would have had no qualms about using her to get to him and to the agency. Do they behead women? He shuddered.

"I am sorry it was so close," George went on. "As soon as I got your SOS, we tried to track down our local agent there, but we had such difficulty making contact with him. His phone didn't ring, and the embassy driver couldn't find his house. It was madness. Phone connections and street addresses in India are ridiculous."

Stephen suddenly remembered the crowd of children in the hotel pool. He had watched them that morning. They had splashed and played with a huge, red beach ball in the aquamarine water of the pool without a care, laughing and yelling. He had been so tempted to jump in and join them. Had any of them made it out alive?

Why had he and George been so in love with the Mumbai-by-sea theory? Right, because fucking Sid had made those reconnaissance trips. All signs had pointed to his interests. Data mining experts had pored over and analyzed intercepts of Sid's data traffic, his physical movements in India, and his calling pattern. All indicated an abnormal interest in marine routes around Mumbai.

Stephen rested his elbows on the desk and squeezed his temples with his thumbs. "I was there. I should have picked up on the signs. I should have had a fucking clue. There had to have been some indication, some misstep. I should have been able to stop them. I failed completely."

For the hundredth time, he looked back and allowed himself to dwell on what had happened. The hotel staffers, most of them in their twenties, so courteous and full of life. "Hello, Mr. and Mrs. James," they would greet him and Nina in the corridors with unfailing cheerfulness. "Welcome back, Mr. and Mrs. James. Did you have a nice evening?" they'd ask. Had all those young people perished, breaking the hearts and lives of those who loved them?

"Stephen, even if you had known or guessed, there was nothing you could have done. The Indians would never allow us to operate on their territory. It would have taken too long to get permissions from our government and theirs. You couldn't have prevented it."

Stephen took a sip of coffee. It tasted metallic and smelled as if it had been sitting on the hot plate for too long. He put the cup down.

"I could have pulled the fire alarm or started a fire or fired a gun and gotten the police to arrest me. I could've done something to distract the terrorists. At least to slow them down."

"Well, you had Nina to consider."

"Yes." Stephen looked down at the shiny wedding band on his finger. Yes, he had Nina to consider. Having dragged her into this murky world, he owed her at least that much. What kind of husband would he be otherwise?

The burly sardar in charge of the morning breakfast extravaganza at Le Méridien had asked Nina that question every day. He presided over twenty long tables covered with Indian, continental, American, Japanese, Mediterranean, and every other cuisine known to mankind yet found time to harangue her. He spoke Hindi and English with a thick Punjabi accent and called Nina *baby-ji*. The sardar made no effort to disguise his disapproval that a nice Indian girl should waste herself on a snooty white man—a *goraa*, as he put it insultingly. He would ask Nina why she was with Stephen. When Stephen tried to interject, he would brush him off, his eyes glued to Nina, and address his remarks solely to her. She would instinctively jump to Stephen's defense until Stephen pulled her away. And even after they sat down to eat, the sardar in his brightly colored turban would shoot looks at them. He would also send delicacies their way, and the waiter would specifically say that they were for baby-ji.

The breakfast sardar drew Stephen's suspicion because of his belligerence toward Stephen. But he had come up clean in Stephen's database search—no match of his fingerprints or face in the catalog of suspected or known terrorists, no known contact or links to any organizations or people on the watch list—so Stephen reluctantly had come to the conclusion that the sardar was just having some fun at his expense. He hoped that at least now the man, who must surely be in heaven, approved and thought Stephen worthy of Nina.

George looked at him with a mixture of sympathy and affection. "Sid will approach you in the near future. Be prepared. Let me know how you want to handle his case."

YOUTHFUL ADVICE

Nina was listless in her parents' home. She was silent, moody, waiting without end. Her mother wondered if Nina was pregnant, but Nina quashed that line of thought. Her father was convinced that Stephen had been up to some villainy to reduce Nina to a ghost of her bubbly self. She would have preferred to go back to Jersey City, but Stephen had asked her to stay with her parents for a few days.

It was oppressive, this constant parental scrutiny. No matter how many times she denied that she and Stephen had a quarrel, the topic would crop up again and again. She desperately needed someone to talk to. Amy was off touring with Jeff. Anyway she was not sure how much she could tell Amy without feeling disloyal to Stephen or reinforcing Amy's disapproval of him.

Nina spent the days in her room, staring at the lovely magnolia in full bloom outside her French windows and exchanging perfunctory e-mails with Stephen. Resentment bubbled inside her with no way out.

The house came to life when her kid brother Neel came home from college for spring break. He was the baby of the family; his grandmother, mother, and sister spoiled him rotten. Their father was left to be the stern disciplinarian, but he was equally indulgent of Neel in his own way.

Nina peeked into his room, which had gone from tidy to chaotic in a matter of seconds. It was a corner room guarded by Nina's room on one side and their grandparents' on the other. A large suitcase lay open on the rug, with books, clothes, and toiletries spilling out in an unruly mess. A pair of jeans and a T-shirt drooped on the back of a chair while a towel lay damply crumpled at the foot of the bed. The top of Neel's curly, black head was visible under the comforter, which heaved gently with his breathing. The bum! He was asleep within minutes of coming home.

Nina shook him.

"What?"

"Wake up! Let's go." She shook him again.

"Neenz! I haven't slept in days. I am tired." He tunneled deeper into the comforter.

"Neel, I need to talk to you. Come on."

He didn't answer.

"Please."

That got his attention. Since when did his big sister plead with him? He sat up. "OK, OK," he agreed and put on his jeans. He and Nina slipped out before anyone could stop them and make them stay for lunch.

The Indian restaurant they went to was packed with the lunch buffet crowd. A teenage waiter seated them with surly nonchalance. Their booth was in a quiet corner—a miracle given the incredible decibel level of the place. Neel, after months of bland dorm food and endless rounds of Chipotle, Subway, and Panera, inhaled the aroma with Homer Simpson's dreamy doughnut gaze. *Matar paneer, alu gobhi,* and *daal* filled up his plate in a colorful mound, with *naan* and *jeera* rice balanced precariously at the top. He dug his spoon into this intricately layered meal like an archaeologist and ate until he finally had to come up for air.

Nina had been waiting impatiently for him to pause. She said immediately, "I need to tell you something, but swear you won't repeat it to anyone, ever."

He sat back with a sigh of contentment and stretched. Neel was athletic, with the slender build of a soccer player. To outsiders he appeared impressively dignified and composed for his twenty years, but in reality he was a complete imp.

Nina got up and sat next to him in the booth. It was easier to talk that way. They looked like twins in gray sweatshirts and blue jeans. Once she started, the story poured out. She told him everything: how Stephen had woken her up in the middle of the night at Le Méridien, the gun, the sprint through the garbage field, the private flights, and finally the truth about Stephen. Tears tripped down her cheeks when she got to the part about how she felt deceived and that he might have married her to use her as cover for his job and—who knew?—might leave her once it was done.

Neel listened, slack-jawed. *Good God!* Nina could have been one of those unfortunate bodies flung out the windows of Le Méridien, shown in an endlessly re-peated clip on Fox News. His beloved, much admired sister would have been killed but for Stephen.

When Neel first had met Stephen, his reaction had been to wonder why Nina wanted to marry this uptight, stuck-up guy. There were plenty of Indian guys inter-ested in her, including that insufferable Samir. Neel had always thought she would marry a nice Indian boy and make their parents happy while he would bring their disapproval on his head with some exotic choice. What did she see in Stephen? He was decent looking but nothing special, your typical clean-cut, corpo-rate America look, though admittedly he was in great shape. And at first glance, he looked older than Nina. It couldn't be his money that attracted her because, in Neel's opinion, she didn't have the imagination to spend her own considerable money, let alone lust after others'. Anyway she was too proud to ask for or accept anything from anyone.

But as Neel had gotten to know Stephen, he'd first been impressed by what a good athlete he was—a quality Neel held in high regard. All his heroes were athletes. Stephen had routinely drubbed Neel at squash and tennis despite being thirteen years his senior. When Stephen had taken him sailing and taught him how to race a sailboat, Neel had become a staunch admirer and devotee. The more he had gotten to know Stephen, the more he had appreciated his principles; his sense of right and wrong; his commitment to whatever he took on, from horticulture to sailing; and his fearlessness. Stephen had grown fond of Neel as well because he was a lot like Nina: bright, good natured, and easygoing only sillier, with a raunchy sense of humor that got increasingly sophomoric with Nina's protests. Neel had been a frequent guest when Nina and Stephen spent time at Stephen's home in Massachusetts.

Now Neel ate his naan, and looked at Nina's drawn face. He was a level headed and deliberate young man, with the same gentleness and compassion as Nina.

"You are being terribly unfair to Stephen," he said.

Nina burst into a fresh fit of tears at this verdict. She had been holding it in and holding it together for so long, she could not control herself anymore. It had been a challenge to act normal around her parents and grandparents.

"Stop it, Neenz. The guy's nuts about you." Neel was alarmed by her uncharacteristic behavior and passed her his napkin to wipe her face. She was one tough girl, and had never buckled under pressure of any kind. He remembered the time when his parents had been away with his grandmother on some pilgrimage. His grandfather, who had stayed behind to babysit the grandkids, had taken ill. Nina had just turned seventeen at that time and had a brand-new driver's license. She had handled everything, including hospitalization, surgery, and discharge, during the two days it had taken for their parents to get back from the remote corner of India they were in. Neel, who had been only ten at that time, had followed Nina everywhere with a worried look, his hand holding on to her backpack. She was his hero.

Neel continued his homily. "I can tell you with absolute confidence that no guy will ever marry a girl for the sake of a job—heck, most guys can't get themselves to marry for love."

Nina knew all this and had repeated it to herself like a mantra over the last few days, to quell her sense of betrayal.

"He must feel awful that he put you in such danger and that he could have tried to save those people had he stayed back."

Nina sat up with a start, as if Neel had slapped her. She had been so wrapped up in self-pity, she had spared no thought for what Stephen must have been going through. She felt ashamed. Stephen's stricken voice haunted her ears: "I should have guessed. I could have saved them."

Nina felt petty and selfish after this gentle but entirely justified rebuke from her kid brother. He looked incongruously childish while he ate *gajar halwa* and examined the spoon for crumbs.

"As for your accusation of deception," he continued, "that is the nature of his job. He couldn't have told you before you got married. I'm sure he would have told you at some point. You've been married just six months, and he might have been worried about your reaction. And he was right—you've been freaking out ever since you found out."

Nina couldn't think of a counterargument. Why had she been in such a snit? The restaurant quieted down as the lunch crowd thinned. The staff started to clean up with an audible sigh of relief. Neel nudged her with his shoulder.

"You know, Nina, from what I've seen of Stephen, he treats you with love and respect, he doesn't fool around. He's a really good guy."

Neel looked at her, but she was lost in thought and stared at her hands linked in her lap.

He threw up his hands. "I don't understand you. What more do you women want?"

He said the last sentence with such comic exasperation that she laughed. She kissed him on the cheek. "Thank you, Neel. Please keep this to yourself."

UNDERSTANDING

Nina woke up to the sound of running water. She always slept poorly at Stephen's place. They had arrived from New Jersey the previous night; he had picked her up on his way back from Virginia. His home had a Gosford Park–like feel for her. Every service and convenience was at her beck and call, yet she was uneasy.

Nina sat up in bed. The sound of running water became louder. Was it raining, or was one of the faucets dripping? She stretched out her hand for Stephen, but he was not in bed. What time was it? She slid off the dizzy heights of the canopy bed and felt around on the carpet for her slippers. That was when she noticed that the bathroom lights were on.

She knocked, but there was no response. "Stephen," she called. When he didn't answer, she got worried and pushed open the door. The enormous room, almost as large as her studio, was swathed in wisps of steam, but the huge bathtub at the center was empty. In the far corner, the shower stall was opaque with warm, humid air. She slid the door aside. Stephen sat on the wide seating ledge, fully clothed, with his head bowed under the steady rain from a swiveling showerhead the size of a dinner plate. He turned off the shower when he saw her.

"Did I wake you?" he asked and wiped the water out of his eyes. His T-shirt and pajama pants were thoroughly drenched. She gathered her nightgown around her and stepped into the stall.

"What are you doing, sitting here like this?"

"Nothing."

The sights, sounds, and scenes of their days at Le Méridien played in his head, and he scanned them for clues, a mere hint, a telltale sign. His fellow intelligence officers had assured him unequivocally there was nothing he could have done to avert or mitigate the New Delhi disaster. But he couldn't absolve himself so easily. There were always signs. No one could plan and pull off such a flawless operation. There had to have been something: an accent, a face, an inconsistency he should have picked up on.

For some reason he kept going back to the breakfast buffet sardar. The agency's image scanners deployed around the world had caught no glimpse of him after the attack. The satellites that snooped on the bits and bytes that whizzed through the airwaves had not intercepted any activity on his phone. Stephen had no reason to believe that the buffet sardar was alive.

But why had he been so interested in Nina? He kept baiting her by referring to Stephen as *phirang*, a disparaging term for a Caucasian. There were many other couples there, some of them multiracial like Nina and Stephen. Why had he singled them out? Anyway the sardar was probably dead, killed during the attack, either by the terrorists or the final explosion that had torn through the hotel and destroyed everyone and everything inside. It was going to take years for the Indian government to identify and tag the remains of the dead.

Stephen's brain had worked itself to a feverish exhaustion; his eyes were red and hot from sleeplessness. He had gotten out of bed to sit in the shower, just as he had seen his grandfather do in times of distress, looking for guidance, looking for peace.

Nina had never seen him so despondent. She had seen him moody, brooding, angry, and upset but never without the undercurrent of arrogant confidence that was such a defining trait of his personality, a trait so many people, including her friend Amy, found off-putting.

She sat next to him and put her arm around his shoulders. With her free hand, she pushed the dripping hair off his face and wiped it dry with her nightgown. Stephen smiled his first smile in more than a week.

Nina's clothes soaked up the water, and soon she was as soggy as he was. But she was warm from being in bed and held him close to transfer her warmth to him.

"I'm sorry I've been so mean to you, Stephen." The magic of the prolonged embrace had soothed and healed the rawness of their recent discord.

"Have you?" He smiled and looked up at her. "Have you been mean to me?" he murmured with his head on her chest. *Stee-phen, Stee-phen, Stee-phen,* her heart sang.

"Yes. I was cold and distant and angry." She pulled his wet head up so she could see his face. "I am sorry." She had tried to say these words to him during the drive from New Jersey, but he had been withdrawn and morose the entire time, his mind still in Virginia, which had made conversation impossible.

"You had a lot to handle. It was natural that you should be upset," he said.

"No, it wasn't. I should have been there to comfort you while you were beating yourself up. Instead I ran off to my parents' house in a selfish huff. I am sorry."

She tightened her arms around him and kissed the water off his tired face, his wet lashes, his cheeks, and finally his lips. The touch of her hand revived him like *sanjeevani*, the magical herb that brought Lakshman back to consciousness in the Ramayana. And now, with his face cradled in her hands, she sent the energy of the entire universe coursing through his body like the goddess Shakti.

AFTERMATH

The couch in the waiting room at Boston Memorial Hospital was lumpy, covered with stains, and full of crumbs that peeked out of the crevices between the cushions. Stephen's boss, George and his wife, Ginnie, sat on it and watched Nina pace. Stephen was in surgery. His left side had been shattered by bullets, and he had lost a lot of blood. Nina's stomach was on fire from the anxiety and the acid released by the coffee she sipped continuously. Neel had suffered cuts to his head, but they were not serious. He was in a heavily guarded room, deep in narcotic sleep.

Ginnie got up and walked with Nina, holding her hand in both hers. Nina was grateful for her company.

She had swooped down upon Nina as soon as she'd arrived and hugged her tightly.

"Honey, he *will* be fine," she had said and almost caused Nina to bawl. Ginnie was a godsend, a stand-in for Nina's mother, who Nina had not contacted yet per George's orders.

Was it just five hours ago that she had been eating popcorn in a movie theater? Her life was just getting back to normal after the New Delhi incident. She had gone out on her own to see a chick flick while her husband and brother bonded over a manly game of squash. A few minutes into the movie, there was a tap on her shoulder, and an usher told her she was needed outside. She was surprised to see George standing in the lobby.

"There has been an accident," he had said. "A shoot-out at your neighbor Sid Ali's residence. An armed robbery."

Apparently Stephen and Neel had rushed over to help. Neel had minor injuries, but Stephen was in bad shape. George had driven her to Boston Memorial, where Ginnie had joined them.

"I know how you feel," Ginnie said to Nina as they made another round of the lobby. "George was in a South American prison for two months during our first year of marriage. I had no idea at all at the time what George did for a living. I thought he was a graduate student, like me. One day there was a knock at the door, and two officers walked in and told me George was in prison."

"What did you do? How did you feel?"

The two women turned to look at George, who suppressed a smile at their accusatory stares.

"I felt like someone had socked me in the stomach. 'As soon as he comes back, it's quits,' I told myself. But the minute I saw him at the door, gaunt and exhausted, all I could do was hold him and cry like a baby."

Ginnie looked at George and relived that moment. He remembered it well too. He had hesitated on the stoop before he'd rung the bell and thought hopelessly, *She's probably not here. She's left me. Gone back to her old boyfriend.*

"He had scars all over his body," Ginnie went on. "His ribs dug into my sides when I held him."

Nina couldn't imagine George in such a state of emaciation.

"I was mad at him but at the same time delirious he was safe."

Old George actually blushed and looked away.

Nina was angry with him even though he had nothing to do with Stephen's injuries. But she held him responsible for introducing Stephen to a dangerous career that encouraged his recklessness. He didn't deserve a kind, generous woman like Ginnie.

A security guard ushered in two men in suits and directed them toward Nina.

"Mrs. James, I am John Barre," said one of the men, "your husband's family attorney. And this is my colleague, Jim Calderbank."

Nina shook their hands mechanically, not sure why they were there.

Barre was in his early sixties, tall and lean. Calderbank was younger, with an incongruous baby face and a shiny, smoothly shaved head. Were lawyers allowed to do that?

"We're sorry to hear about the accident," said Barre. "We hope Mr. James will recover soon. In the meantime, Mrs. James, we need to talk to you."

George, who seemed to know the legals well, showed them to a small room and left, closing the door behind him. Nina sat in close quarters with the lawyers.

"Mrs. James, we have to talk to you about your husband's will," said Barre.

"Why? He's going to be fine." Nina was reluctant. Talking of such matters would only tempt fate, according to superstitions she'd inherited from her grandmother.

"We know, we know," Calderbank said in a soothing tone. "But there are certain things we have to apprise you of since your husband left very specific instructions. Unfortunately it would have been easier if we had had a chance to discuss this under less-stressful circumstances."

"Discuss what?" Nina looked at her cell phone. What if the doctor had come out to talk to her? George had promised to call her if there were any activity.

"Estate planning issues and a living will."

"I have nothing to do with the estate. You should talk to his family."

The lawyers looked at each other in surprise. Nina was distracted; her mind hovered in the waiting room and prayed for the doctor to come out. She tried to get up and excuse herself, but Barre interjected.

"Please, Mrs. James, just a few more minutes."

She sat down.

"Mr. James left very specific instructions for you about his care in case of a medical emergency. We have prepared a summary for you."

She took the sheet from Barre's skeletal hand. Hot tears stung her eyes as she raced down the list: no life support of any kind, do not revive in case of cardiac arrest, all healthy organs to be donated. She turned the page and read "property disbursement, Nina Sharma, sole beneficiary of all estates and holdings."

"When did he do this?" Her voice trembled.

"September twenty-ninth of last year."

Two days before their wedding, the day they had decided to get married.

"I have to go. Thank you for stopping by."

Nina got up and fled to a corner of the waiting room where she could be alone. She couldn't hold it in anymore. She sat down in a chair, covered her face with her hands, and let the sobs explode inside her chest.

Ginnie rose from the sofa to go to her, but George held her back.

"Give her space." He conferred with the lawyers briefly before they left.

Nina wiped her face and returned to the couch to sit between George and Ginnie. The room felt stuffy. Her chest and throat were tight and tense; her nose and eyes felt raw. She was in the same clothes from the night before. George offered to drive her to his and Ginnie's place for a shower and a nap, but she wouldn't leave the waiting room even for a minute. They had to make her go to the restroom and wash her face once every few hours just to break her anxiety.

Ginnie and George spoke in undertones.

"She is tough. She is strong," he said.

"You demand too much from us," Ginnie replied. She had been through the Cold War and two South American coups with George out in the field. There were no words to describe the black, nauseating despair that permeated every minute of the day, every cell in the brain. She had celebrated with champagne when George had grown too old for fieldwork, relieved that he had survived the Russian roulette of espionage.

Another two hours went by. Nina seemed to shed pounds in front of their eyes with her pacing. She checked on Neel a few times, but he was still asleep. Around four in the morning, the doors to the treatment area swung open, and a doctor came out.

"Mrs. James?" he looked around, right past Nina. He was a tall Iranian in his late forties, slightly jowly but still handsome, with a leonine mane of salt-and-pepper hair.

"I am Mrs. James," Nina said.

He had not expected to see a young Indian woman. He recovered from his surprise and turned to her with a professional smile. "It was a complicated surgery, but he did well. The injuries were extensive but, fortunately, not too deep. And thankfully none of the vital organs were hit. He is a lucky man."

And a smart man, with the bulletproof vest, the doctor thought.

"Will he be OK?" Nina asked, tears perched precariously behind her lashes, waiting for the slightest lassitude on her part to come flooding out.

What beautiful eyes, he thought.

"There is no danger to his life," he said kindly.

Nina was giddy with relief, but with an iron will she held back the tears. "Will he regain functionality of his arm and leg?"

He was guarded. "I cannot say for sure, Mrs. James, but there is no reason why he shouldn't unless there's some secondary infection that damages the tissue." He turned to leave, but she had another question.

"What about scars? Will the scars be permanent?"

He faced her once more. "Yes, the scars are permanent, but the good news is there is no injury to his face or neck. The scars won't be visible unless he removes his shirt." This time he waited in case she had more questions.

"When can I see him?"

All her love, distress, and worry of the past hours were concentrated in those hopeful eyes. *What a lucky man*, the doctor thought, *to have someone love him so much.*

"We'll bring him to his room in an hour or so, but he won't be awake for at least another four to five hours. And even then we'll keep him sedated for a few days to ease his pain."

"Will he be in a lot of pain?"

"Yes, Mrs. James," he replied in a gentle voice that he usually reserved for children. "But we'll try our best to see that he doesn't feel it. And with you near him, I'm sure he won't even notice it."

She smiled. The tears flowed freely. "Thank you, Doctor," she mumbled. He shook her hand and strode off smartly.

Nina ran to George and Ginnie and relayed the news.

Ginnie wrapped her in a maternal embrace. "Let's go home. You need to take a shower and come back all pretty for Stephen."

George agreed. He was as relieved as Nina, although he had not shown how worried he had been. He had seen Stephen brought out of the ambulance unconscious, his clothes soaked in blood, and his face an unhealthy gray. He had been attached to IVs through which the paramedics pumped all manner of fluids into him. George had made sure Nina didn't see Stephen until he was cleaned up and on the stretcher under a blanket, so she couldn't know the extent of his injuries. George had allowed her a quick kiss and hustled her out before she could see any more.

"George!"

He shook his head free of the memory of Stephen's blood-splattered face and came back to respond to Nina's words. She wanted Neel and Stephen in the same room.

"I will take care of it." He took her arm and led the way to the garage while Ginnie stayed back in case Stephen or Neel needed help.

Neel. Now there was a surprise. George had met him at Stephen's Indian wedding and had written him off as a pleasant but frivolous youth. He was a natural with people and had an easy and engaging manner but nothing more. But today George was awed and amazed by him. It took balls to do what he had done. For a twenty-year-old pampered child—because that was what he was—who had never seen a gun in his life, to do what he did. It had taken courage, confidence, and utter devotion. Stephen would have bled to death if it weren't for Neel.

George hadn't told Nina the real story. It hadn't been an armed robbery gone wrong. Stephen had been lured away from the squash game into a meeting at Sid's home, where he was ambushed by two of Akhtar's men. They had been interrogating Sid. Neel, who had returned home after the squash match to pack, had heard the gunshots and rushed over to see what happened. Stephen had managed to incapacitate the two men by then, but he had been losing too much blood and had become unconscious. Neel had run into the glass-strewn house, searched around among the bloody debris, pulled Stephen to safety, and called for an ambulance. Meanwhile George had also dispatched his team to make sure Akhtar's men and Sid had been spirited away before the local authorities could get to them.

But he couldn't tell any of that to Nina.

RELIEF

S tephen tried to open his eyes, but they felt glued shut. His whole left side felt numb and raw at the same time, like a thousand knives had had their way with his limbs. He couldn't move. His eyes finally managed to open a slit. He was surrounded by flashing, beeping screens. A soft light filtered through the translucent shades on the windows.

The last thing he could remember was Neel's face over him. He had felt his blood soaking through the bewildered young man's clothes. "I am so sorry," he remembered saying to him. "Tell Nina." And then he must have fallen asleep.

Stephen tried to concentrate. Where was he now? He tried to move but couldn't. He must have been tied down. The bastards had gotten him! As his eyes adjusted, he saw a figure in a chair next to him, slumped over the bed near his hand. Friend or foe? Across the room there was another bed, the patient in it hooked up to gizmos just like he was. Looks like America at least, not some goddamned cave in Tora Bora.

Nina! He hoped Neel had given her his message. Had the kid made it? Neel had been bleeding from the head pretty badly. Stephen's head throbbed as he tried to get his bearings and remember what had happened.

Nina, in the chair by the bed, woke up. She had felt movement. Stephen was squirming and trying to sit up in bed.

"Stephen!" She climbed in next to him and covered his face with kisses. Crying and laughing, she drenched him with tears. He opened his eyes a little wider and tried to smile. His skin had a bluish-gray pallor, and his eyes were dulled by the pain and the drugs, with big, gray circles around the sockets.

"I am sorry, sweetheart," he said.

She grinned 'til her cheeks hurt and hugged him with joy, careful not to crush his injured side.

"How is Neel?" he asked groggily after a pause. Every word required effort.

"He's fine. He's right there." She pointed to the other patient.

"Thank God." Stephen fell back on the pillow in relief and held on to her hand with his good one.

During the following week, Nina hardly left Stephen's side. George worked miracles for her and arranged for her to stay in the room with Neel and Stephen. He transported her clothes, talked to her parents, and arranged a special wireless Internet connection for her in the room. Stephen channeled his will through George and made him attend to Nina's every need.

Neel was discharged after a few days and went straight back to school, parents none the wiser. All they and the general public knew was that there had been some kind of an armed robbery at the Ali residence, which Stephen had tried to stop. His injuries were downplayed in the press as well as to Nina's parents. They had no knowledge of Neel's involvement. As far as they were concerned, he had stayed back to help Nina. George had complete control of the story and had not allowed a single unintended detail to get out.

Just before Neel's departure, George took him aside.

"Call me whenever you want. Don't hesitate. There are people already stationed on your campus. They will babysit you. Don't worry. You are safe. You did an amazing job, and we will stay in touch."

Nina saw Neel off with a heavy heart. His presence had been a huge help to her. She and George followed

Neel to the door of the hospital. Nina had a list of things he should and shouldn't do, sounding exactly like their mother. Neel gave her a long, solemn hug and got into a taxi. George and Nina watched until it disappeared from sight.

"George, I don't want him involved in this," Nina warned. She didn't want Neel getting mixed up with this crowd. She had more to say, but she wanted to get back to Stephen.

The hospital staff doted on the couple. He was some hush-hush hero. His room was under constant guard. She was his devoted wife, the sweetest thing you ever saw, with a ready smile for everyone. The nurses were smitten by the romance, how she slept with his hand to her heart, and how he smashed the doctor's prognostications with his rapid recovery. It had to be because of her constant touch, they sighed.

George stopped by every day on his way back from work. Sometimes Ginnie joined him. They usually found Nina curled up next to Stephen on his good side, working on her laptop if he was asleep or lying next to him if he was awake, reading aloud from a newspaper or magazine. Or they would catch her singing to him—old Hindi film songs, hopelessly romantic, sentimental ballads of love and yearning. Stephen looked happy with his head on Nina's breast, comforted by the steady beat of her heart, his good hand wrapped around her waist while she cradled him in her arms.

Her voice came from deep within her belly, traveled up her lungs and throat, and poured sweetly into his ears. She stopped as soon as she saw George, abashed.

"What have you done, Nina?" George pretended to scold her. He was delighted for Stephen. This was typical—trust him to zero in on the one woman on the planet who was his perfect complement, who would adore him and worship him and put up with all his madness.

When the handsome Iranian doctor pronounced Stephen well enough to be discharged, Nina was ecstatic. They had just completed four weeks in the hospital, and she was desperate to go home. Stephen had started a painful physiotherapy regimen and was able to get around on crutches.

Nina ran around in a frenzy, gathering the names of specialists, doctors, nutritionists, physiotherapists, and trainers in the New York-New Jersey area. She wheedled a cell phone number out of the Iranian doctor. Stephen felt helpless in the unaccustomed role of a spectator, sitting and watching her take charge of his life. It was a frightening and emasculating experience.

On their last night in the hospital, he woke up around midnight. Nina was asleep and occupied hardly any space next to him in the bed. The nightlight shed a ghostly glow on her. As he watched her peaceful face, suddenly and without warning, his tears flowed. The anger, frustration, and guilt that had begun on that night at Le Méridien and culminated in blood and fire at his doorstep finally extracted their price. He shuddered to think what would have happened to Nina if he had been killed. Worse, he had put Neel's life in danger.

When Nina felt him move, her fingers instinctively reached for his face and found his damp eyelids.

"Come here." She drew him to her and caressed his cheek with maternal tenderness.

THE DECISION

"**I**'m on my way."

Stephen was stuck in Manhattan traffic en route to meet George at the Museum of Modern Art. Four weeks had crawled by since his homecoming from the hospital. He and Nina had moved to a two-bedroom apartment on the Upper West Side to be closer to the medical facilities he frequented.

During those initial hectic weeks, his in-laws had been invaluable. They had helped them move, arranged for the sale of Nina's Jersey City apartment, driven him to appointments to lighten Nina's schedule, and taken embarrassingly good care of him. In the beginning he had felt uncomfortable and highly obliged. But this was their way—the family clustered around those in need. When Stephen had suggested a professional caregiver, Nina had been outraged at the thought of a stranger taking care of him. He didn't have the energy to argue with her. Besides, she was the one in charge of his life right now, and she had every right to handle it the way she wanted. The only reason she allowed even the nurse to come and change his bandages twice a day was that she was afraid she might mess up, and the wounds would get infected.

During the first week, both his in-laws had stayed over. They had been discreet and considerate and kept to their bedroom to give Stephen his space. After the initial awkwardness, he had found the sound of their voices in the apartment comforting and looked forward to lunch with them every day. One of them had taken him to the appointments (Nina would meet them at the doctor's office) while the other had taken care of running the household—sorting the mountains of mail for Stephen or Nina to look through, organizing the medical bills and insurance documents, making Stephen's appointments, keeping his medical supplies stocked, and ordering groceries. They had done it naturally, without making it seem like a favor. To put him at his ease on his very first day at home, his mother-in-law had said to him with a smile, "One is a parent for life, and you kids are our responsibility for as long as we live."

Stephen had spent the first week in a fog, sleeping for long stretches. Physiotherapy and bandage changes had been the main punctuation points every day other than lunch and dinner. His wounded arm and thigh had occupied his attention constantly in those first few weeks. They had throbbed under the bandages. *Zia's calling card—the marks of Zorro*, he had named them in a fit of bitterness. Zia Akhtar had sent the two men to question Sid because he'd suspected Sid of working for Stephen.

George sent Stephen snippets of information on memory sticks through the nurse—a transcript of Sid's debriefing, details about the two men Akhtar had sent, their backgrounds. Nina, of course, had no idea.

Sid was in a real mess. He had started off with the best of intentions, seduced by Tariq Rehman's elegant oratory and his credentials as the head of South Asian studies at the nearby university. Rehman had gotten Sid involved in several foundations and their boards. By the time Sid had woken up to the reality of these outfits, it had been too late. However, instead of contacting the FBI or even the local police, Sid had made the active choice—and this was an important sticking point for Stephen—to go along with Rehman's plan of scouting for potential targets for a terror attack in India. And even at that stage, Sid had not informed the authorities, knowing full well that hundreds of innocent people were about to be killed in cold blood.

Unconscionable, Stephen thought, and just for that he should hang.

Of the two jihadis sent to interrogate Sid, one was a newbie, probably sent to observe only—a field trip at Sid's expense. He was a student and had been summoned for this mission. The main interrogator, Asad, had come all the way from Michigan, Sid's childhood stomping grounds. He had looked vaguely familiar to Stephen, who had George's analysts simulate different hairstyles and beard and moustache variations, and finally it struck him: Asad looked like the breakfast buffet sardar! But it couldn't be because the fingerprints didn't match. He listened to a snippet of Asad's voice. The nasal, irritating, high-pitched voice was unmistakable, except this time he had used an American accent.

"Check for siblings," he told George. "A twin brother, perhaps."

There was another development that worried Stephen: Neel and George were in regular contact.

"Leave him alone, George. Don't get him involved in this shit."

"I didn't do anything. Neel is the one bugging me for an internship. He is incessant."

Stephen shouted, "Send him away! Don't encourage him."

When Stephen got tired of George's files, he moved to the living room to watch TV. His father-in-law joined him if the news or a sports show were on.

They stuck to safe topics like literature, movies, and sports and carefully avoided politics. The whole family was firmly to the left of center as Stephen had discovered—no surprise there. The mere mention of the word "gun" got them worked up. How could a civilized society condone gun ownership? It was a relic from the Wild West days. Terrorists were taking full advantage of the lax gun rules. Mark my words, his father-in-law pronounced, we will be killed by terrorists with the very guns we let them buy!

And when he had exhausted all the possibilities television had to offer, Stephen amused himself by studying his in-laws. Ravi, his father-in-law, traveled frequently, and spent ninety five percent of his time on the phone with clients, lawyers, suppliers, and engineers. He loved nothing better than a crisis.

"I don't understand why it is so fucking hard to cut a piece of steel to specifications!" Stephen heard him yell on the phone. "And don't tell me you're going to charge me again because you couldn't get it right in the first place."

Ravi left after the second week, and Deepa, Stephen's mother-in-law, came to cover the third. She was the head of the drug discovery group at a pharmaceutical company. A big part of her job was to manage the egos of her researchers and herd them toward a common goal. One minute Stephen overheard her cajoling a guy into running experiments, and the next she was hectoring another to "bloody finish the paper already." Lawyers figured prominently in her conversations; she was on the phone for hours with them and hated them with a passion. But above all she was Mother Goddess, as Nina called her with irreverent affection—a force of nature in the most subversive way who ploughed down the defenses of boys and men.

Stephen had gotten a taste of it firsthand during that week. He had hobbled into the kitchen, where Deepa was busy making tea, to get a drink. (This was a family of tea drinkers; they drank it in prodigious amounts.) She had offered him a cup, and he had sat down on a stool at the counter to drink it.

Halfway through a sentence, she exclaimed, "Stephen, your bandage is leaking!"

He looked down at his arm. The wound had oozed and soaked the sleeve of his T-shirt.

"I'll change it." He got up, embarrassed by another reminder of his weakness. He knew full well he couldn't do it by himself but was too proud to ask for help.

"Rubbish! I'll do it. That's what I'm here for."

The nurse had set up a bandaging station in the bathroom with a chair that had an armrest and a cabinet full of supplies next to it. Deepa sat on a stool across from him. She unwrapped the bandage slowly and stopped, staggered by how violent and extensive his injuries were.

"You poor boy!" The words flew out of her mouth with a spontaneity that caught Stephen in the gut. She was in such distress, as if he were her own child. She cleaned the wound and applied the ointment gingerly. It stung terribly; the wound throbbed, and suddenly there was a tennis ball lodged in Stephen's throat that made it impossible for him to swallow or take a gulp of air.

She put the gauze in place and wrapped the bandage with geometric precision, lips pursed in concentration. When she was done, she flashed Nina's smile and put away the paraphernalia.

"Try to stay out of trouble." She looked into his eyes and put her hand on his. He was like her. He hadn't had a consoling maternal presence in his life for the most part, someone who would wipe away the tears and say everything would be fine, just you wait—a presence that would have filled him with safety and protected him from the cruelty and senselessness of the world around.

Deepa handed him the walking stick and helped him to his feet.

"You seem to have a lot of practice." He tried to stop his voice from shaking.

"Yes. Neel was a most injury-prone kid. I don't know how many bandages I have changed."

"You must miss him." They walked back to their tea, which had become tepid.

"I do. He is my baby." Her face was bright at the thought of Neel.

Stephen reddened, taunted by his conscience: *See what you've done? Her baby is walking into a life of danger thanks to you.*

"Nina is not your baby?" he asked.

Deepa had a clipped Indo-British accent with a touch of Jersey that he found charming. "She is, but she is Daddy's girl through and through. Even when she was a baby, as soon as she finished nursing she would bawl for Ravi to pick her up. They were very close, those two, until you came along." She gave him a sidelong glance, full of mischief. "Now it is Stephen this and Stephen that. Poor Ravi. He didn't know what hit him for several weeks after Nina first mentioned you."

Now, sitting in the taxi, Stephen tapped his walking stick impatiently. George would be annoyed by having to wait. Outside, the traffic was a mess. The president was in town, so roads were blocked off, and there was gridlock and utter chaos everywhere. Damn! He couldn't even get out and walk. His leg was much better, but he could not risk straining it.

To Stephen his in-laws were impressive on many levels. He found them to be quite different from what he had expected. Nina's parents were hyperliterate, from distinguished families. They were both well read and widely traveled and had imparted a decidedly global and cosmopolitan outlook to their children. Ravi never missed an opportunity to impress Nina's intellectual and cultural pedigree on Stephen.

But more than qualifications and achievements, Stephen was intrigued by their relationship. Deepa and Ravi had met as freshmen in college in India and married as soon as they had graduated, before they had come to the United States for graduate school. Twenty-eight years, two kids, and two careers later, they still found each other interesting and talked constantly. Stephen had tracked their communication patterns out of professional curiosity. They talked on the phone an average of twelve times a day; he assumed there had to be text and e-mail traffic. And they always had dinner together, during which they would have energetic discussions about the most trivial matters.

"No, we should not plant mandevilla this year."

"But why not?"

And they would debate that for an hour. Nina had told him they had always been this way, worse than teenagers. She and Neel had found it exhausting to be around them at times with this incessant communicativeness, having to tell each other every little thing as soon as it happened. But Stephen thought it very sweet that they still turned to each other so much after so many years. His gruff father-in-law, who was a bit of a hard-ass, thought nothing of driving an hour each way in the middle of the night to pick up his wife at the office because he didn't want her at the wheel when she was tired. He wondered how Nina and he would be in ten years, let alone twenty-eight.

The taxi came to a halt in front of MoMA. As usual the museum was packed with tourists. Stephen could always tell them from the locals even without the cameras. He bought his ticket and walked slowly to the sculpture garden, leaning on his walking stick for support. The café, the venue of his rendezvous, overlooked the garden.

George was already there, gazing meditatively at the goat and the naked lady lying by the pond. He got up to meet Stephen when he saw him come up the steps.

Not bad. Stephen had good color, the steely-gray light was back in his eyes, and he was moving quite well. Not bad at all.

"You look good, Stephen."

"Thanks." He was not particularly warm in his greeting. He leaned his walking stick against the table and took off his raincoat.

The café was not crowded. A solicitous waitress hovered and waited for their order. She turned to Stephen, ready with a big smile and practiced patter, but he quelled her with a cold look. George ordered for both of them and gave her an extra-bright smile to make up for Stephen's rudeness.

"I can't do it, George," he said after she left.

"Why not?" George was curious. He had made an offer to Stephen, a very special mission that would help him get to the bottom of the New Delhi disaster and track down Zia Akhtar, Stephen's nemesis. Akhtar had landed the first vicious punch that had almost crippled Stephen.

"I don't think I can put Nina through something like this again."

George frowned. Women do this to the best of men. They leeched the juice right out, sapped the killer instinct. Marriage spelled the end of all good men.

"But you don't have to go out into the field. You'd just run the operation."

"That's bullshit. You have to do whatever it takes, and sometimes you have to stick your neck out all the way. You can't let your guys take the heat while you sit comfortably in an office. You know it."

George looked at the very expensive but tiny sandwich on his plate. He knew that Stephen wanted to accept the assignment but was trying his best to be fair to his wife.

"Have you mentioned the possibility to Nina?"

"Of course not. She'll go ballistic."

"She might surprise you. I think you underestimate her. I suggest you talk to her before you turn it down."

The rain sprayed the goat and the naked lady with a fine mist. The glass pane lost its transparency under the assault of water and shielded the statues from

Stephen's moody scrutiny. He longed to be back on his dock, ready to set sail for the open sea in his beloved sailboat, ocean spray in his eyes, that feeling of utter stillness and peace. He wondered when he could sail again, when the doctor would let him. He was fed up with this inactivity.

"OK. Let me think about it."

Stephen returned home and fell into bed, exhausted from his outing. He was still asleep when Nina came home from work. He woke up to the smell of potatoes sizzling in sesame oil. Nina was busy cooking dinner and warbled along to some blues song about a heartbreaker. She was clad in a blinding-pink, glitter-covered T-shirt and black gym pants, with her hair tied up in a knot. He leaned against the doorway and watched her, and as usual just the sight of her made him smile.

He walked over to where she was and stood behind her, reaching over her shoulder to eat the potatoes out of the pan until she smacked his hand away.

"I met George today," he said.

The singing stopped. She turned off the stove and turned around to glare at him. George's name got her hackles up even though she was the first one to admit he had been a huge help during the hospital days. Unable to find words to express her ire now, she slammed down the dinner plates, dumped the food down, and sat across from him, ready for battle.

"What did he want?" she asked. "To send you out somewhere to get killed?"

"He offered me a job."

Stephen had recovered well. His confidence and cockiness were back to their original, near-offensive levels. His wounds had dried up. The focus now was on physiotherapy and exercise to get strength and tone back in his thigh and upper arm muscles. The blank, tired look that had bothered Nina more than anything else had finally disappeared. Pain was still a factor, especially with sudden movements, but it didn't suck all the life out of him, as it used to.

She put down her spoon. "What job?"

"As a military attaché to the US consulate in New Delhi."

"What does that mean?"

"It's a common CIA ploy. On paper, I will be a consulting expert on military surveillance. It allows me to be a part of the diplomatic mission. I will have the status of a US diplomat even though I have no foreign-service background. Isn't that great?"

Nina wasn't impressed.

"Why New Delhi?" she asked.

"It's my opportunity to get to the people behind the New Delhi attack."

"Shouldn't you be looking in some godforsaken cave in Pakistan?"

"According to Sid there's an Indian end to the operation, and it's better to start there."

"Sid? What does he know about this? Don't tell me—he works for the CIA too. Since when do we look to Sid for advice?" She was being sarcastic.

"Since he made a plea bargain to help us," Stephen replied in his most soothing voice.

"What?" Nina stared at him. Of course. How could she have been so stupid? "That wasn't an armed robbery at Sid's place, was it?"

"No."

"Stephen, you promised. How could you lie to me again?" And then she remembered Neel. "You risked my brother's life!"

"No, Nina, no. I would never hurt Neel." He tried to reach for her, but she recoiled in her chair. "Nina, honey, you know there are some things I just can't tell you. We discussed that."

"Tell me what happened. Tell me the truth, damn it."

"Nina, I did not involve Neel. I swear on everything I love. Sid wanted my help. I went alone to meet him. But two thugs were already there. They ambushed me. Neel heard the gunshots, called 911, and rushed over to check on me. If it weren't for him, I'd be dead. I owe my life to him."

"Why should I believe you?" She was calmer now.

"You don't have to, but that's the truth. I would never hurt you or Neel. Never. Ever. You know that." He reached for her once more and held her hand across the table.

"Why did Sid want your help?"

Stephen hesitated for a second and then plunged ahead. "I never told you this, but he was the one who tipped me off at Le Méridien to leave at once. He wants me to return the favor."

"How did he know?" she asked, puzzled.

"He had a big part in planning the attack."

She looked at him wide eyed. "What? Our neighbor? Amy's friend, Sid?"

"Yes. Sid is in a lot of trouble. The Pakistanis are after him for helping me get away. He wants to buy protection for his family and for himself by helping us out."

"I can't believe it! How is that possible?"

"People have complicated reasons. He might have thought he was doing it for a just cause. Who knows? But he saved our lives. And if it weren't for him, I'd never have met you. For that I am grateful."

He meant it even though he had said it in part to get on her good side. She was the one thing he had focused on and held on to, the prize that had spurred his recovery. She lay on the bed next to him in the hospital twenty-four hours a day and willed her strength and health to flow to him. It had moved him deeply even though to her it seemed the most obvious and natural thing. To him it was the sort of devotion and commitment Indian mythology was made of, right out of the stories from the Mahabharata and Ramayana that she told him during those terrible days and nights when the pain wouldn't let him sleep. He could never tell her in words how much of an effect it had on him.

Stephen stretched out his injured leg, which had begun to cramp up. She saw him grimace; despite being mad at him, she got up to help him massage his leg.

"Where did you get this hideous T-shirt?" he asked to distract from the topic of Sid.

She ignored the question.

"Now…now you want to go back to Delhi." The sight of his scarred leg reminded her of the danger once more. She stood up with renewed anger. "You are going to get killed at this rate. Why don't you just shoot me? It would be much kinder."

"Nina, come on. Don't be like that."

She shook her head from side to side like a child. "Why not? Sitting in that wretched Boston Memorial lounge, waiting for the doctor to tell me whether you were going to live or die—that was the worst, lowest moment of my life. You have no idea what it feels like, how impossibly wretched and miserable."

"Actually I do," he replied in a low voice, almost a whisper. "That was all I could think of while trying to get you out of Le Méridien. That is all I wished for: that you should make it out of there alive."

Nina stopped, arrested in the middle of her melodramatic declaration, chastised by his emotion.

He tried to put his arm around her waist and get her to sit down near him. He knew that words were futile given how agitated she was. She pushed him away.

He continued. "Nina, they knew who I was. They picked that day because I was there. And Sid tried to play both sides by sending me the note. They sent those assassins to take him out. And now I have to see it through. There is no peace for you and me until those people are put away."

She turned away and walked to the bathroom. Before she could close the door, he slipped in behind her and watched as she brushed her teeth with unnecessary vigor.

"Talk to me, Nina." He said her name so sweetly, she couldn't stay angry.

"Does it really matter what I think?" She was frantic with anxiety but knew that the deal was done; she had no say in it, and he just wanted her to agree and go along with it.

"More than anything else," he replied.

It was true. During the cab ride back home, he had already decided to move ahead. But it mattered to him how she felt about it. He wanted to reason with her and convince her that in the long run, it was better to take care of it now rather than to run from Akhtar all their lives. It could snowball into something worse, and the benefit of pursuing it now far outweighed the risk. His getting shot had been a freak occurrence that happened under a highly complex and unlikely set of circumstances that would most probably never be repeated. He wanted her permission, and he wanted her to go with him willingly and understand that it was the right thing to do, the best thing for both of them. And above all he wanted her to be happy about it.

She sank down on the edge of the bathtub. It was a wrenching moment for her. His ashen face, the lifeless eyes, lips contorted with pain and parched from all the detestable medications being pumped into him—all of that was branded in her memory, as were the long, bleak days she had sat by his bedside while he'd struggled to recover his health and strength. It was barely ten weeks ago.

He knew he was selfish, but he needed her and wanted her with him. He couldn't do it without her. He loved his work and wanted it as much as he wanted Nina. He couldn't give up either.

"I have to see this through," he repeated softly and lifted her chin with his finger.

She brushed it off. "I know," she said hopelessly.

"I can't do it without you. You are my strength. I need you."

She looked at him, only half believing him. This was quite a speech for Stephen.

Her hands—small, with long, slender fingers—rested on her knees. He took them in his hand and sat next to her on the bathtub. It was not safe for her to be there by herself. He wanted her near him, where he could watch over her with a thousand eyes. That was the only way he would take the job, he had told George. And damn George, he could bloody well pay for Nina's security guards in India.

She snatched her hands away from him and braided her hair furiously. He could feel her relenting, melting at his touch, but she was still angry enough to sit stiffly instead of hurling herself into his arms, as she would normally do. He pulled her closer and, with his cheek against hers, murmured, "Won't you come with me to New Delhi, my lovely Nina?"

NEW DELHI

Nina waved excitedly when she spotted Amy in the trickle of people emerging from Indira Gandhi International airport in New Delhi. The airport, with its bizarre décor and throngs of people, was a dazzling swirl of glittering glass and bright lights. Amy and Nina fell into each other's arms.

"You look lovely!" Amy hugged her.

Nina was thrilled to see her friend after six months. The driver took Amy's luggage and held the car door open for them. It was more an armored vehicle than a car. A security guard sat in the front passenger seat with a rifle across his knees. Amy raised her eyebrows in surprise, but Nina merely shook her head and shrugged her shoulders as if to say, "Don't ask."

The night was chilly, cooler than typical November weather, unusually cold even for Delhi. It was the ghostly stretch of time between late night revelry and early morning newspaper delivery runs, and the roads were empty. An occasional bonfire in a metal drum pierced the thick fog, with dark figures swathed in blankets huddled around it for warmth.

"How is everyone back home?" Nina sat sideways so she could see Amy, ignoring the driver's pleas to put on her seatbelt.

"They're all fine. Your mom sent a ton of stuff and told me to tell you she wants grandkids soon."

Nina rolled her eyes. "She shouldn't have bothered you. You have enough to lug around the world without her foisting more things on you."

"I don't mind at all. I love your mom."

Amy and Jeff were on their way to vacation in Bhutan and Nepal. They wanted to spend time with Nina and Stephen before they left. Jeff was scheduled to arrive in Delhi in a couple of days.

The car entered a spacious suburb where the homes were hidden behind high compound walls and tall trees. The streets had remote-controlled gates at various checkpoints that creaked open at the press of a button. Nina and Amy drove through a maze of interconnected streets and alleys and pulled up to a heavily guarded, two-story white bungalow sequestered behind white walls topped with electric wire. The guard who sat in the sentry box opened the solid metal gates and shut them with a noisy whirr as soon as the car slipped inside the compound. The driveway took them to the front of the house, where another security guard stood watch. He saluted smartly and opened the double doors at the entrance. Nina gave instructions in Hindi and dragged Amy inside the house, pulling on her arm like an excited little kid. Even though it was dark, Amy could see and smell the lush garden.

The house had been built around a square courtyard of grassy paths, potted plants, stone benches, and flowering climbers that snaked up stone pillars. An inner veranda bordered the entire perimeter of the courtyard.

Nina and Amy raced down the veranda and up the staircase to the guest bedroom on the second floor. It had a view of the terrace garden on the other side and the courtyard below, lit at this hour by landscaping lights. The fragrance of night-blooming jasmine and *chameli* filled the air.

"Wow, this is paradise," Amy said in a hushed voice.

"You haven't seen the half of it. Uncle Sam treats his diplomats very well. The embassy arranged this official residence for Stephen." Nina grinned. "Are you hungry? What would you like to eat?"

"Nothing. I just want to take a shower first. You should go to bed. Stephen must be waiting for you."

"He isn't around. He'll be back home tomorrow evening."

"How's he doing?"

Amy had heard about the shootout, but all she knew was the publicly circulated story about an armed robbery at the Ali home that went sour. Sheri had totally dropped off the face of the Earth, incommunicado, and hadn't responded to Amy's e-mails or voicemails. Sheri's parents had sent Amy a note saying she had gone abroad. And there were vague rumors about Sid, but no one could help her get in touch with him. Jeff and Amy had visited Stephen at Boston Memorial and had been shocked by how badly he had been injured.

"He is doing well. He's almost one hundred percent recovered, but sometimes he'll strain himself, and the pain comes back for a few days. But he is doing well."

It was true that Stephen was almost completely healed, but he pushed himself beyond reason, fueled by an absurd rage and determination to go after Zia Akhtar. As a result he suffered setbacks and had to go back to physiotherapy every few weeks. But each setback doubled his tenacity to catch the people who had massacred innocents and scarred his limbs. His body functioned perfectly well, but the injured muscles cramped up at inopportune times and frustrated him with newfound limitations.

Nina showed Amy the bathroom and the hot-water controls.

"You don't mind being by yourself in this huge place?" Amy asked while she unpacked her toiletries.

"By myself? There are at least eight or ten people around at all times. Security guards, housekeeper, cook, driver. I *wish* I could be alone."

"Yeah, what's with the guards? It feels like a maximum-security prison."

"Stephen is a part of the diplomatic mission here. He advises the American government on joint projects with the Indian Corps of Engineers. As a US diplomat, his official residence gets standard embassy security. Plus, he has his own paranoid security arrangements. American citizens are targets for kidnapping, particularly diplomats and business executives."

"I don't blame him."

To Amy's eyes, from what little she had seen on the street and at the airport, the crowd in New Delhi was rather rough, particularly the way some of the men stared at the two girls. As soon as she had stepped out of the airport building, before Nina could get to her, a crowd of taxi drivers, porters, and tour guides had pressed around her and waved their hands in her face to catch her attention. She had been quite frightened until she'd caught a glimpse of Nina cutting through the mob with a security guard at her heels.

While Amy was in the shower, Nina asked the cook to send up sandwiches and tea. She sat on the bed and sorted through all the things her mother had sent. Deepa had packed Nina's favorite Indian snacks and pickles. Only a mother would do that—send Indian snacks to India. Nothing came close to Mom's cooking, no substitute for it; she was suddenly awash in sentiment. She missed going home to see her parents every other weekend, but she couldn't complain. She had Skype.

Amy emerged revived and cheerful. There was a soft knock on the door, and a young woman entered with a tray. Nina thanked her and closed the door after she left.

"This is quite a setup!" Amy marveled while she toweled her hair dry.

"It gets better. You'll see." Nina munched contentedly on the snacks Deepa had sent.

She watched Amy scarf down her sandwich. It felt just like high school, hanging out together. After Nina and Stephen had gotten married, Amy and Nina had tried the couples-dinner thing a few times. It was pleasant enough, but Jeff and Stephen did not have the same interest in meeting as Amy and Nina. After Stephen's injury Nina was too preoccupied, and her and Amy's time together became even shorter and more infrequent. Those lovely long, delicious days of endless gossip, where they tore to shreds old acquaintances and haunted their favorite restaurants and movies, were impossible to come by again. This break—a few days together, just the two of them—was a great luxury. Stephen had discreetly disappeared on a trip to give them their privacy.

"So Nina, my love, are you happy?" Amy asked. She was refreshed and fully functioning now, with the terrible smell of airplanes and airports out of her hair and nostrils.

"Of course I am." Nina beamed from the couch, where she had got comfortable in a pile of pillows.

"You don't miss your work?"

Nina had taken a year's leave of absence to join Stephen in New Delhi. Nina's ambition and diligence had always been a big part of her personality. To Nina, anything worth doing was worth doing with every fiber of her being. She would fuss, agonize, and obsess over every test, every term report, every word she committed to paper. In her senior year of high school, universities had lined up with scholarships. BigSearch made her an offer for a permanent position at the end of her summer internship, even before she had started her senior year in college. And more recently BigSearch offered to pay for her to earn an executive MBA.

When Nina decided to accompany Stephen to India, everyone, including Amy, had thought she was throwing it all away. Ravi was particularly upset that his love-struck daughter, who had such a promising and phenomenal future ahead of her, had jeopardized her career in deference to Stephen's. While he had great respect for Stephen's physical courage in stopping the armed robbery, Ravi couldn't find any details about it on the local TV channels or in newspapers. A cat stuck in a tree would have gotten more coverage. There was something fishy about the whole story, but he didn't want to confront Stephen because that would make Nina furious.

Ravi was also wary of Stephen's inexplicable influence over his normally level-headed daughter. She had jumped into marriage after barely a few months' acquaintance—and without the approval of her family. She had brought Stephen home one day after a lone phone call on this important matter to inform them, for the first time, that she had been seeing this man for a few weeks and had agreed to marry him. Ravi and Deepa had had no say in the matter. Luckily Stephen seemed to be in a hurry to get married and brought it up almost as soon as he and Ravi were introduced. *Not surprising*, Ravi had muttered angrily. Stephen must have been worried that Nina would get away if he didn't seal the deal.

Both Deepa and Ravi were surprised by Nina's choice. They found nothing remarkable about Stephen, a serious man who looked at first sight quite a bit older than Nina. His family name didn't carry the same weight with them—Indian immigrants with a pecking order of their own—as it carried with the incestuous New England community that dominated the corridors of power on the East Coast. In fact when they found out his family history, Nina's parents were not too happy. A broken family, they cautioned Nina—alcoholism, adultery, suicide, rived by property disputes. *Are you sure,* they'd asked. But Nina seemed completely infatuated, determined to marry Stephen. They knew that stubborn streak too well to try to stop her.

As soon as Nina and Stephen had left after their first visit, Deepa had told Ravi, "They seem very close. We should get them married immediately."

Ravi had noticed it too: Stephen held Nina's hand constantly; they sat too close together on the sofa. Deepa had accidentally glimpsed them kissing with embarrassing abandon, bodies indistinguishable in an ecstatic embrace.

Nina's parents were unaware that Nina and Stephen had already been married for several weeks. So they went ahead and threw a roaring, red-blooded Indian wedding at short notice for their precious daughter. The efficient team that they were, they went turbo speed with preparations. Within two weeks they had the wedding hall, priest, and caterer booked. Thanks to the goodwill of and the clout they carried in the community, everyone came to their aid, printing invitations, stuffing envelopes, tracking down musicians and DJs, booking hotels and airlines, and hosting the guest overflow in their homes. Nina was a model young woman and the beloved of the local Indian community. All her parents' friends wanted to help despite their perplexity at her choice of suitor.

After that wedding it had been just one crisis after another for the young couple. Nina's parents watched as their daughter rushed between hospitals and her office, pretending to be tough for their sake while her heart was sick with anxiety over Stephen's health after the shooting. And now this move to Delhi. It was the last straw for Nina's father.

"What's wrong with her? How is he able to make her do this?" he ranted at Deepa. "Why does she have to go live in India? Why can't she just visit him once every few months?"

Amy too had doubts about Nina's move to India.

"Don't you miss your work?" she repeated now, and threw the damp towel in the laundry hamper, looking expectantly at Nina for an answer.

Nina stretched out on the sofa and looked up at her. "I do miss my work, but it's only for a few more months. I've been doing some legwork in the meantime. I travel with Stephen to all kinds of remote places. The world around here is frightening—the need is so great, and we can do so little."

Those sad children outside Mumbai—Amy could not even imagine their lives. They were the children of sex workers, surrounded by pimps and whores. They had no hope unless they were placed in a school, particularly the girls. They would be raped and sold by the time they were ten years old. But Nina kept quiet. She didn't want to steer the conversation to such a dark place.

"What if Stephen has to extend his stay?" Amy asked.

"I don't know." Nina shrugged. "We'd figure something out."

Amy was amazed by the power Stephen had over Nina. Her friend had broken every one of her rules for him—rules she had cherished and lived by for twenty-six years. She had married him, a man she had barely met a few times, at two days' notice without the knowledge of her family, and here she was, throwing away a career she had worked so hard for since middle school.

"What are you getting out of this relationship, Nina?"

She sat down on a big rattan chair. Her fine, blond hair flowered into cheerful curls as it dried. She knew it wasn't money, because Nina had very few material needs. Besides, she had enough of her own thanks to BigSearch's meteoric fortunes. Her parents were affluent in their own right as well and didn't need her help.

Nina sat up. "Love?"

Amy snorted. "You seem to be doing all the loving, Nina dearest. All the sacrifices seem to be on your part. You spent the first few months of your marriage playing nursemaid, and now you follow him around the world like a groupie at the cost of your career."

Nina didn't take offense. She knew Amy too well for that. "Wouldn't you do the same for Jeff?"

"Yes, I would take care of him, but I am not willing to run off to remote corners of the Earth while he chases a poisoned toad. Anyway I knew him for a lot longer than a few months before we got married."

"You *have* to trust me on this, Amy. I know you think Stephen is aggressive and controlling, but that's simply not true where I am concerned. He hasn't bullied me into coming with him to India. In fact, he couldn't stop me if he tried. There's no way I'd have stayed back. I'd miss him too much."

Amy watched Nina closely and tried to read her body language. She sensed no sadness. She knew Nina's distress cues better than anyone. On the contrary Nina was positively radiant and continued her explanation enthusiastically.

"I don't know how to put it into words, but I feel I have known him all my life, and I felt that the very first time I met him. This year that we've been married has been very complicated and difficult. We've had our fights and arguments, and I was devastated when he was injured, but I am happier than I've ever been. And

I know he feels the same way. And, strangely enough, when I'm with him I feel completely safe, untouchable. I can't imagine my life without him."

She smiled at Amy's intense examination. "You have to trust me. I know what I'm doing."

⋖⋗

The next morning Nina took Amy on a tour of New Delhi. It was a bustling, jostling, elbowing city full of young people; their energy, brashness, and laughter filled the air with electricity. Trucks and cars jammed together in undisciplined chaos, snarled by dense smog that didn't melt until midday. With their incessant honking, the noise level was unbelievable. Corny advertisements for matrimony, tea, shampoo, electronics, and insurance flashed from the medians of the busy streets in a cryptic mixture of American and Indian idioms.

Nina loved the city and its energy and showed it off with great pride. She was a walking encyclopedia on all things Delhi. She excitedly pointed out her favorite landmarks, little gardens ablaze with dahlias and chrysanthemums, fountains, bookshops, and restaurants. They drove through the sprawling Central Secretariat, with its wide, tree-lined avenues and majestic sandstone buildings, and stopped at the imposing Rashtrapati

Bhavan and the Indian parliament building to take pictures.

Two bodyguards accompanied them wherever they went and kept the snack and tchotchke vendors at bay. When Nina started to walk toward a spicy *chana* seller, the driver stopped her, and one of the bodyguards bought the snacks for them.

Amy looked puzzled. "Why did they do that?"

Nina just shook her head. "Security measures."

It was broad daylight with at least a million people around. What could possibly happen? The bodyguards were just a few feet away in case there was a problem. It seemed mystifyingly excessive. She said so, and Nina replied with a smile, "Stephen's rules. I don't make them."

For the next several hours, they shopped, haggled, bargained, and bought several bags of clothes and jewelry. They were an odd couple: the five-foot-eight, athletic Amy with her golden hair, gray eyes, and pale skin, and the five-two Nina, tanned to a toffee brown by the Indian sun. People stared at them without any qualms.

At around three in the afternoon, the girls felt insanely hungry. Nina leaned forward and gave the driver instructions in Hindi. When they arrived at the destination, Nina said excitedly, "You're going to love this, Amy. The best South Indian food in town."

They stepped into a modest restaurant packed with patrons. Would-be diners hovered around the seated ones, ready to scoot into their seats as soon as they were vacated. Waiters flew around with steaming mounds of white rice in big, overflowing dishes. The commingled aromas of ghee, basmati rice, and sizzling onions permeated every corner. Excited customers shouted over the din.

The waiters hustled and kept up a steady conversation with each other:

"Out of my way."

"Here's the order for table four."

"Where is the water?"

"You there! Wipe that table."

It was unlike any restaurant, diner, or fast-food place Amy had seen.

One of the bodyguards spoke to the manager and got them a table in a corner. The two men stood watch while the women ate.

"That's disconcerting," Amy said.

"I know," Nina replied. "It took a while, but I'm used to it now."

"Do all embassy spouses have such security?"

"Well, most of them don't leave the compound, or they stick to country clubs, so I guess it's not an issue. I love being out in the city. This security is a Stephen special."

Amy was about to say it was a bit overdone but kept her opinion to herself. It was a way to exercise control and to circumscribe Nina's movements. Perhaps Stephen was jealous. But Nina was not one to rush into another man's arms; he should have known that by then.

But right now, in New Delhi, it wasn't jealousy that drove Stephen—not that he was immune to that emotion. He was worried that Nina would be kidnapped. That was why she had the entourage when he wasn't around to be her protector. He didn't tell Nina in so many words, but George did. He had dropped in on her at work a few days before her departure for India and taken her out to lunch.

"Gee, George," she had said, "you want to take me out to lunch? What's next, flowers?"

They had found their angle of repose at a polite state of mutual disagreement. Each had enough respect for the role the other played in Stephen's life and shared affection for him that kept them from falling out completely.

"Nina, I know you don't approve of what we do, but there is no other way. This is the best we can do without all-out war. We have made mistakes, no doubt. But we're well intentioned, and we really do care about not hurting innocent civilians. These terrorists don't. They use them as fodder."

Nina listened without any reaction.

"You have to cut Stephen some slack. He drives himself crazy worrying about your safety. Don't make it harder for him."

"Why would I do that?"

George smiled at her, a slightly mocking gesture that he reserved for annoying her. Some of her opinions were stereotypes—black or white, red or blue.

"Round-the-clock bodyguards might be involved, and an ever-present security staff to watch over you at all times. Privacy might be a rare commodity, and I know how much you love your privacy."

"Why do I need so much security?"

Because you are his Achilles's heel—a most dangerous vulnerability. But he didn't say that aloud. He gave some vague reason about general security for Americans abroad, particularly the families of intelligence officers. Thanks to George's forewarning, Nina took Stephen's arrangements in stride, without her usual arguments and endless debate, much to Stephen's surprise. The bodyguards were now a part of her daily routine in New Delhi.

To walk off the calories of their carb-heavy lunch, Nina and Amy made the rounds of some obscure, little bookshops Nina had discovered in her six months in New Delhi. Dust, dim lighting, and a musty smell were the standard décor. Startled old men in thick glasses jumped up, annoyed by being disturbed in their solitary vigils.

It was almost seven in the evening by the time their car turned around to head home. The city flew by, glittering with brightly lit malls, bazaars, and vegetable markets.

"Stephen's home!" Nina clapped when she saw his car in the carport as they drove up. Amy was moved to see Nina so happy. Nobody could fake such a spontaneous expression of joy.

Stephen was with a group of people in the upstairs office. Nina and Amy could hear voices and see shadows on the curtains. Nina ran up the stairs and poked her head in the office door to say hello. Stephen came out immediately, grinning at her.

"Amy! Welcome," he said warmly and extended his hand to her, his other arm around Nina. "I hope you had a comfortable trip."

"I did, thank you. Nina has been showing me around."

Stephen and Amy beamed at Nina like proud parents of a precocious child. She loved it, this moment when her closest friend and the love of her life were united in peaceful camaraderie. She knew it wouldn't last long. But for now she was happy.

Even though Stephen smiled, he managed to be distant. Amy had tried her best to dissuade Nina from marrying him. During his objective moments, he could see the logic in Amy's disapproval, but it was too personal for him to stay objective for long. Amy could have killed his long-awaited chance at happiness. But it was important to Nina that he and Amy get along, and he was determined to be at his most charming.

What a nice couple. The sight of Stephen and Nina together touched Amy. He was thinner than the last time she had seen him, but he looked well, very proper in a white shirt and dark pants. This was the uniform of the consulate, apparently; everyone was dressed that way, the no-nonsense, all-American look. And he was a totally different person when he looked at Nina. His mouth relaxed involuntarily into a soft smile, and his prim lips were released from their prison. A sweetness suffused his eyes and face, and he always seemed on the verge of bending down to kiss her. Nina was the exhibitionist of the two and clung to him with her arms around his waist, grinning from ear to ear as though she had just won the lottery. She was dizzy with relief each time he returned from a trip, and grateful that he was unhurt and had come back safely from whatever dangerous errand he had been on.

"I have to get back to my meeting. I will see you at dinner." Stephen waved and disappeared into the office.

Nina and Amy went to the guest room and dumped all their bags on the bed to review and evaluate the fruits of their shopping. Soon the young woman who had brought the sandwiches the previous night came in with tea and cake.

"Wow!" Amy couldn't believe her eyes.

"Ma'am, *aaj kya khaana banayen*?" the girl asked Nina.

"*Gobhi paratha, kadhi, chole aur raita. Sahab ke liye* egg curry. *Aur matar pulao. Khaana nau baje beechwale garden mein table daalke vahan pe lagaiye. Theek hai*, Paro?"

"*Bilkul*, ma'am." Paro flashed a big smile and left.

"What did you say? I heard 'gobhi paratha.'" That was a favorite of Amy's. Growing up she would knock on Nina's kitchen door right in time for brunch every Sunday, dying for Nina's mother's soft, fragrant parathas stuffed with spicy cauliflower or potato mash, soaked in ghee and just-off-the-pan hot. Amy and Nina would wolf their share down and run off to play while little Neel would complain to his mother that they wouldn't let him join them.

"I told Paro to serve us dinner at nine in the courtyard."

"Nina, baby, this is the life!"

"Tell me about it."

Dinner was mellow, lit by a bright autumn moon, with Punjabi food cooked in the heart of Punjab by a Punjabi chef whose blood was half ghee.

"This is obscene," Amy joked.

Nina was too full to talk. She just smiled in agreement.

Stephen was almost asleep; he had gotten up at four o'clock that morning and driven ten hours to get home from Jaisalmer.

Amy was feeling the jet lag kicking in. "I'll go to bed now."

After she left, Stephen came out of his doze. "Did you two have fun today?" He got up from his chair to go to bed. Nina took his proffered arm and chattered on as they went up the stairs and walked through the terrace garden toward their bedroom. The garden was beautiful and quiet. The foliage glistened with a frosty glow in the moonlight.

"Where did you girls go?" Stephen asked. He was awake now and sat down on a rattan armchair near the jasmine climber. She squeezed in next to him.

"The Secretariat and India Gate, and then we went shopping. It was a lot of fun, but never mind all that. I'm so glad you are back safely."

"Me too." Stephen rested his head on hers. They sat like that for a long time, in complete stillness, peaceful and contented, watching the brilliant, silver moon make its way across the sky.

The next day Nina took Amy to see the glories of Mughal architecture that Delhi was famous for: Humayun's tomb, Qutb Minar, and Jama Masjid. The warmth of the winter sun had seduced the denizens of Delhi to skip whatever they were supposed to be doing, to go and laze in the sunshine on the acres of green lawns. The rowdy crowd drank tea and ate roasted peanuts, gossiped, chattered, and laughed. They looked curiously at the group of four—Nina, Amy, and the two brawny security guards—and wondered if Nina or Amy were a movie star or a VIP to merit such security. But when the girls didn't meet their expectations, they lost interest.

At Jama Masjid, however, a young man with an impressive camera followed them, undeniably interested in them. One of the bodyguards went over to warn him off, but after a brief conversation with the man, the bodyguard returned to Nina and said something. Nina nodded. The young man approached them. The bodyguards watched him.

"My name is Mohan, ma'am. I overheard you discuss Mughal architecture, and I want to tell you a bit of little-known history about this place, if you will kindly permit me."

They sat inside the mosque, on the steps of the vast interior courtyard, in total serenity compared to the noise, smells, and crowds just outside. Mohan spoke with a casual eloquence with a typical Indian turn of phrase now and then, his voice reverberating pleasantly in the wide-open hallways lined with intricate prayer carpets. The hush of the holy place accentuated the young man's words. Hundreds of pigeons roosted there, wagging their behinds as they waddled as fast as their little legs could carry them.

A bearded old man watched the girls from a distance and smiled.

When they were ready to leave, Mohan recited an Urdu poem on the miracle of friendship to them and wished them both a lifetime of its blessing. Amy was taken aback by this serenade, but she was getting used to how friendly and chatty people were, even toward strangers. Nina looked at her phone and realized they had to leave right away.

"Thank you, Mohan." She waved as they ran to the car.

Stephen was supposed to meet them at a well-known Tibetan restaurant. And after lunch they were scheduled to go to the airport to pick up Jeff. The restaurant was near an arterial road that housed the offices of almost all the major national newspapers and magazines. Artists and journalists were frequent patrons; it was a fashionable meeting place, a place to see and be seen. Stephen was already there, mingling with the journalists he knew. As soon as he saw Nina and Amy, he went over and led them to a corner table. He sat between them, facing the door.

Amy found it very grating, this take-charge attitude. Nina played along like a stereotypical South Asian wife—no opinion, no protest, just do as your husband tells you. Amy held her tongue and fought down the sarcastic comment that struggled to jump out and bite Stephen.

But Stephen had his own reasons for being security obsessed—almost a dozen reasons that nestled inside his office safe like a clutch of scorpions. The photos had begun appearing as soon as he and Nina had arrived in Delhi. They came in the mail, always mailed from the main post office in Delhi, Gol Dak Khana, in plain white envelopes with generic, printed labels: "Mr. Stephen James." No fingerprints, chemicals, or any other identifying marks. With a rapacious intensity, the pictures caught the subjects at their most unguarded, open moments, like the one where Nina and Stephen laughed, eyes locked, while they walked down a pavement near the art galleries in Hauz Khas, or the one of Nina and Paro as they giggled at some joke and bought flowers. Beautiful, studio-quality photographs that turned his blood to ice.

George was sure it was done at Zia Akhtar's behest, to intimidate Stephen and get him off the case. Nina, at her unsuspecting, trusting best, was at the center of every photo—smiling, laughing, the goddess of happiness. There was nothing subtle about the message. Stephen was not willing to take any chances. Akhtar was bound to get more desperate as he drew closer. Stephen was convinced that a denouement was imminent.

He looked around at the diners. The restaurant was a total dive—bare, white walls, spartan metal tables and chairs. There was no menu. The waiter brought the courses one by one.

"Why does everyone stare at you?" Amy asked Nina. They were between courses.

"Thank you!" Stephen exclaimed in agreement. "Yeah, Nina, why is that?"

It was true. Several men, young and old, all Indian, stared at Nina and Stephen in turn, but mostly at Nina. Stephen had commented on it many times to Nina, but she had dismissed it.

She glared at him with a flash of the old Nina. "Since you seem to have a theory, why don't you tell us?"

"Gladly, my dear Nina." He turned to Amy. "The men here don't approve of an Indian girl being with a white guy. The fact that we are married seems to carry no weight. They think she's a…you know, a woman of easy virtue." He couldn't get himself to say a vulgar word with regard to Nina.

Stephen found the staring maddening, his protective instinct in full fettle. Nina, of all people, didn't deserve such disrespect. The ultraconservative faction of the society, which was also the most vocal one, frowned on public displays between men and women, and he was very careful to respect that. But he had no choice in crowded public spaces where he wanted to make sure she stayed near him. Despite his best efforts, they were met with uncouth stares and occasional muttered obscenities. Nina would continue to walk forward, expressionless. He would sometimes stop walking and return the stares until she dragged him away. He carried a gun, and she was terrified he would be provoked into using it.

For Nina such experiences, while uncomfortable, paled in comparison to the times when Stephen disappeared on missions for George. He would simply say, "I'll be away for a few days." Two special bodyguards, not the day-to-day ones who accompanied her into the city but two deadly serious ones, would materialize out of thin air like hulking genies with guns. One was an ex-marine from the embassy, and the other was a retired Indian special ops officer. Both were older and tough, men of few words. They barely spoke to her or looked at her but shadowed her the minute she stepped out of the bedroom, even inside the compound. Stephen didn't trust the preexisting staff he and Nina had inherited with the house.

On such occasions, time expanded to an unbearable scale for Nina, filled with anxiety and boredom. She had no idea where Stephen went or what he did. All she had was a number to call—George's—in case of an emergency or if she needed anything. So far, due to the grace of God, Stephen had returned safely, barring minor bruises and sprains. And each time he came home from such a trip, when she heard his car drive up, she would shut herself in the bathroom and cry in relief.

After the shootout at Sid's, after seeing Stephen so close to death, Nina's emotional strength was eroded by anxiety for his safety. Without her work to keep her busy, without a tangible goal to work toward, she focused all her energies on worrying about him. Stephen knew the price she paid. He watched over her with a ferocity that could easily be mistaken for possessiveness, as Amy had done. As far as he was concerned, Nina walked on water. He found it difficult to say such things to her, but his actions spoke for him. Fragrant rajanigandhas, mangoes and sapotas, tickets to concerts—he surrounded her with things that made her happy.

Nina couldn't explain any of this to Amy. Her friend's opinion of Stephen was unfair and completely off the mark but, hopefully, the passage of time would convince her otherwise.

MISCALCULATION

"Look at him, Jeff! He's always hovering over her. As soon as any of the crew comes up, he immediately runs close to her. He is so insecure. And Nina simply goes along with whatever he wants."

Amy, Jeff, Stephen, and Nina were on a weeklong vacation together on a private schooner. It was a beautiful, Turkish-built vessel made of teak and mahogany, a Gullet with two masts, spacious suites, and a crew to sail the boat and wait on the guests. Stephen had felt he could control the environment better on a boat than at a resort or hotel. They sailed along the coast of Goa and stopped at small, isolated beaches to swim and snorkel. The November weather was perfect and gave them a great week of sailing. The schooner anchored off bends in the coastline that sheltered white-sand beaches, away from the maddening tourists, hippies, and hipsters.

"Come on, Amy. Give the guy a break. He likes being with his wife, that's all."

"He's a control freak, that's what he is. We went for lunch the other day, and *he* decided where she should sit. I'm surprised he doesn't cut up her food into small pieces and tell her how to eat it."

"Sweetie, I'm sure Nina can take care of herself."

"I hope you're right. Her free will seems to have disappeared."

Amy kept up an incessant stream of complaints to Jeff about Nina-Stephen interactions. And on the face of it, they appeared justified. Nina was even more compliant than usual, almost docile. Stephen seemed to shuffle around her, never giving her a moment to herself, especially on the deck or when they stepped off the boat to visit the beaches where they anchored. Even when she was with Amy, Stephen was barely ten feet away, always within sight of her. Amy found it very abnormal. She wanted to talk to Nina in private, but with Stephen always in the picture it was impossible.

Stephen could sense Amy's irritation but couldn't have cared less. He wasn't going to risk letting Nina out of his sight.

"They are going to try to get to you," George had said over the phone that morning. From the photos it looked as if they were going to go after Nina. The closer Stephen got to Akhtar, the more jittery and determined the terror group became. Stephen's investigation had to be foiled and his path to Akhtar blocked. They would do whatever it took to accomplish this. Stephen thought they wouldn't dare hurt a US diplomat or his wife and especially not on Indian soil.

George was skeptical. "All it takes is one maniac," he'd said.

Ever since Stephen and Nina had arrived in India, Stephen had poured all his energies and anger into tracking down Zia Akhtar. He traveled the length and breadth of India, working closely with Indian intelligence, RAW, and the border security force officials. The CIA had extracted valuable information from Sid—sources, contacts, chain of command, informants, couriers, locales. Analysts examined and checked every little scrap and used the information to fill in the jigsaw puzzle. They were getting to the heart of Akhtar's empire. But Asad the interrogator, the man sent to torture and kill Sid, was yet to talk despite the agency's persuasive powers.

Stephen followed every lead; scoured the Indo-Pak border from Jaisalmer to Kashmir; and, in various guises, talked to locals, informants, arms dealers, the Indian mafia, and anyone else who had the slightest potential to help. He had acquired a deep tan from his field trips, and now he could almost pass for a Kashmiri or an Afghan. His most recent tryst had led him to a contact in Srinagar who would provide the ultimate link to Zia Akhtar himself.

Now that Stephen was close, the enemy had become more daring. The photos got progressively personal, with tight close-ups that upped the psychological ante. It was clear that Nina and he were being watched constantly. The camera could get frighteningly close. In one particular photo of Nina and Stephen at a restaurant, he could see his own reflection in her eyes. It had to have been shot from behind a curtain or door fewer than five feet away from where they had sat. He was surprised he had not heard the camera shutter.

George had been sorry he couldn't think of anything more specific. "Anyway, try to enjoy your vacation," he'd said.

Today the schooner was anchored at Khola Beach in Cancona, with a wide, isolated stretch of sand that gave way to palm trees and, farther inland, a steep, verdant hillside.

Prior to the trip, Stephen had been paranoid about the boat's crew, who would be milling around Nina. The agency had vetted all members, but one could never be sure. His mind returned constantly to the glossy photos in his office: Nina and him walking along a busy pavement; Nina going for a run in the park with the bodyguards. Under normal circumstances he would have enjoyed those poetic, evocative records of their life together, but he could not forget the purpose for which they were sent to him.

The past few days had been a welcome break. The water had its usual calming effect on him. He was actually beginning to enjoy himself.

Nina and Stephen returned to the boat after a swim while Amy and Jeff stayed back to explore the beach and the hills and village beyond. There was still half an hour to go before lunch. Stephen looked through the mail that came in daily through a courier. A large, white envelope lay buried beneath the other items.

Not another one. Stephen grimaced and looked around to make sure Nina wasn't nearby. He broke the seal and opened it.

The image took shape as he slid it out slowly. As soon as he recognized it, he paused. He covered his face with his hand, inhaled deeply, and opened his eyes to the inevitable. It was an intimate picture of Nina and Stephen on a private section of the schooner the previous day. They were crushed together on a lounge chair, Nina in a short, cotton dress and Stephen in his swimming trunks. The cameraman had a clear shot of Stephen's face as he bent down to kiss her, but the centerpiece was Nina's shapely thigh, which Stephen's fingers caressed as they reached for the white lace of her panties, the scar on his arm an angry, violent red.

Whoever had taken the picture had to have been barely a few feet from them. Who had done it? How had he or she gotten on the boat? Could it be one of the crew? And what else had they seen and captured?

The blood rushed to his face, and his brain went numb. Nina was going to die of embarrassment if these pictures got out. Soon another thought struck him: could the terrorists have planted something on the boat? How was he going to search the huge vessel without alarming everyone?

This meant he was really close to finding Akhtar, just as George had said. These clowns had some powerful people behind them. Politicians, Bollywood types, and half the Mumbai underworld were all in bed with these guys. No wonder they were spooked.

"What's wrong?" Nina asked when she came upstairs a few minutes later. He looked distracted.

"What?" Stephen tried to stall.

"What's going on?"

The last few days had been idyllic, with Stephen in an uncharacteristically relaxed and happy frame of mind. He loved being on water. He and Jeff had helped the crew sail the boat. The two New England boys couldn't stop talking about the beautiful wooden schooner. But today the grim mood was making a comeback.

Stephen stole a look at Nina. She sat next to him, fresh from the shower, glowing in a white dress. The heat and humidity of the Indian climate loved her skin and invested it with a sizzling luminescence. A clip held her damp hair piled up in dripping, black ringlets on top of her head, to keep it off her neck.

Stephen was worried. Something terrible was about to happen; he could sense its approach. According to George, Akhtar would spring something soon, but what? The last link to the man had been tantalizingly within Stephen's reach for the past month. He had traveled twice to Srinagar, but the person who was supposed to help him get to that final link had been a no-show on both occasions, either dead or in a dungeon somewhere. Akhtar's people were closing ranks, plugging the gaps, and getting ready for battle.

He tried to fight the uneasy feeling. What could possibly happen on the boat? "Nothing," he said to Nina with a smile.

The words were barely out of his mouth when his ears picked up the familiar sound of a speedboat. He stood up and scanned the horizon. A black speck in the distance moved rapidly toward them.

"Damn!" He turned around, grabbed Nina by the arm, and raced belowdecks.

"What's happening?" Nina asked as she tried to keep up with him.

"You stay here," he told her and pushed her inside their suite. He pulled out a box from under the bed, grabbed a sniper's rifle and binoculars, and ran out.

Where did he get them? She paused in confusion for a split second and then ran up after him. She tripped in her panic and scraped her knee badly.

"Nina, stay there!" he shouted down at her.

"No!" she yelled back.

He was irritated, but she had already come up. He dropped down flat on the floor and pulled her down with him.

"Stay down. If any of the crew tries to come up, warn them off."

She nodded. Her knee smarted and burned. It was bleeding profusely.

Stephen looked through the binoculars and saw a small speedboat headed directly toward them. There were two men in it. One was at the wheel; the other stood next to him with something that looked like a long camera lens in his hands, but it could have been a gun. Could it be a suicide mission? A boat packed with explosives? Unlikely. Too expensive, and Akhtar wouldn't waste two men. The one at the wheel was probably armed. As Stephen searched for signs of a hidden holster, his blood rose in a hot fury.

"I need to teach these assholes a lesson," he muttered. Propelled by a blind rage, he raised his rifle and took aim.

Nina was down on the floor. She couldn't see anything other than Stephen taking aim. She was terrified he would get shot again. Her stomach churned as she prayed like never before.

Whenever she tried to raise her head, Stephen would bark, "Head down *now*." She placed a restraining hand on Stephen's leg when she heard him release the safety latch.

The speedboat slowed as it got closer. The cameraman—it was indeed a lens—raised his camera in preparation. *For what?* Stephen began to panic. What did the man want to record? What was he waiting for? Did they want to lure him into a shootout and leave him no choice but act in self-defense?

Just then a single shot rent the air. Birds took flight from the beach and surrounding hills in raucous chaos. The shot had come from behind Nina and Stephen, aimed high above the sails. The marksman could have picked off Nina and Stephen easily while their attention was riveted by the speedboat in front of them. But the shooter had chosen not to. This was just a warning: get off the case now. Stephen grabbed Nina by the arm and raced down the stairs once more, conscious of the camera shutter clicking relentlessly as they stumbled down.

It was dark by the time the schooner turned around. Amy sat on the couch in Nina's suite, next to Nina, who looked surprisingly calm. Jeff and Amy had rushed back when they had heard the shot. They had found the boat in turmoil, the staff hurrying around preparing for departure while Stephen grimly bandaged Nina's leg.

As soon as they arrived, he handed Nina's first aid over to Amy and took Jeff aside.

"I need your help."

Jeff was not surprised by Stephen's confession. He had always suspected there was more to him, some crazy, secret life—particularly after the armed robbery incident. Jeff was no stranger to intelligence work, and on Stephen's suggestion, George and Homeland Security had tapped him on several occasions when his travels took him to places and people of interest.

Jeff and Stephen examined the boat from top to bottom. They interviewed the staff to find out if anyone had seen or heard anything that could help identify the location or identity of the shooter or the speedboat hooligans, who had sped away while Stephen dragged Nina to safety downstairs. No one had a clue. The boat showed no signs of a suspicious break-in or tampering or any unfamiliar cargo.

"Did you by any chance hear or see anything while you were out there?" Stephen asked Jeff.

"No. I wish we had paid more attention, but we were too wrapped up in ourselves."

Stephen showed him the photo.

"Wow!" Jeff whistled.

"Yes."

"This is not the first one, but it is the most brazen one." Stephen looked down at his sandals. "Ever since Nina and I arrived in New Delhi, I've been getting these pictures in the mail. They're usually of Nina or sometimes the two of us, but always in public places. I guess they've been trying to warn me off. This is the first time I've seen one so close and in a private setting. The photographer must have been on our boat."

Jeff looked at the photo again. "Yes, it must have been taken from halfway up the staircase. It is a perfect shot. It had to be a professional."

For all they knew, it could have been one of the crew or anyone with a few thousand rupees to bribe an obliging member. Perhaps the speedboat cameraman had come in the previous day for reconnaissance and hit pay dirt when he found Nina and Stephen there.

Stephen didn't say anything for a while, lost in the contemplation of his feet. Jeff felt sorry. He wished he could help him. Then he remembered.

"Stephen, Amy brought her little camera with her, and she shot tons of video and photos. Maybe there's something there that might help."

Stephen looked up immediately. His grey eyes were full of hope. Jeff went to his suite and came out with Amy's camera and laptop. They went down the hallway to a corner and sat down on a bench.

The computer booted up and synched with the camera. Jeff said, "There's some really personal footage in there. Amy will kill me if she finds out I showed it to you."

"We'll be even, after what I showed you just now," Stephen muttered.

The pictures finished loading. In them, Amy strutted across the beach, lay in the sun, hugged a palm tree, sat on Jeff's Speedo'd lap. Stephen looked away, unable to stomach the voyeuristic glimpses of their private life that flashed by every three seconds. There were five minutes of additional footage, with Jeff clowning around before he dived into the water from a small cliff.

They did a second pass over the visuals, this time very slowly. Homes and hotels populated the areas behind the beach. Some of the photos showed people walking in the distance. Stephen was interested in the diving footage and photos from around that area because he felt the gunshot had been fired from an elevation.

Jeff was a magician with photos and image-manipulation software. He broke down the video into still frames, and they scanned the shrubbery carefully for anomalies, as he called them. And behold, just as Jeff had prepared for his swan dive, in the distance a black smudge was circled in red by the image recognition software. When they zoomed in on it, the smudge transformed into the top of the head of a sniper, and his rifle poked out like a branch from one of the bushes.

Now that they knew where to look, they pored over the sequence and watched in amazement as the sniper snuck up the hill and nestled in the bush. He was too far away to have seen Amy with her camera, and he was too low to the ground for her to have spotted him.

The sniper wore a checked shirt and had an unusually big build for an Indian. Stephen looked at him closely and tried to match him with his mental database of terrorists. The guy looked familiar. Yes, he remembered with a burst of recognition—the ring on his finger. It was the burly sardar from the breakfast buffet at Le Méridien, except he was no Sikh. Here he was clean shaven, with close-cropped hair, looking quite young, but the build and ring were unmistakable. And he looked almost identical to Sid's nemesis and interrogator, Asad.

Stephen was stunned. The fake sardar had studied Nina and Stephen at leisure during their daily breakfasts at Le Méridien. Now he had been sent to finish the job that Sid's note had foiled. But why didn't he shoot them? Perhaps Stephen and Nina were not worth risking bigger plans Akhtar might have had. Perhaps the consequences would have been too much to handle: the fury and wrath of the mightiest nation in the world would be upon the shooter and his terror colleagues. They wouldn't want such close scrutiny from the United States. And the Indians could be ruthless if they got hold of the sardar.

What a fucking mess. How would he explain all this to Nina? But he *had* to tell her about the picture. She needed to know before it showed up in some sleazy tabloid. After all, American diplomats, however low-ranking, were still interesting fodder for the America-baiting Indian media.

He went to their suite, where Amy and Nina sat watching a movie. Amy got up to leave as soon as he came in. For the first time, she understood the complexity of Stephen's situation and viewed him with a mixture of sympathy and respect. She had misread him all these days.

To Stephen's surprise she came over to him and said with the utmost earnestness, "Please, let me know if I can be of any help."

As soon as Amy left, he said to Nina, "I want you to see something."

His tone gave him away.

"What's wrong?" she asked. She was attuned to his every inflection.

"You need to see this."

He handed her the envelope and watched her face. She looked at the photo for a long time. He couldn't make out what she was thinking. There was none of the anger or fear he had expected. Or even embarrassment. She appeared puzzlingly indifferent as she chucked the picture aside and turned to him.

"Is that all?" She put her arms around his neck and leaned on him.

"You do realize that photo can be published anytime."

"I don't care."

"Your parents and grandparents will see it."

"I don't care."

"And your colleagues," he added as an afterthought.

"Still don't care. We can do what we want on our boat." They had almost gotten killed, after all, and there was nothing like a good dose of fear to put things in perspective. She was just glad he hadn't gotten shot.

Stephen was truly speechless at this metamorphosis—at Nina, who used to jump three feet in the air if he walked in on her while she changed her clothes, and who now so casually dismissed the prospect of being plastered half naked across the covers of gossip magazines, caught in the middle of a very private moment.

"It was foolish of me. I should have known a vacation out in the open is risky. But I was so tempted." He hugged her close. "I am sorry."

During the following days and weeks, the Indian media came unhinged. Each newspaper, news agency, and television channel tried to outdo the other in hyperbole, melodrama, and jingoism. Editorials bemoaned the subjugation of Indian sovereignty at the hands of a power-drunk, imperialist United States. The gall of the diplomat, headlines rued.

"Expel Stephen James!" was a constant refrain. TV channels ran the same set of pictures in a mind-numbing loop, interspersed occasionally with stock footage of Stephen and Nina at various embassy functions.

Two things mystified Stephen. The photo that had been sent to him was nowhere to be seen in the media, nor were there any others like it. Was the enemy holding them in reserve as a threat if he didn't cooperate? The pictures that appeared in the media were of poor quality, grainy and overexposed but following a sequence. The sniper in the hills had probably snapped those photos. The first was a picture taken from behind of Stephen raising his rifle at the cameraman in the speedboat while Nina lay on the floor. The last showed him, rifle still in hand, dragging Nina in a bloodied white dress. The two men in the speedboat were visible in the background of the photos. What about the pictures taken from the speedboat? Those would definitely show the sniper in the hills. The two must have faced each other in almost perfect alignment, with Stephen and Nina snared in the middle. Had the speedboat cameraman been just a decoy? Or was he the real stalker, the one who had followed them, snapped the pictures, and mailed them to Mr. Stephen James in plain white envelopes?

One particular media conglomerate stood out in the intensity, volume, and frequency of its attacks. Its newspapers, TV channels, magazines, and Internet portals stayed on the story, relentlessly demanding the resignation of the foreign minister and prime minister for letting a US diplomat get away with threatening an Indian citizen's life on Indian soil. Newspapers and TV channels in all twenty-one national languages ran human-interest stories about the cameraman's humble life. Who would have cared for his wife and kids if Mr. James had callously killed him? Thankfully that Good Samaritan had fired a warning shot that sent Mr. James scurrying for cover and put an end to his bloodlust.

Stephen shielded Nina from the media feeding frenzy and didn't allow any of the newspapers to come into the house. She wasn't interested either and didn't even bother to turn on the TV. Then one day she received a photo attached to an e-mail sent by a long-abandoned high school friend.

"Are you OK?" the friend asked.

Nina stared at the picture: Stephen aimed his rifle at the cameraman, she lay flat on her face on the deck near his feet, and there was the cameraman, about to raise his lens. It was a little fuzzy, the picture quality was poor, but she recognized the face.

She went in search of Stephen and found him in his office, grimly at work on the computer.

"I know the cameraman."

Stephen stared at her. "What cameraman?"

"The guy in the tabloid pictures. The guy in the speedboat," she replied impatiently. "I know who he is."

"How?" He pushed back his chair and frowned at her.

"Amy and I were in Jama Masjid. He followed us around and told us some touristy stories. His name is Mohan, or at least that's what he said it was."

"What were the bloody bodyguards doing? They are not supposed to let *anyone* come near you."

"They checked with me. I said it was OK."

Stephen was stunned by this revelation. What had the fucking bodyguards been doing? Even if she said it was OK, they were not supposed to allow anyone near her. They should have figured out who this guy was, and at least now, after seeing his picture in the newspaper, they should have come to Stephen. But they hadn't. They had conveniently disappeared once the storm broke. Then it struck him. Of course, the guy had bribed them.

"Come here, Nina."

He seemed angry with her. Nina went closer. He was entirely justified in being mad at her.

He made an effort to soften his expression when he saw her hesitate.

"It's OK, sweetheart. I am not mad at you. I just want you to tell me everything you saw."

He made her sit in front of him and leaned forward, his eyes drilling into hers while she talked. It had taken her a few months of living with him to get used to his intensity, but this was at a completely different level—must be his professional interrogating mode.

Nina described the encounter, feeling guilty that she had done something foolish and caused him additional worry. She recounted every detail, and he made her repeat the story multiple times, stopping her at the part when the old man with a beard smiled at them from a distance. How tall was he, how far away, what did he wear, did he say anything?

Akhtar. He was dismayed Zia Akhtar had been barely ten feet away from Nina. No wonder all of Stephen's leads had dried up. His last contact had not shown up, and people had become suspiciously coy. Akhtar could have done anything—grabbed Nina— and those good-for-nothing bodyguards would have keeled over. He should have had his special-ops bodyguards with her at all times, Stephen thought, not those nincompoops.

But the good news was that Akhtar had *not* grabbed Nina or threatened her in any way. What had stopped him? How had he come to be in New Delhi? He must have crossed the border in Kashmir, which was like a sieve. Maybe Akhtar was afraid the Indians would be furious if he grabbed an American diplomat's wife on Indian soil. Since when did he care? Maybe he knew he could do more damage by putting Stephen in the media limelight, having him discredited, rather than by kidnapping his wife and risking drawing the attention of the whole world.

Stephen couldn't sleep that night thinking about it—that Akhtar had been within feet of Nina. And Akhtar wanted Stephen to know that. Akhtar was notoriously publicity shy, and he would never have revealed himself like that otherwise.

There were massive protests outside the US embassy. The usual gaggle of communist party representatives, students, social activists, and hired hooligans showed up with banners, placards, and noisemakers. They ceremoniously burned effigies of the US president and Stephen. The usual stone throwing and tire burning ensued. Two people were killed in a stampede when the police fired tear gas and water cannons at the crowd.

A mob of camera crews and reporters camped outside Stephen's official residence. They got creative—bribed the neighbors, climbed trees, pretended to be tradesmen or repair technicians. Servants and staff were pounced on as soon as they stepped outside. Reporters swarmed around, foraging for any scraps they could find.

Enterprising news crews went to America to gather more color on Stephen. And that was when they found the Sid connection. The story morphed from an annoying pit bull into a raging monster of mythical proportions and made everything that had happened before seem like a kindergarten field trip. The headlines were out of control.

"Sid Ali, the man behind the New Delhi attacks, worked for Mr. James as a CIA agent. Mr. Ali was two-timing the CIA, because his true employer was ISI, the Pakistani intelligence agency."

"Mr. James has the blood of three hundred and twelve lives on his hands."

"What happened at Mr. Ali's residence in America? Was it really an armed robbery?"

"Where is Mr. Ali now?"

"Is the Indian government a tool of the CIA?"

After a week of this media mania, the Indian government couldn't take the heat anymore. With a general election just months away, the ruling party could not afford to be seen as weak, particularly after the newspapers tied Stephen to Sid, and Sid to ISI and the New Delhi attacks. The opposition party made huge headway in opinion polls once the story broke.

In a press conference, the minister of foreign affairs announced the expulsion of Mr. Stephen James, minor diplomat and military attaché to the embassy of the United States. A stinging letter of rebuke accompanied the announcement. The American government lodged a protest to no avail.

It was brilliant. The enemy had neutralized Stephen without firing a shot (well, just that one warning shot by the fake-sardar sniper) and brought his investigation to a standstill. It was unlikely he would ever be allowed back into India. And the whole world knew who he really was. He couldn't conceal his identity anymore. He had no cover.

LIMBO

T wo limos idled by the fence near the edge of the airfield. Nina got into the first one with their luggage. Stephen stood outside talking to George. Their return to New Jersey was muted, unlike their pyrotechnic departure from New Delhi, where protests and riots engineered by political hooligans had seen off Stephen and Nina. In New Jersey, George and another officer met them at a small airport without fanfare.

The Indian government had lodged an official complaint. The State Department and White House demanded an investigation. Until that was completed, Stephen's fate was unclear. The American press remained quiet about the episode.

"Stephen, I have it under control. Don't worry. It will blow over. We just need to wait it out."

"George, this investigation is unadulterated bullshit, and you know it."

"I agree, but we can't avoid it. Anyway, Nina is waiting for you. I'll see you in a minute." He walked away to the other limo.

Stephen opened the passenger door and leaned into the backseat, where Nina sat. His lips moved but couldn't form any words. With a sigh he got in and closed the door.

He leaned forward with his hands clasped between his knees. Touches of gray had appeared at his temples. His fingers worried his wedding band, moving it up and down. He looked at her and forced a smile.

"Nina, I am sorry I got you into this. I had no right. I was selfish. I have no idea what's going to happen to me now or how long it will take. I'll understand if you never want to see me again."

For a moment he thought she was going to hit him. She had been under almost as much pressure as he had been. However, while he had the luxury of retreating into a cold, introspective silence, she carried the burden of watching over him, to stop him from breaking. She had tried to get him to talk about his anger and frustration, the bitterness of failure as he had watched months of work evaporate in one stroke, so close to the prize that would never be within his grasp again. But talking was not his way. During the last tumultuous weeks in India, he had been distant but polite, made sure she was comfortable but shut her out in every other respect.

The only moment of connection came at night, when he kissed her before she went to bed, before he retreated to his office. He would hold on to her just a bit longer than usual, with all his strength, and mutely communicate the maelstrom raging inside him. He felt betrayed and let down, fearing that his own government was going to investigate him when they knew perfectly well what had gone down. George had assured him it was a charade, and they had to go through with it as a matter of process. But it was a blow to Stephen's pride that his conduct should be questioned when he had shown exemplary discipline and restraint under the most-stressful circumstances—and played completely by the rules.

The look on Nina's face now absolutely killed him.

"Do you want to get rid of me? Will that make your life easier?" she asked quietly while the light went out of her eyes. "What happened to 'you are my strength, I need you'? You don't need me anymore? Is that it?" Her voice dropped further and became almost inaudible.

Stephen watched her, mesmerized by her eyes. This was his punishment, to watch the only person in the world who cared about him look at him like her heart had been cut out. He had done this to her with a few thoughtless words when all the bile and violence in India couldn't shake her.

Nina knew he had not meant for it to come out the way it had. His intention had been to tell her how awful he felt for everything she had been through during the last year on his account: the escape from Le Méridien, the shootout in Sid's house, Stephen's painful recovery, and the recent diplomatic disaster. What he must have meant to say was that he would do anything to make her life better, even giver her up. But it had come out wrong.

She too, in her heightened anxiety, had lost control of what she really wanted to say. Her worst fears had risen harshly to her lips at the thought of parting from him.

He enveloped her in a crushing bear hug. "I'll see you soon," he said and released her. He opened the door and stumbled out.

⟞⟊ ⟊⟝

Nina's limo sped home through central Jersey. Stephen had insisted she stay with her parents until he figured out whether it was safe for her to be by herself in their apartment in New York. She had to wait until she got the all clear from him.

After a three-week stay at her parents' home, and Stephen still hadn't given her the go ahead, Nina decided to go back to the apartment anyway. It was a few days before Christmas, and she wanted to be home. Was it safe? Her mother worried. But Nina was determined. She missed Stephen. She wanted to be where she could be surrounded by their life—his shirts and shoes, arranged with such thought and precision, his books and photos of sailboats and Grandfather James that lined his office. Neel offered to go and stay with her, but she refused. She didn't tell Stephen, naturally. The mere thought of going back home cheered her up. Maybe this was the charm that would draw him home. That was her desperate, superstitious hope.

She was about to go to bed, her bags packed for leaving the next morning, when her phone beeped. It was very late, almost two in the morning. "Open the front door," Stephen's text message read. She flew down the hallway and flung the door open. There he stood under the front porch lights, unable to hide his joy at seeing her after three long weeks. She threw herself into his arms.

"It's OK, sweetheart, it's OK," he soothed her. "It's over now."

"How did you get here? I didn't hear a car."

"I got dropped off at the bottom of the driveway."

The porch light streamed into the front hall through the glass door. He held her at arm's length to fill his eyes with her. She looked ridiculously young in two braids and her high-school pajamas.

"I missed you, missed you, missed you," she said and dug her hands inside his jacket to put her arms around his waist, taking deep, satisfying breaths of the smell of burnt coffee and stale, secondhand cigarette smoke that had soaked into his clothes. He zipped her inside his jacket, and they did a silly little stumbling dance and laughed. On the way to her room, they tiptoed and tried to be very quiet, but Neel heard them. He came into Nina's room grinning and closed the door behind him.

"How are you?" He greeted Stephen with a fist bump.

The little scar just below the hairline on the left side of Neel's face was inconspicuous, but Stephen noticed it because he looked for it—full of guilt and regret for being responsible for its existence.

"How is school?" Stephen asked.

"Great! It was a nasty semester. I'm glad it's over."

"Staying out of trouble, I hope."

"I try, but trouble finds me."

No, Neel was out there looking it. Why was Neel so determined to work for George? Stephen wanted to ask him, but Nina was around. George had already signed the CIA's offer letter to Neel.

"Maybe you should try dating one girl at a time," Stephen said while he hunted for his toothbrush. Nina relayed to Stephen, in excruciating detail, an ongoing account of Neel's love troubles.

Neel merely grinned and said good night.

By the time Stephen woke up the next morning, the family was about to sit down for breakfast. Neel pulled out a chair for him at the central eat-in table, where Grandma and Grandpa were already seated. The kitchen was a big affair, sleek and modern with a concealed design where everything—fridge, dishwasher, storage—was hidden behind wooden panels.

"*Dadaji, dadiji, namaskaar,*" Stephen said in Hindi to the grandparents.

"*Jeete raho, beta.*" They blessed him in unison.

"Good morning," he called out toward where the others were standing. Nina was in the process of making coffee; Neel rolled *alu* parathas, and their mother had them sizzling in a pan. Stephen could hear Nina's father on the phone somewhere in the recesses of the house. The master suite was in the other wing, away from grandparents and kids, separated by the huge living-library-family-kitchen-dining hub in the middle.

"Good morning, Stephen," they sang back at him. Nina finished with the coffee and started to set the places.

"Hello!" Stephen's father-in-law bustled in, showered, dressed, and ready to take on the world.

Stephen rose and shook his hand. "Good morning, sir." They sat down next to each other.

"So how are you, Stephen? Is everything under control?" Ravi poured orange juice for both of them.

"It's OK so far," Stephen replied. Nina placed a mug of coffee in front of him. "I could have got it," he said to her.

"That's fine." She was thrilled to see him with her family and talking to her grandparents in Hindi.

"Give these to Stephen," Deepa told Neel.

Two sizzling parathas stuffed with spicy potato filling landed softly on Stephen's plate next to a glazed sweet-and-sour ginger pickle and a small bowl of ghee. The aroma brought back memories of their Delhi days.

"Would you like yogurt with it?" Nina asked. Stephen nodded.

Deepa was flushed from the stove, a little harried but delighted to have her flock around her. She was dressed in the family uniform of black gym pants and a white T-shirt.

"When these two boys are around, I can't even get a glass of water," Ravi complained good-naturedly. Nina jumped up and got him the water. She had returned to her usual bubbly self, singing and laughing, being silly.

Ravi was glad to see her smiling face. Stephen made her happy. That was all there was to it. But the scar on Stephen's arm distracted him. It peeked out from under the sleeve of his T-shirt whenever he moved his hand to eat.

Stephen concentrated on his parathas. He had developed a taste for spicy food during his year of living with Nina.

"Stephen, I have to take off now. I have a meeting in the city." Ravi patted him on the shoulder when he tried to stand up. "Please don't get up. I'll see you later. Bye, guys." He waved to Deepa and the kids and went downstairs to his car.

"Ma, why don't you eat? We'll make the parathas for you." Nina nudged her mother away from the stove.

Deepa poured herself some coffee and came around the table to sit next to Stephen in the chair Ravi had just vacated.

"Would you like some more coffee?" she asked.

"I'm fine, thank you," he replied, and smiled at Mother Goddess.

"How are you doing?"

He considered the question for a few seconds. "I don't know. I have to wait for things to get sorted. I have no control over them. I wish I could look into the future and get it over with."

Please say everything will be all right. He looked at her hopefully.

She stared at the plate Neel had just placed before her and nodded briefly to thank him. Stephen's words and the emotion that accompanied them touched her. Deepa had always worried about the kind of man Nina would marry. She had hoped it would be someone who could appreciate and respect Nina's quirky combination of academic smarts and emotional naïveté, her affectionate nature that occasionally verged on neediness, her stubborn loyalty, and her childish belief in happiness. Deepa knew that Stephen got Nina, and for that she loved him. She picked her words delicately now, eyes fixed on the plate.

"Nina worships you. We are all very fond of you. We can make things a little easier. You don't have to slog it alone. You have us."

There it was again, that lump in his throat. Deepa knew that expression from her son's eighteen years at home.

"Nothing is ever as bad or as good as we expect," she went on. "There are joys to be had in the worst of times and frustrations during the best of times."

Neel poked Nina in the side and pointed at the table. "Ma is in lecture mode."

Bravo. Nina was glad Deepa had decided to say these things to Stephen. He had the habit of shutting out Nina in times of trouble, to protect her. Someone needed to shake him up a little.

"I know we come from different cultures, and you are used to being on your own," said Deepa. "But that is such a hard, lonely path. So unnecessary."

She interrupted her lecture to tell Nina she was done with the parathas and didn't need any more.

"We all need help at some point, and we are lucky to have people who love us to lean on." She looked at Stephen, but he remained silent. "Anger, guilt, pride, regret—all useless emotions. Let go of them. Do whatever makes you happy."

He stared at his food impassively, but her words had found their mark.

"Well, that concludes the lecture part of today's entertainment," Deepa said and got up from the table. On her way to the sink, she patted him on the shoulder the way he had seen her do a thousand times with Nina and Neel, and the lump in his throat grew bigger. He found it difficult to swallow his food.

HOMECOMING

The apartment in New York felt like paradise after so many months of the staff-filled bungalow in New Delhi, where they'd had hardly any privacy. The sun streamed in through the large windows and lit up a vase of flowers Amy had left for them along with a fridge full of goodies. Deepa's parathas were still traversing their digestive systems and made them helplessly drowsy even though it was not yet noon. They fell into bed, under the freshly laundered sheets and comforter, and instantly slipped into a deep, restful sleep—the kind that can be had only at home.

It was around three in the afternoon when Stephen woke to the smell of coffee. He continued to lie there but emerged a little from the comforter and propped himself up with Nina's pillows in anticipation. He could hear her singing in the kitchen, happy as only she could be. She had a sweet voice, ideal for Hindi movie songs that had barely any range and needed no vocal dexterity.

Nina came in with two cups, and they drank their coffee with legs entwined, looking out the window at the waning sunlight. No security guards tramped up and down. No Paro to ask, "What to make for dinner, ma'am?" No noisy phones, fax machines, or incessant stream of visitors. Just the two of them.

She turned to him and said, "Let's get a Christmas tree and ornaments, lights, stockings, the whole deal."

"Now?" he asked.

Her hair was still damp from the shower, and a fine mist landed on his face whenever she tossed her head to get the wet strands out of her eyes.

"Yes. There are only a few days left."

"We didn't have one last year."

"Well, we didn't need a tree last year. We had a wedding to go to last Christmas, if you remember."

Of course he remembered their Indian wedding. It had been the most psychedelic experience of his life— the outfits, the food, the music, the people, and the endless dancing.

"Come, Stephen. Let's go see the Rockefeller Center tree. The city looks beautiful." It was getting late. "We have to go out to eat anyway," she said.

Nina finally convinced him to get out of bed. Deepa's parathas had yielded their calories long ago. It was time to leave their cocoon.

A couple of hours later, an icy wind smacked them as they stepped out of a restaurant after dinner.

"Did your parents always have a Christmas tree?" Stephen asked. He was surprised by her enthusiasm.

Nina laughed at the recollection. "No, they actually started doing it the year I left for college. Before that they were just too busy running around with us—soccer, ballet, track, tennis. The first time, during my freshman year, my environmentalist mother insisted on a real tree that she was going to plant in the backyard afterward. It was a disaster. There were needles all over the floor, and it was half dead by Christmas. From then on we have always had two artificial trees—a small one in the living room and a larger one in the family room. We've added odd little ornaments to them over the years: football helmets, handmade cloth fishies, beaded dragonflies. They are very peculiar trees."

"But you love them?"

She nodded. "Of course. It took us a long time to collect that weird set of ornaments. We have a Ganesha made in Chennai. My grandparents brought it from India."

Stephen smiled. He had to fight hard to keep his spirits up these days, to repel the black moods that waited in the wings for a cue, ever ready to pull him into their dark embrace.

"What about you?" Nina asked. She shifted the bag of leftovers from one hand to another in order to hold Stephen's hand. But there was no joy in holding gloved hands, and it was too cold to do without the gloves.

"It was fun while my grandfather was alive. Everything was done on a large scale—huge tree, tons of presents, parties, relatives."

When he'd lost his grandfather, he had lost his childhood, his family, and his traditions. He had lost everything.

"After he died there were two horrendous Christmases. Mrs. Brown oversaw the half-hearted preparations. My brother and sister came home but refused to speak to me. They thought I had schemed and convinced my grandfather to cut them out of the will while he lay on his deathbed. Perhaps my mother felt the same way. I was so young—just a teenager when my grandfather died, you know. I was very hurt, and my mother was no help. She could barely manage her life. How could she possibly deal with three obnoxious, unhappy children?"

He turned to look at Nina, to draw comfort and alleviate the memories of those miserable years.

"After that I never went home for Christmas. I would go sailing in Australia, the Bahamas, California, wherever I felt like. At least my allowance was generous enough to let me do as I pleased."

"You never reached out to your siblings?"

He shrugged. "We were never close. They were grown up and out of the house by the time I was old enough to remember anything. And I am very different from them. I think we must be from different fathers. My grandfather was convinced I'm my father's only real child."

Nina was shocked by this cynical comment. He had never spoken in this vein before. But the past few months were beginning to catch up with him now that he had no more depositions to give, no debriefings to attend. The frustration of failure was hard to keep at bay. And there was nothing to keep him busy. He just had to wait, wait, and wait some more. It drove him mad and drained them both.

"You are very lucky to have the family you do," he said gently, to make up for his harshness.

"I know," she replied.

New York City was ablaze with holiday lights and full of shoppers and tourists. Traffic was a nightmare despite the police force that herded jaywalkers and recalcitrant drivers with loud whistles. Except for the cold, which felt worse after their balmy India days, it was delightful to be out walking on the streets.

Their trip to a department store on Broadway proved to be very productive. Nina wanted a huge tree, but Stephen talked her down to a manageable seven feet. Ornaments, ribbons, and lights took another twenty minutes of discussion. Why was Nina being so picky about this? She wanted Christmas stockings now.

"We don't have a mantel," he said.

"I will find a place," she replied.

She was unstoppable. He gave in. Clearly it was very important to her.

"We can spend Christmas at your parents' if you miss home, Nina."

She didn't answer, too preoccupied with her search for a treetop ornament. Nothing matched whatever vision she had in her head. They ran out of time as the store began to close.

As soon as they got home, Nina unpacked the tree. Stephen leaned on the kitchen counter and ate ice cream while he watched her heroic efforts. She got the tree to stand up; it was a remarkably real-looking fake, with little golden lights wrapped in its branches. The ribbons proved to be a tough bunch. They enveloped Nina, the stepladder, and the tree in a tangled mess. She had absolutely no idea how to do it.

"Would you like me to help?" he asked without making a move. She nodded and tried to get off the stepladder without bringing the whole thing down.

He took the spools and scissors from her and walked around the tree, sizing it up. Soon he had the gold and green ribbons swirling down in graceful alternating spirals around the tree, from top to bottom.

"You are my hero!" Nina beamed.

"I know." He gave a rare smile and helped her put up the ornaments, the big ones recessed in the inner branches to catch the twinkling lights, the smaller ones on the outside.

"Would you like me to plug it in?" he asked.

"Yes, yes, please," she replied. Her face glowed with anticipation. He expected her to start skipping from one foot to another at any minute.

"Close your eyes, and don't open them until I tell you to." He was beginning to be infected by her enthusiasm.

He plugged it in; positioned it properly, careful not to disturb the ornaments; and switched off the room lights. It was glorious. The gauzy ribbons glittered with the reflections of the little golden lights. The ornaments sparkled like magical, mysterious fruit, with a flash of red and gold in the dark-green branches. He paused, unable to take his eyes off the tree. Memories he had buried for years, in order not to miss the people and times associated with them, rose to the surface in a bittersweet rush. He recovered with a shiver, walked over to Nina, and covered her eyes with his hands.

"Are you ready?" he asked.

"Yes, yes."

He removed his hands from her eyes and hugged her close to him.

"Oh my God! It's beautiful. I love it." She looked up at him.

He didn't say anything, just stood rooted to the spot, holding on to her. And thanked a god he didn't believe in that this sparkling, happy woman loved him.

The next day Stephen went out after lunch. Nina stayed back because she wanted to prepare for the following day's Christmas Eve dinner with George and Ginnie.

She was halfway through her preparations by the time he returned. His cheeks were red from the cold, and snow sat like powdered sugar on his brown curls. He wandered into the kitchen and marveled at how someone so clumsy could slice, dice, and cook with such skill and precision. The counter was covered with bowls of chopped yams, pumpkin, carrots, cabbage, snow peas, beans, peppers, spinach, and tomatoes all neatly sealed in plastic wrap for tomorrow. The piecrust was rolled and ready in the freezer.

"Where did you go?" Nina asked him.

"I was looking for something." He took her bowl of carrots.

"What were you looking for? Did you find it?"

He nodded and slid a gift-wrapped package the size of a shoebox across the counter.

"For me?" She was surprised. It wasn't Christmas, and anyway they had agreed they didn't need any gifts. "Would you like me to open it now?"

He nodded again. There was so much he wanted to say to her, but his natural reticence and ingrained habits from decades of being a spy were hard to overcome despite being married for a year. He still tended to deal with issues on his own terms or not deal with them at all, letting them simmer and harden into indifference, anger, skepticism, any number of negative things that took the joy out of life. Even though his mother-in-law's words were well-known pop-psychology mantras, they had stayed with him because they'd come from her. He wanted to let go of the anger and bitterness because for the first time, there was someone in his life he trusted completely—someone who offered him unconditional love. He couldn't afford to screw it up.

Nina washed her hands and dried them. She was very curious. Stephen was in a peculiar mood. The fancy bow and the green-and-gold gift wrap came off easily. The box's lid slid open to reveal an object wrapped in pale-green tissue paper with tiny gold stars. She looked up at him, but he was inscrutable, watching her with an expression she couldn't decipher. She was a little afraid. What kind of extreme gift was this? She removed the tissue.

It was a treetop ornament—an angel with wings, dressed in a sari with a red bindi on her forehead. It was exquisite, a minor work of art, a dusky angel with a sweet, happy face.

Nina was tongue-tied. All she could do was shake her head in amazement. There was a card at the bottom of the box. She fumbled in her hurry to open it. It read, in Stephen's unmistakable, precise handwriting, "To my darling Nina, my guardian angel. There are no words to describe what I feel for you. Yours always in this life and next, Stephen."

Nina steadied herself against the counter. She looked around for him, but he had gone to lie down on the couch.

"Everything OK?" She looked down at him.

He was tired and melancholy but made an effort to smile at her and look normal.

"I'm fine, just a little tired."

She squeezed in next to him and wrapped him in her arms. "Thank you for the angel." She turned his face toward her.

He received her in his arms with a wistful hug. "You smell nice," he said and inhaled the aroma of fresh mint that lingered on her hands. He settled his face in the crook of her neck. This time her perfume greeted him and transported him at once to the night he had wiped the pollen of scented stargazers off her cheek, the moment when, like Superman, he had plunged into the abyss of the future with her in his arms.

"Sing to me," he whispered. "The saddest song you know."

Nina smoothed his hair back and thought for a while. It was a complicated song, and she was sure to mangle it, but she wanted to sing it for him because the melody was heartbreakingly sad and because he loved the sound of Urdu.

> When the sun goes down,
> My eyes come alive,
> With the light of hope.
> But the dark night taunts with a cruel tongue:
> "The one you wait for
> Will disappoint you once again,
> The one for whom you tend this fire,
> These futile flames of desire."
>
> I am all alone
> With my loneliness.
> It holds me in its grim embrace
> Through the lonely night,
> The night comes and leaves on silent wings.

By the time she finished, they were both close to tears. Into that doleful song of parting and heartache, into those elongated, quivering notes, she had poured all the pain and sorrow they had endured. They had weathered more in one year than most married couples did in ten.

REHABILITATION

Nina fussed around and tried to straighten the already immaculate apartment. Between Stephen's restless energy and her cleanliness fetish, the place was tidied up several times a day and polished to a spit-shine. Stephen had taken to prowling around the flat and devoted his engineering skills to fixing, mending, spackling, and painting. No other apartment in the building was in such shipshape condition.

George and Ginnie were due to arrive at any minute. The Christmas tree was a twinkling tower of green and gold and stood in a corner, bookcases on one side and a bank of windows on the other. Angel Nina surveyed the room from atop. Stephen sat in the guest bedroom that served as his office. Nina's enthusiasm was out of sync with his mood, but he didn't want to get in her way or discourage her. He looked out of the windows at the muddy river encrusted with dirty ice. *How much longer, for God's sake?* He was going raving mad. He would have liked to go home to Massachusetts, but he hated being there during the holidays.

George and Ginnie arrived red nosed from the cold. George looked around him. It was ironic—he'd never expected to see Stephen in a domestic setting like an ordinary mortal, taking the coats from his guests and hanging them up in the closet. George was accustomed to seeing him in his huge mansion, waited on by Mrs. Brown or conferring with the groundskeeper. To see him in a small Manhattan apartment offering them wine was quite a turn of events.

After a few minutes of polite standing around, Stephen marched George into his office. He was impatient to find out if his fate was any closer to resolution.

"You look well," George said.

It was true. Stephen had recovered almost completely, with near-normal movement of his leg and arm. He exercised like a maniac—swimming, climbing, running—to stay busy more than anything else. He looked younger and healthier than ever.

"Never mind my looks. What's happening with my case?"

"I need a smoke. Shall we step outside?"

"I'll open the window. You can lean out. Don't dance around the topic, George. Tell me what's going on."

George perched on the windowsill and tipped his cigarette outside. After a minute he slipped his hand into his jacket pocket, took out a letter, and handed it to Stephen.

"What does it say?" Stephen ripped it open.

George didn't reply but looked down at the unsuspecting people below whose heads were getting dusted with the ashes from his cigarette.

Stephen read and reread the letter.

"Happy?" George threw away the stub and stood up.

The commission had cleared Stephen of all charges and found he had not violated any diplomatic protocols, American laws, or Indian laws. He was reinstated retroactively to avoid any break in service. In fact he was even honored with an award for exceptional conduct. The letter included an appointment to a new job.

"About fucking time! They knew the truth going in but put me through this crap anyway, like a common criminal."

"You know how these things work. We had to have this investigation to make the White House feel good. They know the truth. The president wrote you a nice letter."

Stephen merely glared at him in reply.

"Take a vacation and start in the new year."

"I don't know. I think this is as good a time to quit as any."

"Come on. What are you going to do? Sit around and play golf? You have to finish what you started."

George wondered how long it would be before Stephen got restless and bored with his recently found domestic bliss. George knew these demons well and the will and commitment it took not to rock the marital boat. Stephen was too self-centered and too accustomed to doing what he pleased. He would find it confining to stay in Nina's domestic orbit. Poor Nina. Her heart would be broken. On the other hand, Stephen had stunned George by getting married at all.

He could see why Stephen was so taken with Nina. She was bright and articulate, pleasant and easygoing, with a wide smile and a pealing laugh. And every few minutes, her eyes would rest on Stephen with undisguised adoration. It was enough to turn any man's head.

But how long could that ardor last? It had been almost two years. George gave it another year at the most. He chewed on a fresh, unlit cigarette while Stephen reread the appointment letter.

"Thanks, George." He put away the letter in a drawer.

"Take the job, Stephen. I want to retire. Take over from me."

"I'll think about it." He shook George's hand. "Let's go have dinner."

As soon as George and Ginnie left, Nina corralled Stephen. "Any news?"

"Yes. They cleared me of everything. They even threw in some stupid award." He smiled. It had been an ego issue for him, that his integrity had been questioned by a bunch of wonks who had never stepped outside the safety of their offices.

"That's great! Congratulations."

But from the way he stood, she knew there was more.

"And?"

Stephen sat down on a stool across the counter from her. She examined Ginnie's almond cookies in search of the best looking one. There was a pile of gifts on the counter from her parents, from Neel, from Amy and Jeff. Stephen took them over to the tree and arranged them underneath.

"And I have a new job." He deliberately had his back to her so as not to react to her reaction.

"What sort of job, please?" Nina became very polite when she was angry. She could guess what the job was.

"I will be running the operations on the Indian subcontinent from here, to finish what I started. In fact, I'll be in charge of all of South Asia."

He got done with the presents and, when he didn't hear any response from her, turned around. Nina had disappeared. He found her in the bedroom changing out of her dress. She didn't look up when he came in.

"Are you upset?" He leaned against the doorframe and tried to assess how long it would take to talk her out of her mood.

"What do you care? It's the same story every time." She flung the dress on the bed and went into the bathroom, ready to slam the door. But as usual he was too quick for her.

"Talk to me, Nina. Tell me what you're afraid of. There's no point in behaving like a child."

"That you will be lying in a ditch blown to pieces, and I won't even know where to find you. Is that good enough?"

"Don't be so dramatic. This is a desk job. There is no danger."

He said it lightly in the hope it wouldn't devolve into a long argument. She brushed her hair violently and braided it so tightly, it was stiff as a walking stick. They were supposed to attend the Christmas service at a Presbyterian church she had found on the West Side. To humor her Stephen had agreed. In her family special occasions were marked through customs, traditions, and rituals, to single out a special day from the everyday. She had struggled to find an equivalent for the two of them in the absence of any guidance from him. She desperately wanted that structure.

Stephen stood immovable in the bathroom doorway, determined not to let her go past him.

"Please, I need to change. Let me pass," she said without looking at him.

"Look at me."

The top of her head bobbed just below his chin. "You should get ready too. The service starts in an hour," she said.

"Look at me, please."

"No!" She turned away in a sulk and sat on the closed toilet.

"Well, I guess we're stuck here then."

He closed the door behind him and settled down on the bathroom floor in front of her. She picked up the *New Yorker* lying nearby and tried to read it. Her satin slip was too flimsy to keep her warm; the hair on her arms stood up, and she shivered.

"It's a strategic job. I will plan and run the operations, but I will not be out in the field. I can do this—I have to do this. These assholes have to be stopped." It was rare for him to use coarse language in front of her. "You know it needs to be done."

Nina didn't reply. *Why did he have to do it?* Was there no one else? Did he forget that his whole left side had been shredded by exploding bullets less than a year ago?

"I have spent the last five years of my life studying the region and these guys. The director has asked me to take this job, and I want to. I have to."

She bit her lip. How come she didn't have a say in any of this? She was afraid she would either fly into a rage or burst into tears if she tried to say anything, so she remained silent.

Stephen's wounded thigh was not accustomed to the lotus position. Stretched beyond endurance, it went into a spasm. He got up awkwardly in an effort to ease the cramp but stumbled into the door.

Nina looked up and hurried to him. "What's wrong?"

"Nothing," he replied and leaned back on the door with a grimace. When he tried to release the recalcitrant muscle, it caused so much pain that his face turned red with the effort. Nina turned on the hot water in the bathtub, soaked a towel, and then pulled down his pants and wrapped the towel around his thigh. She pushed him down on the toilet to massage the area near the scar.

"Divine retribution," he said, "for harassing you."

She relented and looked at him, at his tired, sleepless face. "Go easy on him," her mother had said. "You're the only one he can turn to."

"Let's forget the service. We can go tomorrow."

"No, I'd like to go. I feel better."

They got dressed in a hurry and took the subway to Park Presbyterian Church. It was close to seven at night. The old church was lively, with smartly dressed people, chattering children, and candles everywhere.

Stephen and Nina sat in the back. She had never been to a Protestant service before, and she waited in anticipation. The candles and the ceremonial lighting cast beautiful shadows.

The minister started with an address and announced the passage he was going to read. Everyone around took out the holy text and turned to the page to follow along. This was new to Nina. In traditional Hindu services, the priest recited and chanted from memory, but recently many temples had started providing worshippers with prayer books and texts, so they could chant along. Then the choir sang, and Nina sat up in delight. The angelic voices washed over her as they rose and fell in harmony. There was much standing and sitting, and singing and reading in between. It was quite different from what she was accustomed to, with the Hindu priests singing the *shlokas* and chanting hymns but never delivering sermons. But it inspired the same sense of gratitude and peace, of being blessed.

Stephen remained still for the most part, though he caught himself humming along once in a while. Despite his not having stepped into a church in twenty years, everything was familiar and comforting. His mother in pearls and his sister in a poufy silk dress appeared like ghosts in the distance. His grandfather sat next to him in the pew with a lingering whiff of the cigar he had just discarded at the door of the church.

Stephen was said to be his grandfather's spitting image. When Grandfather had entered a room, crowds parted respectfully, and people clamored to catch his eye and talk to him. Even as a little boy, Stephen had wondered why his father never had that effect or commanded the same respect and authority as Grandfather James.

Stephen's alienation had begun when his grandfather became ill. Stephen had sat by his bedside during his months of awful suffering, doing schoolwork and entertaining his grandfather with stories of sailing and the girls in his class. Grandfather was sedated most of the time but attempted to stay awake when Stephen was around. Toward the end Stephen lay on a cot next to Grandfather's bed, unable to sleep, dreading the moment when his labored breathing would stop forever.

After his father's suicide, Stephen's parents' lives became public fodder with the formidable patriarch too sick to keep the gossip hounds at bay. Stephen simply could not relate to the petty, squabbling members of his family. It would be a relief to go away to college, and he waited eagerly. And then everything exploded. His grandfather died, and the family scattered across the globe in the aftermath. His mother went into hiding in Cyprus; his brother married an Argentinean heiress, and his sister settled in California.

Memories he had refused to acknowledge for so long now held him in their thrall and played across his mind's eye like a bad, bitter movie. Nina's hand rested gently in his. He gripped it tightly as he tried to stay afloat while the flood tossed him around for the duration of the service. Nina turned to look at him now and then, sensing he was on a faraway journey. She moved closer to him in the pew and put her head on his shoulder. He looked down at her and was brought back to the present.

They stepped outside after the service and walked to the subway. The air was bitingly cold, aided by a brisk wind that penetrated their jackets. Stephen enveloped Nina inside his coat to keep her warm, and they walked in the peaceful night like a two-headed monster created by a facetious god.

AN INCIDENT

Settling into his new job as head of South Asia operations took more time than Stephen had expected. He had to deal with innumerable intelligence agencies, attend endless meetings, conference calls, and sign reams and reams of documents. He had been at it for more than six months now. The politics were vicious; the rivalries between sister agencies were obnoxious, and the egos! Resentment was high that he had been promoted over other more qualified people. Just because of his connections, the office grapevine declared.

That day, it was almost six thirty in the evening by the time he got a chance to breathe. *Shoot.* He had forgotten to return Nina's call. He tried her cell, home, office—no answer.

Old fears are hard to shake, worse than old habits. "I hope nothing's wrong," he muttered as he raced to the subway station. Was she hurt or lying on the floor in a faint? Had she been in an accident? Terrifying thoughts lurked at the edge of his consciousness, but he ignored them with grim determination. He thought of calling Nina's mom, Deepa, but he didn't want to alarm her unnecessarily. Still, it was unusual for Nina not to call or text back within minutes of missing a call from him.

Taxis were scarce at that hour, plus they could get stuck in the evening traffic. He jumped onto the subway for a quick ride, but his train took its sweet time, idling on the tracks in between stations while other trains whizzed by. When it finally pulled into the station in slow motion, he rushed out and ran all the way home, incongruous in his tailored suit and immaculate, shiny shoes, his briefcase flying.

"Nina! Nina!" he called once inside the apartment, but there was no answer. Everything seemed to be in order—no signs of a struggle, break-in, or assault. Her cell phone was right there on the counter with all his missed calls dutifully registered. She must have come home early and then forgotten to take it with her when she went out. But she hadn't mentioned any plans to him. It was unlike her. She never went anywhere without letting him know. Her keys and handbag were missing. He looked in the closet. Her black fall jacket and black boots were also missing.

The bedroom looked normal except for her pajamas flung carelessly in the bathroom doorway. He walked to the bathroom and stood over the garment, tried to determine if she had thrown them or some other, more sinister hands had dropped them inadvertently. There were no unusual odors, no telltale hints of an unwelcome presence. He was about to bend down and pick up the pajamas when he heard a key turn in the front door. He walked to the living room and waited silently, braced for the unknown.

It was Nina. She hurried in and chucked her handbag and keys on the sofa.

"Where were you? I couldn't reach you at any of the numbers," he said and finally exhaled and began to loosen his tie.

"I went to see the doctor." She hung up her coat in the closet, removed her boots, and went over to where he stood.

"Why? What's wrong?"

"Two months!" She smiled at him. It took him a minute to figure out what she meant. When he did, his heart raced even though he had known it was likely to happen sooner or later, just a matter of time.

"Really?" His hand flew to his hair involuntarily and fussed with it. "Are you sure?" he asked, a silly question given that she had been to the doctor, who must have confirmed it, otherwise she wouldn't be telling him. But he couldn't think of anything to say. His brain had been rendered dysfunctional by the pleasant fog that had descended on it.

She nodded vigorously. "I managed to get an appointment with the doctor after I called you."

After such a long time, her face was bright with happiness. Stephen hoped they wouldn't run afoul of fate. A hesitant joy lit up his melancholy gray eyes, and his lips smiled without prompting, unable to resist the thrill of the moment.

Stephen and Nina had gotten absorbed in their outside lives, and when everything ran smoothly, there was no place for the raw, wrenching emotions that had gnawed at them during the insanity that descended on their lives in the past two years. But they were both grateful for the reprieve. They wanted safety, predictability, and as much normalcy as they could possibly get. And now there was going to be an excitement of a happy sort in their lives.

The next evening Nina came home early and tried to make grilled cheese sandwiches for dinner. The smell of butter made her sick. *Forget it*. Cold sandwiches would have to do.

When she heard Stephen's key in the front door, she called out, "Sorry, cold sandwiches for dinner."

He smiled at her from the doorway. "No problem. Give me a minute to change out of these clothes," he said and disappeared inside the bedroom.

She had finished setting the table by the time he came out clad in pajamas.

"I'm going to ask you for something really big. It's unfair, and you have every right to say no, but I'd be very happy if you agree," he said as soon as he sat down at the table, as if he had been waiting to get those words out the whole day.

Nina looked at him in surprise. Stephen never asked for favors. He never asked, period. He took it for granted that he would get what he wanted.

"What is it?" she asked.

"I want us to move to Massachusetts and raise our child there, in my home."

Nina put down her fork. He watched her expression intently to figure out what her first reaction was. She would eventually agree—she always did—but he wouldn't want to do it if she really hated the thought.

The haunted James mansion, that traitor Sid had called it. Nina did a decent job of maintaining a neutral expression, and in fact she really didn't care about it one way or another. There were many positives. It was beautiful, and it clearly meant a lot to Stephen. That was a good enough reason. It was within a reasonable distance of New York if she needed to go there a couple of times a week. It was an ideal distance from her parents—not too far, not too close. And Neel was next door in Connecticut. But. There was always a "but." There was so much bad karma associated with that place.

However, she didn't want to dwell on it. "I am fine with that."

Stephen's face lit up. She had never seen him like that before. Even at his happiest, there was always a shadow of sadness to him, but not today. He jumped up, went over to her, and enveloped her in a big hug. He kneeled by her chair.

"If I die now, I will die completely happy," he said with his head on her chest.

"Don't." She smiled down at him. "Before you get too happy, I have a favor to ask too."

"Ask away." He got up and walked back to his seat and his sandwich.

She tried to pick words that would not elicit a knee-jerk refusal. "Just as you feel it's important that your child feels connected to your home, don't you think it's important to be connected to people too?"

He knew where she was headed. "Nina, sweetheart, we have discussed this ad nauseam."

"I know, but it's your baby, a part of your family. Don't you think he or she would want to meet his or her grandmother, aunt, and uncle?"

"You have a great family. She will have excellent grandparents and great-grandparents and a totally cool uncle. That's plenty. That's a lot more than I ever had." He looked at her and shrugged his shoulders.

She, Nina was amused. He had decided that the baby would be a she.

"You know I'm right. Please, think about it, Stephen."

He didn't answer.

"Is it because they'll disapprove of me?"

"No, it's because they're substandard human beings, and I don't want them in the same room as you."

"That was a long time ago. Things change. And you've given most of the estate away. They can't hold it against you."

"That's precisely the reason they'll hold it against me. They'll say I chose to give it away rather than let them touch it."

"How about your mother? I'm sure she misses you."

He ate silently for a while, chewing with great concentration, his eyes glued to the crumbs on his plate.

"What she did to my father was reprehensible, even if he deserved it. Simply walking out would have been the decent thing to do instead of doing what she did—sleeping with every man who crossed her path."

It was a terrible exaggeration. "That's not fair, and you know it," Nina said. "Also it was a long time ago, Stephen, people change."

But he didn't hear her. He was fifteen again, sitting at the table between his feuding parents, muttering under his breath, "Shut up, shut up, shut up, both of you; just shut the fuck up."

Nina was startled by his expression. It was a look of pure misery. He didn't notice her looking at him. He was too deep in his past. She would never be able to understand what they had done to him.

"Sorry. Whatever you want is fine with me," she said gently.

He nodded but did not look up.

Three weeks later Nina had an appointment with the doctor at 1:00 p.m. She took the afternoon off from work and took a taxi to the Upper East Side, Seventy-Ninth and Lexington. The doctor gave her a thumbs-up: everything was progressing well. She was into the twelfth week of the pregnancy.

She decided to take a taxi back home. The driver weaved through the crosstown traffic, headed back to the Upper West Side. Nina removed her seatbelt to reach for her handbag, which had slid across the seat. She searched in it for her cell phone. She couldn't help smiling with anticipation—her mom would be totally thrilled. But first she had to call Stephen. He had wanted to come along for the appointment but couldn't make it.

Bang! She felt a big jolt as something rammed the taxi from behind. She went flying and hit her head on the plastic partition, crumpling forward at an awkward angle. Bang! It happened again. This time she was doubled up, hurled into the side of the taxi. Her head hit the window. The taxi braked suddenly, and the driver jumped out. There was a huge altercation outside. Angry men shouted at each other.

Nina looked through the rear window. The drivers of the two vehicles were trying to punch each other. The limo driver looked vaguely familiar. She had seen him somewhere, his big, burly, football-player physique. In the midst of the argument, he turned around and caught her eye. He looked at her for a good twenty seconds without blinking, as if to say, "We did this on purpose, and we are not going to stop until we get you."

Nina was truly frightened. Stephen had been right all along. He had warned her, wanted to get her a bodyguard, but she had refused. That look from that driver was pure evil.

Even though her head hurt from the impact, she wanted to get away from the scene. She flung a twenty-dollar bill on the driver's seat, hurried to the pavement and hailed another taxi. She was sore and tired. She had gone to work early that morning in order to take the afternoon off. All she wanted to do was go home and lie down.

When she woke up after a few hours, she heard Stephen in the kitchen. He was on the phone. Her body was dull and achy. She didn't feel like moving, but she had to go to the bathroom. She swung her legs down and sat on the edge of the bed for a few minutes. When she tried to straighten herself into a standing position, a crippling abdominal cramp doubled her over. The bed was damp and sticky.

"Stephen!" she screamed. He came running into the bedroom.

Nina stood by the side of the bed, holding on to the headboard, bent over. Her pajamas were soaked in blood. Stephen's eyes were riveted to the crimson pool that was beginning to collect at her feet.

"Nina! Sweetheart. What's wrong?" He rushed to her.

"The baby!"

RECKLESSNESS

Stephen watched Nina while she slept. It seemed so pointless, the pregnancy that had thrilled them both but ended almost as soon as it had started. Nina didn't tell her parents. There was no point now other than to spread the unhappiness.

Nina had wanted to get away from the apartment so they had driven up to Massachusetts to Stephen's home as soon as Nina was able to travel. Stephen stayed with her day and night. He had no words to comfort her, just his constant presence and shared sorrow. He didn't have to endure the physical pain, but he was as heartbroken as she was. It was like his grandfather had died again.

Mrs. Brown ministered to them silently. Amy came to visit that weekend and sat with Nina to relieve Stephen. He aged in front of her minute by minute, a new line on his face for every tear Nina shed.

After she had watched them for two days, Amy warned Nina, "You're going to kill him if you don't pull yourself together. Get a grip."

That was the wake-up call Nina needed. As usual she had been too wrapped up in her own drama to pay attention to Stephen. It was as much a loss for him as it was for her. Perhaps more so because this was the first time he had felt a blood connection. She was overcome with remorse; she turned her energies on him and to getting their life back to normal.

"Let's go back to the city," she said that night after Amy left.

"Are you sure? We can stay for another couple of days if it helps."

"No, I'm fine. I will be fine," she corrected herself.

"We *will* have a baby," he consoled her. "If we can do it once, we can do it again."

She gave him a smile, but it wasn't her usual high-voltage smile. "I know, but I don't want to think about it right now."

She stared at his haggard face. He looked like he had when they had fled Le Méridien—angry, sleep deprived, full of guilt and regret. She hadn't stopped for a minute to wonder whether he too was in need of comforting. She felt terrible. He made it worse because he blamed himself for what had happened.

"I'm probably the worst thing that could have happened to you." He lay on his back, his head resting on his hands clasped underneath, staring up at Grandpa James on the mantel.

Nina smiled, this time with warmth and affection. "I wouldn't have it any other way. We just have to figure out how to stay out of trouble."

A familiar tightness gripped his chest and throat. She removed his glasses and bent down and kissed him.

He was one lucky bastard. He should be shot for what he had put her through. "I've figured out a way of doing just that," he said.

"What?"

"You'll see. Don't worry. It will be good."

They returned to the city. Her parents never came to know about the pregnancy, but Neel was a frequent confidante during their weekend Skype sessions.

"Hey, Neenz."

"Hey, you. How's it going?"

Neel's stubble-covered face smiled from her computer screen. "Where's the boss?" Stephen was off camera, reading in bed. "Hey, Neel." He walked over to the screen and stood behind Nina's chair, like an old fashioned portrait. After exchanging pleasantries with Neel, Stephen went to the guest room to allow them to talk freely. Snippets of their conversation floated into his hearing.

"Stephen was convinced it was going to be a girl," he heard Nina say. "We were going to call her Uma." She did most of the talking in an even, quiet voice. She told Neel about the renovations they had planned, to make the old Victorian mansion more baby-friendly.

Neel worked on his project reports while he listened and looked up at her now and then to smile or make a silly joke. He remained there patiently as long as she needed him. Stephen was amazed that someone so young and irrepressibly immature on the surface could be so full of compassion and generosity.

Nina's body and mind started to heal. She threw out all the baby-related paraphernalia—vitamins, books, pamphlets. The apartment got a major spring-cleaning even though it was already in perfect order. Bright colors and big prints were suddenly unbearable to her. Stephen watched, initially with concern but later with increasing respect, as Nina marched through these rituals, putting the past to rest. There was a new solemnity to her, a maturity that dimmed the spark of happiness that used to burn so bright.

That's it, Stephen decided. He had to go after these fuckers. He had to get them before they could hurt her again. Akhtar's men were not going to stop until they killed her. He needed to convince George, who would say, "We need to plan it; we need to time it." But they didn't have that luxury. They needed to get fucking Sid to help them get these bastards if they had to pull out all his teeth to make him talk.

Ten weeks later he put his plan in to motion. He called Nina at work.

"Nina, I need to go away for around ten days starting next week. Is that OK with you? Can you manage?"

"Sure. Where are you going?"

"I'll be in Virginia most of the time. I have to finish some administrative training."

"No problem. I'll be fine."

"Good. Thanks."

That evening when she came home, he was waiting for her. He was sitting on a stool at the kitchen counter, at work on his laptop, surrounded by piles of papers. It was highly unusual for him to come home so early and for him to let even a scrap of paper leave the security of his office.

He looked up when she entered and gave her a smile she hadn't seen in months: a wickedly playful smile he reserved for cajoling her when he wanted something. She threw her bag and keys on the sofa and went to him, wondering what had caused the change in current.

"What *is* it?" she asked with hands on her hips.

He drew her closer, to stand between his knees. She looked very corporate in a white silk blouse and a black pencil skirt. She had a week full of meetings where she had to present her funding recommendations to BigSearch executives. He wished she would dress like that more often; it suited her. But she favored a style that could only be called bohemian—comfortable but a complete disservice to her figure, hiding it under layers upon layers of baggy, loose clothes. Therefore it was a treat when she let him watch her undress. It was magic: out of layers of sweaters and scarves and T-shirts and vests and camisoles would emerge this stunning Venus with bountiful breasts; a narrow waist; and full, curving hips that gave way to shapely thighs, legs, and ankles.

Stephen slid his hands around her hips and squeezed her closer to him. His face nestled between her breasts. "I plan to quit my job at the end of this month."

"What? I thought you're going on some training trip." She shook his shoulders.

"Yes. That's part of the quitting process."

"Really?" She was thrilled but rather puzzled. "Why do you want to quit?" When he didn't answer, she asked, "New threats?"

"No, not at all."

"Then why? You love your job."

"I know." He sighed and sat back. "But there are younger, smarter people now who can continue my work." Like Neel, who had been with the agency for almost a year.

"Stephen, are you…are you going to quit?" She didn't believe a word of it.

"Yes. I want to go back to being a real engineer and run my company. The time has come. The time is now."

"Well if it's true, then more power to you. But I hope you're not doing it on my account. If you are, you'll regret it all your life. And hate me for it."

"You're a part of the reason but not all of it."

She stared at him and wondered what he was plotting.

"Kiss me," he said.

"First tell me the truth."

"Quitting my job, that's all." He grinned at her, happy as could be. "Come on, kiss me." He moved his face close to hers.

"What's come over you?" She ran her fingers over his lips while she bought time. She was perplexed by his behavior. He had made a big decision to give up something he loved. He should be pensive and conflicted, but here he was, flirting with her without a care in the world.

She was still trying to find clues to his strange mood when he couldn't wait anymore and kissed her, and pressed her to him with such urgency that she could barely breathe. She pushed him away and held him at arm's length.

"Are you on something?"

"No, nothing." He gave a funny laugh. It was just that he had to leave the next day for a few days. He had no idea whether he would return in one piece or in many, but he had to accomplish this one last mission for her, for both of them. But right now he didn't want to think beyond the next few minutes.

She turned his face toward her and continued to examine it for evidence of intoxication. But his eyes and speech were crystal clear, in fact even more so than usual.

"Show me no mercy." He pulled her down to sit on his thigh.

"Are you on painkillers?" she asked. *And maybe a cocktail or two to wash them down.*

He paused and looked at her with sudden sadness. "Oh, my sweet Nina, if it were only that simple."

"How do you mean?"

"You don't have to worry about drugs or alcohol where I am concerned. My vices, as you know by now, are much worse and harder to cure."

Could it be that these strange mood swings were caused by this job-quitting nonsense? It was too abrupt and wrenching. That was his vice: his job. "Don't quit," she was about to say when he broke into one of those mischievous grins.

"Come on, woman. Kiss me. Don't make me beg."

DÉJÀ VU

Nina was in the middle of watching *Daniel Deronda* when the doorbell rang. Whenever Stephen was away, she indulged her fondness for period dramas. He found them insufferable, with their interminable dialogue, repressed love, and yearning looks.

"Why don't they cut to the chase and just do it? Where are the explosions, the action? How long can people make goopy eyes at each other?" He would tease her. "And what's with the tinkling music?"

She switched off the TV and went to the door to look through the peephole. George loomed outside like a specter.

"Hello, Nina," he greeted her when she opened the door. He was subdued, not his usual smug, condescending self.

"Hello, George," she replied. He walked past her into the apartment. She closed the door and returned to the living room.

Something wasn't right. His eyes looked flat and expressionless.

"George, what is it?" She couldn't stop her voice from trembling. It was past ten o'clock, way past George's bedtime. This was obviously not a social call.

"Nina, please sit down."

"Is he OK?" She knew the answer before George could open his mouth.

"I don't know."

"What happened? Has he been in an accident?"

George looked away. He couldn't stand looking at her worried face. She had no idea where Stephen really was. She was under the impression that he was in Virginia.

"Sit down." He took a deliberately stern stance to preempt any hysterics.

Nina slumped onto the sofa. *Here we go again.* She never learned. Why did she fall for it every time? She had believed him when he'd said he was going to Virginia to quit his job. What a gullible idiot she was. What a complete idiot.

"Where is he?" She had trouble forming that sentence. The words flew away just as she was about to reach for them.

"Nina, you need to be strong."

"About what, damn it? At least tell me that!" She gave a harsh laugh. It disconcerted George.

"Stephen is in Pakistan, but I have lost contact with him."

"No. No. He is in Virginia," she said. She was relieved—it was just a misunderstanding. "He's going to quit his job." Stephen would never go to Pakistan without telling her. Would he? Nina wasn't sure anymore.

"I haven't heard from him in two days. Have you?" George asked.

"I haven't heard from him in a *week*. He said he couldn't stay in touch while he was being cleared to resign. Did he really quit, or did he lie about that as well?"

"He did quit, which actually complicates matters. I can't help him in any official capacity. He's out there with no resources, no backup, and no support." George was worried. "He didn't want the agency to be blamed. That's why he quit."

"Blamed for what?"

George didn't answer.

Nina jumped up and yelled at him. "Bullshit, George! I have a right to know. Tell me."

He got up and pushed her down on the sofa. "Calm down, Nina. You can't lose it now."

He went to the kitchen to get her a cup of water. While standing at the sink, he debated how much to tell her. What the hell, she had been through so much already. She deserved to know.

George placed the cup of water in front of her on the coffee table. "Drink up."

"Tell me what is going on." She was calmer but didn't touch the water.

"He went to look for the people who caused your accident and miscarriage. They are in Pakistan."

Nina blinked at the mention of her miscarriage. She hadn't thought of it in weeks.

"He felt you couldn't get on with your lives unless they had been accounted for. They will keep trying to get to you until they succeed in hurting you both."

But without telling her? He couldn't leave her like this whenever he pleased. What if he died? Or worse, just disappeared? She jumped up again.

"Nina, my dear, please sit down. There is more." George was plaintive.

She sat down, expecting the worst. He was dead. He was dead. *Shut up*, she yelled at herself.

"Since he's not there in an official capacity, I cannot use the agency's resources to find him."

"George, you can do whatever you want. I know that."

He fixed her with a look and forced himself to speak slowly even though he wanted to rush through it and get away so as to not see the look on her face.

"I had to find someone who was willing to follow him and find him, but off the books, completely deniable. And it had to be someone who could pass as a local."

"Yes?"

For the second time, George felt wretched. What he was about to say would be a total shock to her.

"A new recruit, a young man who joined us less than a year ago, offered to go on this errand. I agreed, and he is out there as we speak. Looking for Stephen."

She looked at him. At least there's hope. They were looking for him. All she needed to do was pray like crazy.

George sighed and braced for another eruption. "You know him well."

"Who?" She had never met any of Stephen's colleagues. How would she know?

"Your brother."

"George!"

"It's true. Just after he graduated, Neel contacted me and said he wanted to join the agency. He's been working for us for almost a year now."

"But he works for a submarine company in Connecticut." Nina remembered how much Neel had wanted that submarine company job even though he had much more lucrative offers from Wall Street firms. The family had been puzzled but proud of his dedication to engineering.

"Well, that's a front for us," George said.

Nina laughed until tears rolled down her cheeks. This was too unreal—her husband and her brother playing superheroes.

He looked at her in alarm. "Hang in there, Nina. We *will* find him."

For Nina it was déjà vu: the terror, the black fear, and the waiting. The worst part of the day was lying to her mother that everything was fine when she knew that Neel was anything but safe. She couldn't even talk to Amy.

Nina went to work but was hardly productive, unable to concentrate or really care. One weekend Ginnie and George found her still in bed at four in the afternoon—unshowered, hungry, her hair uncombed, unkempt. Ginnie pushed her into the shower and, while Nina returned to a semblance of normalcy, made her dinner. George and Ginnie watched her stare at the food, not a morsel going in.

George was exasperated. "Eat!" he said.

"I am not going to eat until Stephen and Neel come home," she said, as if it was the most obvious thing to do.

George was fed up with her tantrums. She was cranky and argumentative and picked fights with him constantly, like a teenager. But Ginnie she loved. Ginnie was her mother in times of crisis.

On the fifth day, Nina had a brainstorm. She hounded one of her colleagues and got him to write a script that would crawl the web and find any news item related to Pakistan, however insignificant. The script sent her updates every few minutes in English, Hindi, and Urdu. She pored over them, combing them for any unusual occurrences. She found an altercation, an unidentified man arrested for gun possession, an abandoned vehicle, a minor grenade explosion, gunshots, a dead prison guard, two unidentified men who stole a vehicle, explosions in a secret stockpile of ammunition and firearms, more stolen vehicles, break-ins in grocery stores, another abandoned vehicle, a water main break, and so on.

There was an interesting pattern. All these events traced a zigzag path westward to Peshawar from Khairpur, a little town west of the Indian border. Nina was convinced these incidents were related to Stephen and Neel and whatever ridiculous mission they were on. As long as there was some activity, she was optimistic. She knew it was crazy and barely within the realm of possibility, but she desperately needed something to cling to, something that gave her a sense of participation and hope. And this was her magic trail of breadcrumbs. She made up stories to fit the events. At one point she started typing them up as log entries. Just typing the words "Stephen" and "Neel" gave her comfort. "Stephen and Neel, Neel and Stephen, Stephen and Neel, Neel and Stephen," she typed.

⇌ ⇋

Nina was alternately hysterical and artificially bright. She couldn't sleep, barely ate, and paced incessantly to release her nervous energy and anxiety. The name Daniel Pearl danced in front of her eyes whenever she closed them. The clocks were paralyzed, and the Earth's revolution had slowed to a crawl.

George felt personally responsible for her. Despite his rough manner, he did everything in his capacity to soothe her. On weekends he and Ginnie brought her groceries and cooked for her. She sat in front of the TV the whole day, watching it dumbly without any sign of brain function. When they rang the bell, she would open it and, without even looking at them, go back to her seat and continue staring at the TV. George had suggested she visit her parents, but she said, "What am I going to tell them? Stephen is busy? Neel is busy? I decided to come by myself?"

It was now almost four weeks since Stephen's departure, twenty days since George had had any contact with him. Soon Nina would have to tell her parents about Stephen and Neel, a double whammy. She'd have to tell them and watch her mother cry. Her grandmother would sob, and her father would be beyond anger and grief. He would go mad.

A MIRACLE

After a restless night, Nina fell asleep around three in the morning. She was frequently shaken into wakefulness by uneasy thoughts and nightmares. Once she thought she had heard something, but when she switched on the light, as usual it was nothing, nobody. No Stephen, no Neel.

An hour later she woke up again. This time the breathing in the room was unmistakable, as was a strong, stale odor. What should she do? She was petrified. She remembered the gun Stephen had thrust on her before he'd left for Virginia. It was right next to her, in the bedside table drawer. She slid it open silently and gripped the gun in the dark. Its cold, hard feel sent shivers of revulsion down her spine. She felt the familiar rush of self-pity over having been put in this position by her reckless husband, but she pushed the thoughts away quickly, alarmed by a movement on the bed. She steadied her hand and, with the other hand, slowly reached for the light and switched it on.

A man lay sleeping on top of the covers—a dirty, smelly, bearded man in a stained, filthy Pakistani-style *salwaar kurta*. Flat on his belly, his grimy hands resting on either side of his unwashed head. She aimed the gun at him. A weight crushed her chest, and painful sobs caught in her throat as she tried to push them back down. She released the safety latch the way Stephen had taught her. At the sound of the click, the man raised his head and turned toward her, his eyes a startling pale gray against his brown skin.

"I didn't realize you're that angry, Nina," he said.

With shaking hands she put the latch back on and threw the gun in the drawer.

"Stephen?" She choked on the last syllable.

"Yeah, sweetheart." He smiled and rolled onto his back.

"Neel?"

"Asleep in the guest room."

For a moment there were too many things going through her head. She chose to fixate on the anger. She pulled Stephen up into a sitting position and slapped him with all her strength once, two times, three times.

He didn't resist, ready and willing to be punished as she saw fit. And anyway it was no punishment. It was a pleasure to be near her again, and her hands hardly had any impact on his bearded face. He could have submitted blissfully to her all night.

But there was no more of that left in her. She was done. She couldn't believe he was sitting in front of her, intact, of sound body and mind. She put her arms around his neck and clung to him.

He felt her ribs under his fingers. She had become very thin. They couldn't go on like this. She couldn't survive another misadventure. He hoped he could close the book on this madness. He wanted a safe, boring life for the two of them, with kids and PTA meetings, with silly quarrels and tedious, mind-numbing domestic problems. With his eyes tightly closed, he held on to her, so small and light on his thigh, taut with the effort of trying not to cry.

"Shush, sweetheart," he said softly. "Everything is fine, and this time I give you my word: I will never do anything like this ever again." The beard got in the way when he tried to kiss her. It felt weird, and his outfit gave off a terrible stench.

"You need to shower," she said.

At exactly 4:33 a.m., Stephen Edward James III shaved his beard in his sparkling bathroom, with his clean razor, while his angry but devoted wife watched. He took off his clothes before stepping into the shower and steeled himself for her reaction. There was a big, fiery welt on his back, and his knees and calves were slashed with dark-blue and purple bruises. His feet had cuts from the glass shards atop the Khairpur prison's wall.

She flinched and sat down on the closed toilet bowl.

"How?" she asked.

"Oh, nothing particular," he replied lightly.

At the turn of a dial, clean, warm water rained down on him in a fluent stream. It was heavenly.

"Soap my back?"

He had missed those lovely fingers. They glided down his back, careful to avoid the violent gash that sliced it from below the left shoulder blade to the bottom of his rib cage on the right. It was healing well but had not lost its vividness. Nina's touch sent thrills down his legs, and he still couldn't believe that when he opened his eyes she would be right there, glaring at him with her angry, lovely eyes, unable to hide her relief and love.

"Next time you try a stunt like this, I won't be around when you get back," she said.

"What stunt?"

"You said you were going to Virginia."

"I did go to Virginia." He smiled. "But then I had to go to one more place."

"I'm really mad at you," she said, but the gentleness of her fingers and voice belied her words.

He toweled himself slowly with his face pressed to the soft, freshly washed terrycloth. It smelled so good.

"Why are you mad, my Nina?"

He could not stop smiling. For the first time, he felt that this rented apartment was really home. It was where his mind had flown to during those hopeless hours and days, the place he longed to be back in, the place where Nina was waiting for him.

The part of his face where his beard had been was several shades paler than the rest. He slipped on a dazzling white T-shirt and savored it slide down his chest and drape over his shorts. As a final touch, he slicked back his wet hair with Nina's comb and gave himself an approving look.

"I am ready for you." He stood with his arms wide open for his wife to admire him. But she turned away because she didn't want him to see her in tears again. She tried desperately to stay mad at him, but why bother? She was grateful he was back safely. Why should she hang on to the anger? He was home. That's all she cared about.

"I'll make coffee," she said over her shoulder on her way to the kitchen.

While they waited for the coffee to drip, Stephen rested his damp head on her shoulder. It was just at the right height while he sat on a kitchen stool, his hand around her waist. He was shocked afresh at how skinny she had become, first from the miscarriage and then from his disappearance. He kissed her shoulder in repentance. All the energy and liveliness had been driven out of her face. Her eyes were dull and swollen from weeks of crying, although, a flicker of brightness had just begun to make an appearance. She had completely neglected her health.

The coffee smelled so good after four weeks without it. And she made it just the way he liked it, with sugar and milk. He closed his eyes and followed the hot, pungent liquid's progress over his tongue and down his throat.

Neel came out of the guest bedroom in answer to the aroma's siren call.

"Coffee! Gimme." He settled down on a stool next to Stephen.

Nina's anger returned. Her handsome kid brother was sporting a ragged beard and a filthy regulation salwaar kurta. A bandage around his ankle was speckled with blood.

"Neel, what the hell is going on?" She bent down to examine the bandage. "How could you let him do this, Stephen?"

"Don't look at me," he replied. "I tried my best to get him kicked out. But George wouldn't hear of it."

"Neel?" she demanded.

"This is what I want to do." It was a sincere answer, without his usual flippancy.

"Why? Has everyone gone mad?" Nina threw up her hands.

"This is what I want to do," Neel repeated. "I love it."

"I am fed up with the two of you, your lies and secrets."

"We have to fight the evildoers, Neenz." Neel tried to make her laugh with his reference to the Bush era terminology for terrorists, but it missed.

"It's beyond repair, you maniac," Nina shouted. "There is nothing you heroes can do about it. The assholes in charge of spreading terror and mayhem are not going to stop until we are all dead. Total annihilation."

She flung her coffee mug in the sink and stalked away to the living room.

Stephen followed. "Nina, calm down." He had never seen her so enraged.

"Where do *you* get off telling me to calm down? Maybe I should take off for some godforsaken hellhole without telling you and see how you feel about it!"

He backed away from her and retired behind the safety of the kitchen counter, where he poured himself some cereal for breakfast.

Nina turned on Neel. "Did you bother to think for a minute what effect it would have on your parents?"

"Gee, that didn't seem to bother you when you ran off and got married behind their backs to a guy they'd never heard of."

"Well, I wasn't putting my life in danger, like you are."

"Facts seem to speak otherwise, sis. You have been in constant danger ever since you married *him*."

Stephen nodded in reluctant agreement.

"Whose side are you on?" She turned on him.

"No sides, but he has a point, I'm afraid. And he is an adult. You should let him make his decisions. I'm sure he knows what he's getting into."

"Please! He's twenty-one. What does he know?" Nina scoffed.

"Some of us don't have to wait until we're twenty-six to know what we want," Neel retorted.

"That's enough, you two," Stephen said. "Here, have some cereal."

He sighed happily even though the siblings scowled at each other across the room. It was the small pleasures that made life worth living, like crisp cereal in ice-cold milk.

What had he done to deserve the love and devotion of these two siblings? Stephen was not a religious man, was an agnostic at best, but perhaps his twenty lonely years had earned him this reward. There must have been some cosmic law of conservation of happiness. He was entitled to his arrears now.

After Neel had helped Stephen break out of that terrible prison in Khairpur, they had dressed as impoverished peasants and traveled on small regional buses that crawled at twenty miles per hour at their fastest.

On those long bus rides, Stephen had watched over Neel with deep guilt. It was like a reprise of the flight from Le Méridien. The siblings had the same wide-eyed look of horror and reproach when faced with the cruelty of this world. Once or twice, when Stephen opened his eyes from a snatch of exhausted sleep, he felt for a disorienting moment that it was Nina asleep in the seat next to him. Neel's presence had reminded him of how much he missed her.

In that wretched prison for three long weeks, he had not allowed himself to think of Nina. Otherwise he never would have been able to get through the daily ordeal of beatings and insults. His captors had tormented him because they could. They were born of a cruel environment and hated his pride and strength, hated him because he was not one of them, and because he had stayed defiantly silent through the worst pain and punishment they could inflict. But in that moment on the bus, with Neel next to him, he had allowed himself to wish and hope that he would be with her soon, hear her laugh, and feel her warm legs on his.

When he had finally made it back home, Stephen had stood over his sleeping wife and held his thumping, aching chest. He couldn't get himself to wake her, not while he was dizzy from happiness and exhaustion, afraid to test the limits of reality. He had lain down next to her, thrilled to breathe the same air she did, hoping that she'd still be there when he opened his eyes.

⊷ ⊶

That afternoon, while Stephen took a nap, Nina went downstairs with Neel to say good-bye and see him off. He was headed back to Connecticut. They had gotten over their bickering long ago. As they waited for the cab, Neel turned to her.

"I have a very personal question for you, and I need an honest answer."

"Sure." Nina looked at him. She had never seen him so serious or uncomfortable.

He hesitated, almost embarrassed. Neel couldn't forget the image of the prison guard's body as it shuddered and went limp in Stephen's hands. The thought that those same brutal hands would caress Nina, his unsuspecting sister, the gentlest of people, turned his stomach. But it was the same ruthlessness in Stephen that had kept her safe. He was implacable in his determination to protect her. The whole fantastic expedition had been Stephen's homage to Nina, his love song for her, the ultimate gift of his life if needed. But what was the guarantee that the same temperament would not turn on her?

"When you guys have a fight or something like that, does Stephen ever get violent? Does his anger ever spiral out of control?"

"Of course not. What kind of stupid question is that?"

"He has never hurt you?"

"Never! Neel, you know I won't put up with crap like that. Besides, he's the sweetest, gentlest person where I am concerned."

Neel looked uncharacteristically subdued. Everyone but Nina could see the anger in Stephen, the violence that simmered behind those cold, gray eyes. His brother-in-law had extraordinary qualities in him but scared the heck out of Neel sometimes. Stephen was crazy about Nina, but what if she did something that made him mad?

"Neel, what happened? Did you two have a fight?"

"No. No. I think he transfers his protectiveness to me when you're not around."

"Then what's bothering you? Why do you think he'd hurt me?"

"Nothing." Neel sighed. "I don't know. It's such a violent, ruthless profession. It changes a person. I was worried that part of him might come through when he's with you."

"No, never ever. Absolutely never."

"OK, OK," he said and shrugged.

"Neel, are you sure you want to get into this business?"

He nodded. "I have no doubt at all. I am absolutely sure. But it is such a different philosophy from what you and I were raised on. It takes some getting used to. There is no place for compassion, negotiation, or even reason in the world of these twisted jihadis. I have seen the horrors they inflict on their own people. We have to protect ourselves from them. This is what I want to do."

CONFLICT

"Third in command of major terrorist group killed."

Nina spilled her coffee all over the kitchen counter when she saw the headline above the fold. It was the day after Stephen's miraculous return, one of the rare occasions when she was up before him. Full of anticipation she had slipped the *New York Times* out of its blue-plastic wrap, only to be greeted by the sensational headline. She cleaned up the spill and muttered to herself.

The bedroom door was ajar. She pushed it open violently. Stephen was asleep under the quilt, sprawled luxuriously across more than three quarters of the bed.

"Stephen!" She shook him.

"What is it? What's wrong?" He sat up immediately and reached for his T-shirt on the bedside table. An agitated Nina came into view and waved the newspaper at him.

"Did you have anything to do with this?" She pointed to the news item.

He didn't answer. A slow smile started at his lips and spread to his eyes while he read. Zia Akhtar, the man who had occupied Stephen's mind for so long, had been killed in an explosion in an old, dilapidated building in Peshawar along with two of his associates. The cause of the explosion was not known.

"What makes you think that?" He stepped out of bed and stretched. Nina read the rest of the story aloud as she followed him to the bathroom. He took the newspaper from her and pushed her gently out before closing the door. When he came out, she was still there, like a stubborn child.

"Tell me the truth," she said.

He pulled on his robe and went into the kitchen with Nina close on his heels. A mug of piping hot coffee waited for him with the perfect blend of milk and sugar.

"Bagel?" he asked.

"Just the story, please," she said with her angry politeness and slid onto a stool at the counter.

The toaster took its time to disgorge the bagel. Stephen removed it and lovingly applied cream cheese to it. She watched his long fingers with admiration. She could dedicate a whole sketchbook to them. Why hadn't she done it already?

A perfectly toasted New York bagel with cream cheese—warm, crisp yet soft, salty, creamy, and delicious. What a joy. The stool squeaked whenever Nina swiveled from side to side. She didn't want to kill his bagel buzz. She waited until he finished eating.

"Did you do it?" she asked.

"No."

His prickliness was just below the surface. If she pushed any more, he was sure to get irritated. But she couldn't stop. She had to know.

"Neel?"

"Good God, no! I would never let him do that."

He was still hungry and scanned the stuffed-to-capacity fridge. On his return Nina had stocked it with everything he had ever said he liked.

"Watermelon?" he asked.

"No, thanks."

He carved himself a hefty slice and ate it unhurriedly while the juice dripped down his hand and chin. It was one of the many things Nina had introduced him to, along with super-spicy food and old Hindi movie songs. With a sigh of pleasure, he washed up in the sink.

The couch was covered with various sections of the newspaper. Stephen located the sports section and settled down contentedly. Nina sat down at the other end, the ideal distance for him to lie down with his head in her lap. This was perfect. This was what he wanted for the rest of his life.

Before he could finish the thought, she snatched the paper out of his hands. "Tell me what happened."

He covered his face with his hands in order to hide his exasperation and to gather his thoughts. It would be a challenge, but he had to tell her. She should know. He looked up at her and hesitated. Once he told her, there would be no going back.

"Are you sure you want to hear it?"

She nodded. He sat up and stared at his feet, his hands joined together as if in prayer. How much should he tell her, and how should he tell her?

"When you were in that accident, I knew I had to stop them. I could not let it happen again. They would get bolder with every attempt."

The room filled with his precisely enunciated sentences. What he said was as harsh and violent as his voice was soft.

"I had to go after them. They could not go unanswered. They took our child." He paused to look at her. "I followed every lead I could."

Asad, the imprisoned brother of the fake sardar, had been deceived into providing crucial information.

He had stubbornly resisted the coercion, but when an American officer posed as a Saudi intelligence agent, the man couldn't stop talking.

"Tell your masters what I have done for them," he told the man he believed to be a Saudi agent.

Armed with that information, Stephen and his team combed through petabytes of data and came upon information that placed Zia Akhtar and Tariq Rehman in Peshawar on a particular day. This was the break Stephen needed.

"I am going there," he had told George. "I'll shoot them down in person if I have to."

"Don't be hasty, Stephen. Think it through," George had said.

But Stephen had plunged ahead over George's warnings. He had quit his job to make it easy for George to deny responsibility.

"We persuaded Sid and the other two terrorists we captured at Sid's house to provide us with contacts who could help us track Akhtar."

Nina recoiled at the word "persuaded."

"What does persuasion entail?" she asked.

"Are you sure you want to know?"

"No." She looked away.

"Good. I don't think you can handle it." His voice was curt.

According to the deal, if the information and contacts provided led to a successful elimination of Akhtar,

Sid and the young jihadi would be placed in a witness protection program. George and Stephen were confident that without Akhtar, the organization would crumble, and the smaller players would have neither the leadership nor the motivation to continue harassing Stephen.

"So I took all this information and went to Pakistan."

Nina was unable to hide her dismay. She looked at him with reproach. He had been willing to abandon her at home, after all the promises he had made.

He knew what she was thinking but chose not to address it. "Unfortunately I was arrested by the local authorities on my way to Peshawar. That was when I lost touch with George."

"But you're an American. How could they arrest you? Didn't you contact the embassy?"

"I wasn't traveling on an American passport, and I certainly didn't have diplomatic immunity."

Nina wasn't sure whether she wanted to hear the rest of the story. Outside the window the day bloomed, incongruously gorgeous with golden sunshine and birdsong. The city went about its noisy business. Cars hummed happily on the Henry Hudson Parkway below.

"I told George to send a replacement to finish the business if I couldn't make it because we would never get a chance like this again."

Nina was startled. So he had known at the very beginning that he might not make it. But he had taken the chance anyway, and she'd had no say in any of it.

"What were you going to do?" she asked.

"At first I thought I would teach Akhtar's enemies how to plant a bomb in the place where he was going to stay. But I got arrested, and we ran out of time. So I decided to do it myself." He told her the truth.

They looked at each other for a minute, and she got up abruptly to leave. He grabbed her hand and pulled her down.

"No, you asked for this. You have to hear it all." He put his face close to hers and continued in a hoarse voice. "Do you know how I got the gash on my back?"

She shook her head mutely, terrified of what she would have to hear.

"One of the prison guards swiped me with a knife just for the heck of it. If I hadn't managed to escape with Neel's help, do you know what they were going to do?"

"Please, stop. I don't want to hear anymore."

He grabbed her wrists and removed her hands from her ears. "They would have tied each of my legs to a truck and pulled in opposite directions until my body ripped in two."

It was true. If they had found out who he really was, that would have been his fate. He knew what they did to spies and informants, even their own. He would not have been spared. They had been waiting for the proper papers to arrive from the central jail authorities to mete out that punishment.

He held both her wrists in one hand, and with the other he pulled up his pajama leg to expose the bruises on his legs.

"Every day they would put ropes around my legs just to explain to me how it would work. Just because I was a foreigner. Just for the sport."

He wanted to stop. He knew she was scared out of her wits. It wasn't her fault, and she didn't deserve to be terrorized by him after having spent weeks being worried sick about him, but he could not stop.

"The next time you worry about guns or torture, think about these sick motherfuckers. And the next time you try to dissuade Neel or blame me for getting him involved, remember that if everyone decided they didn't want to get their pretty little hands dirty with such nasty stuff, we would all be murdered in our beds like those poor bastards at Le Méridien."

He released her finally.

"Nobody likes to get hurt or get killed or take stupid risks." He got up. "You seem to think these decisions are made lightly, on some whim."

Her eyes followed him as he walked around the room in agitation. She desperately wanted him not to be angry. She wanted to make up. The window drew him with its promise of freedom and fresh air. He opened it and leaned out for a minute.

"I had to take this risk for you," he said. "I could have sat around and done nothing, but that is not how I am made. I am not capable of that. I can't let what happened to you happen again, or worse, when we have children, allow them to be exposed to danger like you were."

It was so odd to hear him talk about children—their children. Those few weeks that she had been pregnant had been so perfect, so full of possibilities, a glorious peek into the future. That thought made her sadder.

He came away from the window to face her. "It was not an easy decision for me to leave you. But I had to rid our lives of this menace. It had to be done."

She looked up at him, trying to telegraph a message: calm down, don't be upset, everything will be all right.

"I know you don't approve of what I do or how I do it," he said, "but sometimes there is no other way."

"That's not fair. You know I don't think anything like that."

"I'm not sure. Every time something like this happens, all I see is disapproval on your face." He turned his heated attention on her.

Nina looked away, afraid he would misconstrue anything she said. There was a long silence, interrupted by the usual apartment noises of distant conversation, elevator rumbles, and muffled footsteps. But she needed to make a move and diffuse the tension. She had seen her mother do it many a time while dealing with her father. Nina had to take the first step toward reconciliation with Stephen because most men, according to her mother, were not emotionally equipped to do it. A chasm created by a quarrel had to be addressed and repaired before it opened its jaws and swallowed their lives.

There was also the danger that Stephen would bolt out of the house in a bad mood, to walk around the city in a foul temper for hours and return tired and melancholy late in the evening. Nina wanted to preempt that at any cost. She could already see the clouds gathering. He was like an overwrought child who had lost control of his emotions and did not know how to return to normal. She had to be the adult and bring the temperature down. The best way to disarm him was to be honest and not let her ego get in the way.

"Stephen, I'm sorry if I've given you that impression. If I disapprove it's only because I worry about your safety. I am afraid of all the terrible things that could happen. You almost got killed within a few months of our getting married." She spoke calmly and clearly, without resentment or emotion.

Stephen looked at the once happy, carefree girl he had married, sitting in front of him now a picture of anxiety and distress, an inch away from melting down. *What a jerk he was. Look what he'd done.* Not only had he made her miserable and worried half to death for most of their life together, but he had made her feel bad and apologize for things that were not her fault.

It hadn't been his intention that she should apologize. And he knew what motivated her disapproval without her spelling it out for him. She hardly ever complained, and over the one topic about which she had every right to complain he had created a scene at the slightest sign of protest from her because he didn't want to give up the game he enjoyed so much.

When Stephen remained silent, she continued.

"I have the greatest admiration for you and what you do. I just wish it was safer, that's all."

Nina finished her little speech and lapsed into silence, staring at her hands clasped in her lap. *Please come here and sit next to me. Don't be so far away.*

As if he had heard her thoughts, he went over to the sofa and slumped down beside her. She leaned against him, and he immediately put his arms around her. The familiarity and comfort of each other's bodies slowly melted away the rancor, each passing minute soothing them into a mellow togetherness.

"It's over now. Nobody will bother us anymore," he said gently and gave her shoulders a squeeze. Her head lay exhausted on his chest. The quarrel had taken everything out of her. He straightened her hair and combed it with his fingers.

"I can't live without you, my sweet Nina," he said almost to himself.

"What?" she sat up. "Say that again."

"Say what?" But the words had been uttered, and they were out there, hanging in the room like a blinking neon sign, matched by her smile, back at its radiant best.

"I promise that from now on, it is going to be one boring life. In fact it's going to be so boring, you will wish you had married Samir."

Stephen occasionally brought up Samir, mostly as the butt of a joke. He claimed that jealousy was an emotion beneath him, meant for mortals who could not reside on the same plane of excellence he did. But he could not let go of Samir, his old rival, the man whom Nina would have married had Stephen not appeared on the scene.

The look on Samir's face when Stephen had walked into the elevator that morning three years ago was one of his most cherished memories. Nina had introduced them barely twelve hours earlier near that same elevator. And there was Stephen at six thirty the following morning, rushing toward the elevator straight out of

Nina's door. Samir had been shell-shocked, unable to take his eyes off Stephen.

"Hey, Samir!" Stephen had greeted him jauntily, examining his reflection in the polished steel doors of the elevator. He adjusted his shirt collar and jacket, his red tie draped carelessly around his neck. And the next morning, having persuaded Nina to marry him, Stephen had timed his departure to run into Samir again.

"Hey, Samir!" he had greeted him cheerfully again, to be met with the same disbelieving look. It was just too much for Samir.

Stephen looked at Nina now, who was back to leaning on his shoulder.

"There is something I wanted to talk to you about, now that I have decided to overhaul my life."

He had been thinking about it for a long time: the inheritance that had caused him so much grief. He had never touched it once he'd been able to support himself. They say money begets money, and this had been true in his case. Even before he had graduated, his alloy and coating material had received considerable investment. The government hired him as a contractor and consultant. He had given away most of the land to the conservancy, keeping just the house and a portion of the grounds around it as a connection his childhood.

Despite that the bulk of the estate was still intact. He had been looking for the most effective way to put it to good use and had hit on a solution while stewing in the Pakistani prison.

"I want to give away my inheritance." He looked at her see to her reaction.

"To your siblings?"

"Never. I would never do that. They don't need it."

Any mention of his family was a major source of friction between the two of them. Soon after their wedding, Nina had tried to get him to introduce her to his siblings and mother. But he had refused, saying he hadn't had any contact with them in almost twenty years and didn't care to do so now.

How could he be happy until he had reconciled with them? Nina had asked.

"Because I am not you," he had replied sarcastically.

Nina was convinced that much of his restlessness and anger were due to his estrangement from his family. But for now she left that battle alone.

"Would you be disappointed if I gave it away and I were not so well off as a result?" he asked.

"Don't worry. I can support us," Nina said. "BigSearch has been great to me. I have more money than I know what to do with."

"Really?"

It was true. She had very few needs and barely spent any money other than on groceries, movies, books, and minor entertainment. Her parents gave their two children money every year as part of some estate-planning maneuver. And then there was BigSearch, which piled stock on her that kept shooting higher each day. Everything got compounded and added up to an amount that in her mind was obscene.

"Really. We can easily buy a house, cash down, if we want to."

"This is fantastic. I have a rich wife!" He laughed and hugged her.

"Don't laugh. It might not be on the scale you're used to, but it is plenty as far as I am concerned."

"I would never laugh at you. Anyway I'm quite solvent. My company is doing well, and it will really take off if I give it the time and energy it deserves. I can't live off a woman's earnings," he added to get her riled up, but she wasn't biting. She was still basking in his recent declaration.

"I thought I'd set up a foundation in my grandfather's name, with the inheritance as its initial endowment."

Nina sat up, her professional curiosity aroused.

Stephen's tan from the Pakistani sun had not faded yet. During the three weeks there, he had seen such horrors perpetrated on girls due to poverty and lack of education. There had been a young girl, barely in her teens, who used to sweep the area outside the prison gate daily, and he used to wonder how she would live out her life, whether she would ever get out of that hell. The guards and prisoners made crude remarks about her within her hearing. She had no future, no happiness ever in store; she would be lucky if she weren't raped or stoned to death. He remembered Nina's lecture on their sailing date, when she had gotten so worked up about education for rural children. This was the reason why, he had thought as he'd watched that sad little girl, even as his own life and future were uncertain. But he had George behind him. Who would rescue this girl?

"For education of girls in third-world countries," he said now.

"That is awesome!" Nina exclaimed. She reeled off facts like the wonk she was: girls benefited from only two percent of money spent by nonprofits; most girls in third-world countries were married by age eighteen; and the biggest cause of death among teenage girls was complications related to pregnancies. Education is the only way to get them off these paths, she concluded sternly.

He watched her face, completely enchanted. "I want you to run it."

"What?" Nina stared at him as if he had sprouted wings.

"You heard me."

"No, no, no. I know nothing about running a foundation. You should hire a professional."

"We will, to do the actual organizing and day-to-day running. But I want you to oversee it and set the direction."

"Stephen, you are crazy. I know nothing. I can't do it."

"Yes, you can. Take a course, or sign up for an MBA program. Whatever you want. You'll have all the help you need."

Nina shook her head repeatedly. "There are many qualified, experienced people out there. You should hire them."

"We will, but only to help you until you find your legs."

"It is too much responsibility. What if I mess up?"

"Everyone makes mistakes."

"Stephen, I am honored, but if something goes wrong, our relationship will be ruined. It is not worth it."

"My dear Nina, our relationship has endured a lot more than financial loss. What can go wrong? All you have to do is spend money to get kids to go to school."

Nina wavered between excitement and fear, ambition and caution. "How big?"

"Around three hundred million dollars."

"Holy shit! No way. I can't do it."

"It has to be you. No one else."

"Why me?"

"Because." He grinned.

"Come on. Be serious."

"Because you are the only person I trust."

THE HOUSE ON CASTLE HILL

It was a beautiful spring morning, cool and crisp. The fruit trees were weighed down with pink, red, and white buds, ready to burst into bloom at the touch of the sun.

"Want to go for a walk?" Stephen asked Nina.

They had arrived the previous night. It was their first real visit since the shooting incident almost two years ago, not counting the miserable stay immediately after Nina's miscarriage. Those horrendous memories came back vividly to her now, conjured up by the surroundings. She didn't have Stephen's history with the place that could mitigate them for her. The gunshots rang loud in her imagination, and she felt Stephen's blood soak into the ground. But this home was her future, where her children would grow up. She couldn't run away from it anymore.

They walked down the gravel path toward the greenhouses. Crocuses, daffodils, and narcissi bloomed all across the grounds and filled the air with sweetness. Nina relaxed in the face of such a vibrant assertion of renewal and beauty.

Stephen was finally happy. The two forces that had pulled at him so strongly were together at last.

It was almost three years ago that he had come upon Nina sitting on that stone bench, sketching his beloved garden. Stephen had stood in the shadows and watched her. She had been sitting with her back to him, engrossed in her drawing, jabbing and slashing with her pencil. The stone bench must have been uncomfortable, but she sat erect. All he could see was a white cotton blouse bisected by a glossy braid.

His boat had made a racket as it pulled up to the dock barely fifty feet behind her. Yet she hadn't looked up. He stepped out from behind the trees into the sunlight in the clearing and said, "Hello."

She was startled but recovered quickly and said, "I hope you don't mind my drawing your property. It's beautiful."

"Would you like to see the garden?" he asked.

And barely five minutes into the tour, she asked where the rest of the family was.

"My father was an alcoholic," he had replied with uncharacteristic openness. "My parents never got along. I haven't had any contact with my mother or my siblings in more than fifteen years, since the day my father killed himself. That's my family."

"How awful!"

The way she had looked at him in that instant...he had been offended at first. He had mistaken it for pity, but when he watched her closely he saw a deep capacity for empathy, a genuine distress, and an instinctive desire to make things better. He tried to brush off that feeling, but no matter how hard he tried, he couldn't. He simply had to see her again, and George had provided the perfect excuse.

So much had happened since that first meeting. It would take Nina some time to calm down, overcome her fears, and settle down in his home, the house on Castle Hill, as the locals called it. Only the passage of time could reassure her. In the meantime he would rebuild the house from top to bottom, remove the traces of all the inauspicious emotions and events that haunted it, and make it a place Nina would love. A place with electronic security that would make NSA envious. He owed it to her. And he never knew when George would demand that he help with some mission—purely in an advisory capacity, of course, he would say. At such times this would be the fortress that would keep Nina safe in his absence.

They turned around at the greenhouses and walked back toward the dock. The water welcomed them with shimmering radiance. Nina's heart thumped wildly as they approached the Alis' property, awash, in her imagination, with Stephen and Neel's blood, something from a graphic Stephen King novel. She tightened her grip on Stephen's arm.

"It's OK," he said. "You'll see."

They crossed over onto the Alis' land.

"Good God!" She stopped. The property had come into view and…there was nothing there. The house had been razed, and all that was left was brown, leveled earth, soggy with morning dew. No house, no Adirondack chairs that had witnessed their first kiss, no garden, nothing.

"What happened?" she asked. It was shocking. She had expected a deserted house, perhaps remnants of yellow police tape, but not total destruction.

"There's a new owner," Stephen stepped farther into the lot.

"Who?" She refused to budge from where she stood.

"You."

"Me? How can I set foot there? Your blood and Neel's blood are all over the place."

"Don't be so dramatic." He went over to her and gently tugged at her hand. "It's been cleaned up. Besides, it was all inside the house."

Nina stood glued to the spot and stared all around her.

"Sheri had it demolished," Stephen continued. "She called me last month and offered to sell it to us. It's five acres. We can build a guest house, add specimen trees, and connect it to the land we're donating to the public gardens."

He could see his new home so clearly, as if it were already done: the nest for his brood, his flesh and blood, his golden children with Nina's caramel skin, the bloodline his grandfather had wanted.

"I want our children to have the kind of childhoods you did, surrounded by people who love them and put them above everything else."

She listened to him but refused to budge an inch in the direction of the lot. They stood in silence, lost in grim reflections of what had happened but relieved that the worst had not come to pass.

"Did Neel ever tell you what I told him before I lost consciousness on the night of the shootout at Sid's?"

Nina shook her head.

"I was light-headed from losing all that blood, and I was convinced I was going to die. I told him to tell you how sorry I was that I got you involved in my violent life and that I had caused you so much sorrow by leaving you so early on, after promising you a lifetime of love and devotion. I might have even said something quite sentimental."

She listened with no visible reaction.

"While I'm happy that I made it, I would still like to apologize to you for getting you involved in this madness and putting you through so much in the last few years. I had no right to, but I was selfish. I wanted to be with you, and I was afraid you would not marry me if I told you the truth. I hid it from you. For that I am truly sorry."

She heard that long statement with wonder. It couldn't have been easy for him. Apologies and confessions were not in his nature. She looked up at him, at his eyes that glinted with reflections of the lovely spring green of the trees.

"You needn't have worried. You had me hook, line, and sinker when you said my name for the very first time, with that lovely lilt in that soft voice of yours. I was toast." She smiled at last.

"When was that?" he asked, poker faced even though he remembered perfectly clearly.

"We stood right there. I had come outside to escape the party. You stepped out of the trees and asked me, 'What are you doing tomorrow, Nina?' I knew you were totally messing with me, but the way you said my name, I was helpless."

Even now a thrill went through her from head to toe when she remembered that moment.

"I don't remember anything of that kind," he said, but his eyes and smile said exactly the opposite.

A NEW BEGINNING

Two months later, on a gorgeous summer afternoon, Nina was expecting George, Ginnie, and Neel for lunch. She had set the table on the porch outside the great room. It overlooked the dock and the newly visible construction lot now that the hedge that separated the two properties had been removed.

Nina jumped up to meet George and Ginnie when she heard their car.

"Hi, Ginnie!" She ran and hugged her and gave old George a kiss on the cheek. They smiled back at her. She was the picture of happiness in a billowing summer dress. After a few months without crises, she had reverted to her old self and glowed with good health and high spirits.

Stephen waved from the porch. He wore a hard hat and overalls but was just about to go change. He too had filled out a little since his return from Khairpur.

Nina heard Neel's car pull up and once more rushed down the porch steps. Even though it was just a month since she had seen him, he looked so mature and grown up, a man of the world, guarded and measured, not her kid brother. Then he gave her a big grin and morphed into the little boy who used to follow her around the house clutching his blankie, the morose schoolboy who, after she left home for college, sat by the answering machine and played the greeting over and over again because it was in her voice.

After a brief conversation with George and Ginnie, Neel walked up to Stephen. They got to talking, and soon George joined them. There was something peculiar about that picture, the way the three men talked and looked at each other in turn. There was something serious going on. Nina's heart sank. She looked at Ginnie and saw the same look of dismay on her face.

"Shall we eat?" Nina interrupted the men.

After lunch and coffee, George and Nina were left by themselves at the table. Ginnie and Neel had gone with Stephen to check out the construction site.

"How are you doing? You look well," George said.

"What are you planning, George?" Nina asked.

George, the Henry Kissinger doppelganger, smiled at her, not without charm. "What makes you ask?"

"I saw the three of you conspiring earlier."

"That was nothing. Just some loose ends. But there is something I want to talk to you about."

Nina was wary. "I hope you are not going to put him in harm's way again."

"How long do you think he'll be happy playing house with you?" George asked.

"I don't know. How long have *you* been doing it? You seem quite happy."

"Stephen is different. You're doing him a disservice keeping him locked up in this prison of domesticity."

"George, you know perfectly well that he does what he pleases. There is nothing I can make him do."

George paused to hear her out politely but continued as if he had not heard a word she said.

"You know, he has changed a lot since he met you. He is positively likable. Thanks to you, he is not as rough and harsh as he used to be. He is a family man with a pretty wife, and who knows? Little feet may be pattering around the house very soon."

Nina was surprised. Did George just call her pretty?

"Don't you think he should run for public office? A senator or a governor?" he said.

Nina laughed so hard her ribs hurt. "Good luck with that!"

"You have to help me, my dear." George was not at all discouraged.

"Have you ever discussed it with him?"

"Yes."

"And?"

"He won't hear of it."

"Well, then that's the end of that, isn't it?"

She was about to get up and join the others at the construction site. George said in an undertone, "Nina, he will run off to do something rash. He needs adventure and excitement. He has outgrown the engineering company. I doubt it can hold his interest for very long. Think about it."

"I don't think there is anything I can do."

"Yes, you can. You have enormous influence over him. You can convince him. Anyway, this is a long-term plan, but we have to start his political career now. I have no doubt he can run for president of the United States one day."

Nina's jaw dropped. "Are you crazy?"

"No," he replied hurriedly. The others had come into view. "Not in the least bit. With his family name, his philanthropy, and you by his side, he is exactly what the country needs. You and I need to work on him a little, that's all."

"Oh George, you have no idea how little influence I have. Nothing happens unless he wants it to happen. It's a good thing that I want the same things most of the time. And for the rest of the time, I've learned to want what he wants, on my mother's advice. Otherwise, she tells me, he and I will both be miserable."

It was true. When Nina had told her mother that although she had agreed to move to Massachusetts, she wasn't 100 percent sure she wanted to, Deepa had launched into one of her sermons.

"Nina, my baby, I know he does his best to make you happy. He goes out of his way to get along with us. It doesn't matter whether you live in Hyannis or New York. If it means that much to him, you should do it. But once you decide to do it, do it with good grace. Don't make it sound like you are doing him a favor."

She had paused to see what effect it had on Nina, her precious daughter who had never really given her any cause for concern while growing up. Nina listened anxiously, feeling uneasy and restless for some reason.

"There will be plenty of situations where the two of you disagree. Save your energy for the really important issues, for things that really matter, things that you feel strongly about. There is no point in making a fuss and filling your life with petty squabbles."

Nina couldn't tell Deepa that she was uneasy in Stephen's home because of all the bad things that had happened to him and Neel, and because of the bad karma that haunted Stephen's family.

"Happiness is hard work, my darling," Deepa had said. "You have to really fight for it. All the time. It takes a strong person to give in. Unless you feel that it is impossible for you to live there, do not make a big deal of it."

Nina knew that her mother was right, but it had been quite another thing to act on her advice, when every nook and cranny of Stephen's home had made her uncomfortable. But as her mother had advised, she had focused on the intent and the motivation behind Stephen's actions. She had watched him work on plans with the architect to tear out the innards of the house and rebuild it to suit her taste.

And now she knew it was the best thing she could have done. Stephen was a totally different person. This home, the house on Castle Hill, was at the core of his being. It was where he was happiest. It was where he wanted to build their future. She had her family, but this was all he had—the only thing that connected him to his past and childhood. After almost two decades of living in an emotional wasteland, he finally knew what it was to be loved, wanted, and adored. The ice at the center of his heart had melted, and he was at peace. And it showed. As George had pointed out, he was positively likable.

George looked at her. "You have to help me. You know it's the natural next step for Stephen."

He was sincere even though he did have a vested interest. He genuinely believed this was the right path for Stephen.

"George, I'll make you a deal. I will help you if you promise me one thing."

"What?"

"Keep Neel out of fieldwork."

George looked at her. "I can't do that."

"Why not?"

"He's really good, and he wants it. He'll be furious."

"I'm sure you can find a way, George."

He would have done that anyway, but he didn't want to seem too eager to agree. Neel was proving to be brash. He had smuggled a Pakistani child across the border into Afghanistan because her brother, Neel's informant, had been killed by militants.

"We promised him," Neel had said. "We have to take care of this girl. She was shot in the face and almost killed last year by the same thugs."

So George had had to scramble and get the girl to a safe place, flouting every rule. Neel's handler had been livid and bumped him to a desk job.

George and Nina stopped their conversation. The others were within earshot. Ginnie and Neel went inside the house in search of more coffee. Stephen came up the porch steps and sat down at the table next to Nina. He looked at her and then at George and back at her.

"What's going on with you two?" he asked.

"Nothing much. Nina just agreed to help me with my next big project."

"I did not!"

"What project is that?" Stephen didn't put anything beyond George.

"You."

"George, I can't believe you're still going on about that." He laughed.

"Why not? It is the natural next step."

"No. Nina and I will raise a big family and live happily ever after. That is the natural next step."

Nina sat up. Good God! A big family? He could count her out after two kids. Now *that* was something she felt strongly about.

"Really? That's all you aspire to?" George asked.

"That's *all*? I wish I had met Nina sooner. I really like this whole marriage thing." Stephen leaned over to her and put his arm around her. He was not going to let George jeopardize his hard-won happiness.

That night, before going to bed, Nina brought up the subject. "I think George has a point. You'll get bored and then run off to slay dragons."

Stephen laughed. "Of course I won't. George is fear mongering, as usual."

"No, I agree with him. Once you're done with rebuilding the house, what are you going to do?"

"I will putter around in the garden and look after our babies." He smiled at her. "While you run the Edward W. James Foundation for Women." They had named the foundation after Grandfather James.

"Come on, be serious!"

He leaned on the balcony railing and stared into the darkness where the ocean was. She stood close to him and held his hand.

"Come on, Stephen. You know you'll get bored in no time. This is another way of serving your country… without getting blown up."

He could feel her shift her weight from foot to foot like she did when she was excited. He looked down at the top of her head, which rested on his arm for support. He had actually been thinking about it as well. Jonathan Kirk, the senior senator of Massachusetts, was ailing. Word was it would be only a matter of months. It would be a great opportunity, right in Stephen's backyard.

With a sigh he turned toward Nina. "What will happen to my engineering company?"

She twisted in his arms to look at him. "So you'll do it?"

He smiled at her enthusiasm, though there was really nothing to smile about. She had no idea what she was getting into. "You realize our lives will become very public?"

"But they can't say anything about you. It's all classified."

"I know, but they can find ways. Even if nobody touches the classified stuff, you and I will be scrutinized every minute. And our enemies will know exactly where we are at any point in time."

She digested that piece of information. "You're right," she said finally.

"That doesn't mean it can't be done. I think we can manage, with the right planning." He released her. "We'll have to be very careful. I don't think we'll come to any harm on American soil."

She had lost all her enthusiasm.

"Nina, it can be done. I've actually thought about it quite a bit. I think I know how to protect us. But you'll have to follow my rules where security is concerned. No arguments. Can you do that?"

"Yes, but…" She was not sure about the whole idea anymore.

"I wanted to talk to you about it before I discussed it with George. So here's the plan. I suspect that in the next few months, the Commonwealth of Massachusetts will call a special election when Senator Kirk passes away. I want to run for that seat."

She listened in awed silence. This was typical Stephen. He made his plans in utter secrecy and then took her by surprise and swept her along like a juggernaut.

He winked at her. "And you thought you'd have to work on getting me to agree!" He slipped a hand around her waist and whirled her closer. "I'm going to play hard to get, though. I'll make George grovel for it."

When she remained silent, he said, "Don't look so serious, sweetheart. This is going to be fun. We'll find out if I'm really the perfect candidate George swears I am."

ABOUT THE AUTHOR

T. Dasu's impressionable years were spent on multiple continents, and it is these richly varied experiences that serve as inspiration for Dasu's writing. In addition to being a published author of both fiction and nonfiction works, Dasu also translates regional Indian fiction into English. Dasu enjoys classic stories of love and longing like Gabriel Garcia Marquez's *Love in the Time of Cholera*, and literary espionage exemplified by Graham Greene's *Our Man in Havana*.